Silent Suffering

Steve Ellis

TRAFFORD

Note for Librarians: a cataloguing record for this book that includes Dewey Decimal Classification and US Library of Congress numbers is available from the Library and Archives of Canada. The complete cataloguing record can be obtained from their online database at: www.collectionscanada.ca/amicus/index-e.html

ISBN 1-4120-5488-5

Printed in Victoria, BC, Canada

 Printed on paper with minimum 30% recycled fibre. Trafford's print shop runs on "green energy" from solar, wind and other environmentally-friendly power sources.

TRAFFORD *Offices in Canada, USA, Ireland and UK*

This book was published *on-demand* in cooperation with Trafford Publishing. On-demand publishing is a unique process and service of making a book available for retail sale to the public taking advantage of on-demand manufacturing and Internet marketing. On-demand publishing includes promotions, retail sales, manufacturing, order fulfilment, accounting and collecting royalties on behalf of the author.

Book sales for North America and international:

Trafford Publishing, 6E–2333 Government St.,
Victoria, BC v8t 4p4 CANADA
phone 250 383 6864 (toll-free 1 888 232 4444)
fax 250 383 6804; email to orders@trafford.com

Book sales in Europe:

Trafford Publishing (uk) Ltd., Enterprise House, Wistaston Road Business Centre,
Wistaston Road, Crewe, Cheshire cw2 7rp UNITED KINGDOM
phone 01270 251 396 (local rate 0845 230 9601)
facsimile 01270 254 983; orders.uk@trafford.com

Order online at:
trafford.com/05-0386

10   9   8   7   6   5   4   3   2

For you, Jemma and Clare

I am not yet born; Oh hear me…

Prayer Before Birth

Louis MacNeice

(1907 – 1963)

Chapter One

Terror makes you talk....

Both men dressed in black to match the night. Wire-cutters clipped a hole in the perimeter fence for their bodies to bend through. Electrified alarms remained as silent as the still air. It had been child's play wiring alternative circuits and turning off the water supply. Infrared sensors sensed nothing. Easy money for an easy job, they thought. It took precisely five seconds to reach the entrance of the target building.

Several nights of reconnaissance had taught the intruders when to make their move. At midnight one of the two guards always started a round of the site, checking doors and pointing a torch into dark rooms. How often do they need to be told? Never develop routines. Change the timing of your rounds. Vary your route. Simple security was still the best. As the guard checked each of the eight research laboratory blocks an automatic radio signal logged her progress to Central Security Control off site. It took thirty-five minutes to complete the round. They always check for signs of trouble, but they never find any. Boredom was the main enemy of night security.

Back at the front desk the remaining guard was responsible for monitoring 18 small CCTV surveillance screens covering the complex. But after 20 years in the job, with only a handful of minor incidents, former marine Jo Worth couldn't muster the enthusiasm for constant vigilance. And when the toilet light went on, it was the signal for the intruders to make their move, tap in the code to disable the lab's alarm, complete the mission. While Jo's bladder found relief the monitors were unmonitored. A good security manager would spy on his staff throughout the night, simulate an intrusion, discover the weak spots. He'd have noticed every toilet visit was a green light to anyone breaking in. Another golden rule of security had been broken: never let the outside know what you're doing inside.

Darwin House was known as the rat run at the research centre. They lived, depending on the tests being conducted, in steel cages or glass tanks on all three floors of the modern brick building. Drugs and chemicals would be pumped into the white rodents to test toxicity for humans. Compounds would be rubbed onto their shaved skin to check for allergic reactions. Chimpanzees and monkeys, in Rutherford House next door, would have squealed and screeched when the two men entered. If Rutherford had been the target these primates would have been gassed to secure their silence. But caged rats are incapable of raising alarm. They could remain alive scratching and scraping and scurrying around. The men in combat fatigues and balaclavas moved quickly and confidently up the stairs to the first floor. They found the target room conveniently sign-posted Records Office. The first man tapped in the four-digit code to release the lock. The second glanced around to check the coast was clear before the next phase of the operation. They remained undetected, he was certain of that. Yet they were observed, by hundreds of pairs of small, suspicious eyes.

Key labelled #1 opened the office door. On entry, to the left as informed, a bank of grey filing cabinets. Key #2 opened the cabinet with drawers "A" to "D". The taller of the two men removed the target file from the second drawer down. He slipped it inside a small rucksack on his accomplice's back. His hand did not leave the bag empty. He removed a can of spray paint: red, blood red.

Within seconds his partner found the target computer. Touching the space bar awakened the screen. The password worked. They'd failed to change it. She'd told the truth after all. Her instructions, passwords and codes – all of them - had been accurate. He deleted the appropriate files according to the list he'd been given. To guarantee the documents could not be retrieved a worm virus was loaded. It would corrupt traces of the deleted files and obliterate all backup recovery programmes. By daylight it will have completed its task infiltrating thousands of computers around the globe. Even records of the records would be zapped.

Key disks had already been taken, thanks to a cleaner who needed the cash to pay her child's medical bills and her husband's drug habit. Target backup CDs and floppies, stored at the research organization's science centre in Germany, had been secured too. Remaining computer-contained research evidence would vanish without trace. Digit by digit would fall away and be overwritten by *The Complete Works of Shakespeare: Histories, Comedies and Tragedies*. It made the hacker laugh out loud when he was given his instructions attached to the bundle of used $100 bills.

The two men turned their attention to the research paperwork and completed questionnaires. They found the folders on the library shelves at the far side of the office, exactly where she said they would be. Four thick buff files were stuffed into the rucksack.

***

Terror makes you talk and talk fast. For nearly two weeks, speaking through the black hood, she told them all they needed to know. They snatched her on Saturday afternoon in the car park as she left the shopping mall in Tampa, Florida. She kept asking why, why me? Even in the back of the van, handcuffed and strapped to the floor, she kept muttering the question through the tape tight across her mouth. It felt like hours since she'd been bound and bundled into the back of the van before it came to a stop. But she calculated it had been less, perhaps under an hour. She heard the garage door open and the van crawled inside to park. The engine was allowed to purr for a long while and she gagged on the gas fumes penetrating the van. Had they planned to kill her with car fumes? Was carbon dioxide to be her gaseous executioner? No. That would serve no purpose. She was certain, after falling unconscious, they would remove her and revive her for whatever they had in mind. Her abductors simply wanted to avoid a struggle. But the engine then stuttered to a halt. Had it ran out of gas before the fumes anaesthetized her? Or had someone switched off the ignition? She didn't care. The air became easier to consume.

However long the journey she was certain they had taken her somewhere remote. Between coughing and gasping for clean air she heard nothing. No talk. No traffic. No sounds of life, rural or urban, apart from her own heartbeat and hard breathing. She assumed her kidnappers had slipped away to prepare whatever they needed to prepare for her. So terrified of the alternative, her only hope now was to die quickly without pain, unused, un-abused.

Footsteps. Steel capped boots on concrete. Coming, coming closer. Coming, coming faster. Then a second of stillness before the sliding door was thrust open with such force the van rocked on its suspension. Quickly they untied the straps binding her to the floor. Grabbing her arms and wrists, one man either side, they frog-marched her down stairs into what seemed an empty stone-clad cellar full of echoes exaggerating every sound. Packaging tape was wound around and around each arm and each leg to a heavy long-back wooden chair fixed to the floor. The pull-string on her hood was tightened like a hangman's rope around her neck. It denied her the last shaft of light and forced her to fight for air from the world outside the black canvas bag.

Then they departed. Alone, after the turn of a door key and the slide of a bolt, silence became more frightening than sound. When quiet, the imagination does its greatest work. When dark, the mind sees more than eyes in daylight. She tried to steady her nerves by deep, slow, regular breathing. She tried to focus on her situation, think rationally, work out clever lines to negotiate her release. How much money could be raised to secure her release? But the solitude, her thinking time, was short lived. The key turned. The bolt slid.

The door opened. She sat upright, as rigid as rock. A draft of cooler air from the world outside crossed her body momentarily. But the door slammed shut sealing in the staleness of her cell she now shared with persons unknown. She heard their breathing. She knew they were there, staring at her, ogling, enjoying her terror. But they did not touch.

She asked for a bio-break. Her words came out surprisingly clearly considering the dryness of her mouth and the pain in her throat. Thankfully, under the hot hood, the tape across her mouth had worked loose. Despite the clarity of her request there was no reply. She called again for a comfort break, a little louder this time, more assertive. But their strength was in their silence. There can be no counter-argument to silence, no words to get a grip of, no phrase to fight, no voice to assess age or personality, no tone to measure strength or weakness, honesty or deception, friend or foe.

The panic set in. They knew it would. She shook violently. Her headache in the heat of the hood was intolerable. She started gasping for air, hyperventilating. Her arms could not wrestle free. Her legs could not kick. She passed out as she felt warm urine trickle down her legs into her shoes.

She hadn't died. But she was certain death wasn't far away. She tried to think hard about her husband and their two wonderful boys. Would they get to know what happened? She prayed not. She thought of her parents, her brother and both sisters. Hundreds of scenes from her life played in her head compiling an autobiography from memories. Holidays. Schools. The Institute in Massachusetts. Postgraduate years at Oxford. Their wedding. Childbirth. Aaron's broken arm. Sam's prize for sport at school.

The sobbing started. They knew it would. But her weeping was not at the thought of dying. It was the certain knowledge that pain would be inflicted before death. These were tears of fear, not of sadness. She knew she was soon to suffer. This was a shrine for sick minds and she was strapped to their sacrificial alter. Beating. Electric shocks. Mutilation. Cigarette burns. Rape. And worse. She knew this was all to do with perverted gratification. She'd read horror books and watched the movies. She'd seen the news and heard the reports. But this wasn't fiction. This wasn't someone else on the news. This was her, a 35-year-old research chemist, wife and mother of two, about to make the headlines in news she would never see, hear or read. She decided to do whatever they asked of her, however revolting the act. Not that it would save her life, but in the vain hope it would reduce the suffering before death.

When she stopped crying, and they knew she would, they would start questioning. Resistance would have ebbed away. She shuddered when he spoke her name. She expected next a slap, a kick, a fist in the face, a ripped blouse to make her more compliant. Then would come the heat of a cigarette end, the cold of knife steel, the agony of pulled hair, the shock of electricity, the dirty talk and the dirtier deeds. Pain was moments away. In the hours of her abduction she'd imagined their grotesque acts. They were now to start their torture, terrorism and bestiality.

His voice, carefully pausing between each sentence, was rich, deep, measured, more frightening because of its unexpected warmth. "If you cooperate Mary-Ann you will live. Do you understand?"

"Yes."

"If you tell us what we need to know you will see your husband again. Do you want to see your husband again Mary-Ann?"

"Yes."

"Your boys will not be harmed if you tell us the truth. Do you, Mary-Ann, want your boys to stay safe?"

"Yes. Oh god, yes, please. Please don't harm them."

"We could hurt you, you know that, don't you."

"Yes."

His mouth moved close to her ear and he whispered. "You know we could do absolutely anything with you, don't you?"

"Yes…yes."

"We have everything at our disposal from crude mechanics to sophisticated drugs. And you know all about the effects of drugs, don't you Mary-Ann?"

"Yes. It's my...."

"However, we would like to progress without causing you pain or any further distress. Do you believe me?"

She stayed silent.

"Do you, Mary-Ann, believe me?" There was no irritation with her hesitation. And he was patient for her response.

"Yes. Yes I believe you."

"I'm glad. If you believe in me, it will, Mary-Ann, be better for everybody. You and your lovely family will benefit greatly."

She believed him. Unlike with God, she had no choice but to believe.

As the head of clinical research at Darwin House she told her interrogators everything they wanted to know about the laboratory. She told them how and where research results were stored. She gave them codes to all the doors and passwords for the computers. She told them how the research company made backup files and where they were stored and how they could be destroyed.

They held Dr Mary-Ann Quinlan for over two weeks until the data destruction had been completed successfully. Torture had not been necessary. Captivity alone was sufficient to loosen her mouth. The promise her sons would go unharmed and she would be returned home had secured complete cooperation. She had not been beaten, shocked or molested in any way. They'd even supplied a wide range of good quality meals. In fact she believed she'd put on a couple of extra pounds. She answered all their questions honestly without hesitation and enthusiastically offered details. It was clear to her the more she helped the quicker she'd be back home. Indeed one of her captures thanked her for her valuable assistance and she felt relieved, even happy.

Then he shot her. In his mind he'd killed her in a kindly way, cocking the pistol outside the room to save her a split-second of fear. He'd come to admire her over the interrogation period. She'd earned his respect and so a painless death. When he entered with the .45 Dr Quinlan died thinking he was bringing her coffee on a tray. But all he delivered was a bullet from his gun to her head.

Her body was never found. It never would be. It could not be. The way it was chemically processed ensured there were no remains. Her family did not learn what happened and probably never would. Local gossip speculated everything from running off with a secret lover to suicide. One group said Dr Quinlan had been abducted. That Saturday night, they claimed, an alien spacecraft was in the neighbourhood looking particularly for scientists and other intelligent lifeforms from planet earth.

In the quest for clues the police confiscated the shopping mall's video surveillance tapes. Dr Quinlan had been clearly identified visiting various stores and buying groceries, books and clothes. But one vital tape covering Car Park 6, where her abandoned car had been found, was missing or had been recorded over by accident. They'd taken statements from shopkeepers, sales assistants and shoppers. But they saw nothing, heard nothing, knew nothing.

To the cops, after a few days of fruitless enquiries, the missing mother of two boys became just another statistic, one of thousands of people every year across America who disappear without trace. The Captain in charge of the Missing Persons Bureau had convinced himself she'd run off with another man. "She's a goddamn good lookin' woman, that's fer sure," he told his sergeant. "Goddamn brainy too. Yep, if she'd been kidnapped her shoppin' would 'ave scattered all over the goddamn place where he'd snatched her." Somehow the possibility that two *or* more kidnappers, male *or* female *or* both, may have taken her *and* her shopping refused to enter his mind. She could also have vanished of her own free will. And he put down the missing surveillance tape to bad luck, "goddamn bad luck".

***

Security guard Jo Worth noticed the corona of light through a side window immediately the fire alarm started to ring. CCTV camera 5, focussed on Darwin House, confirmed the location of the blaze. Fire fighters were slow to reach the scene. Joyriding kids had crashed a couple of stolen cars right across the main approach road to the science research park. The automatic sprinklers also failed to douse the flames in Darwin. A simple turn of a tap had cut off the system's water supply. Another security blunder, the subsequent inquiry would doubtless find. Lucky rats, in cages opened by the departing intruders, fled the burning building. Unlucky ones remained roasting inside. The research company's insurance would rebuild the laboratory block with its offices and scientific facilities. Buildings and equipment can be replaced. As he looked over the smouldering shell of Darwin House with two open-mouthed security guards, the lab's chief administrator was thankful they had key backup data files downloaded off site.

At first Captain Bob Murray of Tampa's Police Department couldn't understand why the FBI disturbed his sleep at 2.30am. Some agent was ranting down the phone about some fire at some laboratory by some crazy animal freedom fighters. He was half-asleep and fully drunk, thanks to a bottle of bourbon with the boys last night. But when Dr Mary-Ann Quinlan's name was mentioned, he woke up and sobered up completely.

"Wasn't she the head of all that animal research stuff?" he asked while managing to move his overweight frame towards the bathroom.

"That's exactly why I'm calling Captain. Where did you get to on that investigation?"

"Dead end, that's where."

"That's real sad Captain Murray, real sad. A lead to her whereabouts could be mighty useful in tracing these crazy guys."

"Nope. Didn't get a sniff."

13

"My boss is asking if you can get down here to help us out, give us whatever you got."

"What? Now?"

"Sure thing, Captain. 'Now' would be just fine."

Murray said he'd be there in half an hour. But he'd take his time. Surely it could've waited until later in the morning? "Goddamn it," he told his sleep-crumpled face in the bathroom mirror.

An hour later Murray read the slogans sprayed in red on the outside walls of Rutherford and nearby blocks: *"Death to animal torturers. Rats have human feelings."* The message was clear. Murray realised the status of Dr Mary-Ann Quinlan's case had been promoted, from Missing to Murder.

Within days the research company appointed a new director of security. Senior night security officer Jo Worth was offered, according to the letter from human resources, "the opportunity of early retirement". It was an opportunity he couldn't refuse.

Worth's junior that night, security officer Katie Cornell, was questioned the next day by FBI agents at Tampa Police Headquarters. Intelligence files revealed twenty years back she belonged to an animal rights group at high school and had taken part in demonstrations against the fur trade. She was a member of the World Nature Fund and a subscriber to National Geographic. The raid on her one-bedroom apartment found all her cosmetics and personal products had labels specifying they had not been tested on animals.

But for Captain Murray the most damning evidence came from Station Officer Malkovicz. "She don't eat no beef for lunch Captain," he reported passing by with her meal tray from the cell. "She says she's one of those vegetarians."

"Goddamn it, she sure knows more than she's saying."

Chapter Two

A mobile chirped...damn it

Matt's hand reached out from under the duvet. His fingers knew where to feel so his eyes could stay shut a minute longer. Then it would be time to make his move. Seconds before 5.30am the button was pressed. It stopped the alarm assaulting their ears. Silence gave Jane an extra hour's sleep. And darkness would help the quality of that sleep. He never switched on a light to walk from their bed to the bathroom. Matt would sense his way like a blind man. He pictured the hazards on route from previous encounters. An iron bed leg, a chair beside the dressing table, a chest of drawers, were all waiting in ambush. Bruised shins and stubbed toes had taught him where to tread and when to turn. Lessons are gained from pain. His hand found the cord inside the bathroom door and he pulled it. A circle of small bulbs surrounded the flattering bronze-tinted mirror above the sink, although this was no Hollywood dressing room. Matt finally opened his eyes allowing his mind and body to adjust from night to day, sleep to activity, home to work.

In two hours the breakfast meeting would be underway in central London. Their new client had important information to disclose before she returned to Chicago. Matt's presentation and proposal were safely inside his laptop. Hard copies were already printed and bound for their American guest and her board of directors. Peter yesterday was confident she would sign the contract today. Matt had every confidence in Peter's judgement. It was usually right. This corporation needed to get its product launched across Europe. And quick. Time is money, she'd said. Every day's delay cost the company one million bucks. Minimum. We're talking clear bottom-line profit lost like melting snow, she'd said. Peter was one of the few people in Europe who could cut the waiting time and generate the profit.

The central heating hadn't started. Weeks earlier Matt changed the settings to reduce the time it burnt energy – and money. He was willing to suffer a little early morning discomfort for a saving on their gas bill. But bare feet on a tile floor supporting a naked body in December caused a shiver. Even the so-called hot water tap at this hour only delivered lukewarm water, making it hard for his wet razor to cut through a day's growth. But the money saved would be worth the sacrifice. Save pennies, grow pounds.

After a tepid shower he crept back to the bedroom where Jane slept. He dressed quickly and quietly using the line of light from the bathroom. He'd sort out his tie at the office. Matt kissed his wife goodbye on her forehead. This morning she didn't stir. Sometimes she murmurs. Sometimes she manages a mumbled "bye". Sometimes she hooks a hand round his neck encouraging an embrace. Occasionally, when the mood is right and the pressure is off at work, Matt finds himself in bed again. There's always a later train.

But today, when a major new business prospect is hovering with a pen over a contract, Matt's routine to work kicked in. A glass of water gulped in the kitchen. No time to make tea. A brisk walk from their small semi in the suburbs to the station. Newspapers off the stall: one broadsheet, one tabloid. Waiting on the platform. A delay. Eight minutes today, if the electronic notice board is right. Eight minutes. For God's sake it's freezing.

The service to London from the south was routinely criticised by the Railway Passengers Association. Commuters were treated like cattle despite the promises of successive governments and the train company's Commitment to Customer Service Policy. Passengers suffered in silence most of the time. The late running 06.05 Sevenoaks in Kent to Charing Cross, three weeks before Christmas, didn't seem severe enough to start a crusade against the chronic condition of British railways. After all, staff at the station or on the train can't do anything. They're not to blame.

Matt and his fellow daily commuters sat in their usual seats in the second carriage from the front. Sometimes the occasional traveller would take a regular's spot invading "their space" and disrupting the routine. Regulars always knew their place. The talkers reviewed last night's match. No way that was a penalty. Arsenal had been lucky. Newspaper readers discovered details of yesterday's events and consumed speculation about what would happen today.

This morning Matt, like fellow passengers not willing to talk or read at this early hour, looked out of the window, or tried to. It was dirty and full of condensation caused by warm breath inside and cold air outside. He used the arm of his coat to wipe the glass clear. In its defence the train company had acquired new rolling stock over recent months. But today's train was one with old slam-door carriages, reminiscent of the 1950s when men in bowler hats occupied these seats. Today's late-running service used rolling stock from semi-retirement in the sidings "due to vandalism", declared the announcement. Last night the soccer tribes on Special Brew had done their work with the spray can and the knife on the newer trains.

In the carriage newspaper readers were privy to the small print. But newspaper headlines on public transport are shared with everyone:

THREE DEAD IN HOSPITAL FIRE
POUND ON PAR WITH EURO
MORE ARREST IN EU CORRUPTION SCANDAL
MOSCOW ELECTION: COMMUNISTS BACK IN POWER

Whatever the stories, whatever was happening in the world, one man in his well-worn brown suit and black shoes, always turned first to the cryptic crossword. He was short with a perfectly round head on an egg-shaped body. He wore white shirts only, despite his pale complexion. For probably forty-plus years of his working life, Matt suspected he never tried or thought of trying anything other than white. He'd probably consider light blue an outrageous breach of tradition. Matt imagined even the headline END OF WORLD TODAY – OFFICIAL would not detract him from his crossword. Matt didn't know or want to know his name. But he assumed it was something like John Brown. They were on nodding terms. That was sufficient acknowledgement for most of London's commuters. Matt didn't know either what job he had, but suspected something tedious and routine. Even accountancy looked too exciting for him. But Matt accepted he could be wrong. Maybe he's head of some secret intelligence service.

Another stop. More passengers. Standing room only. The condensation increased. Nobody opened a window. Stale air is preferable to cold air in the experience of commuters. Only strangers on trains open windows in winter. Stale air assisted sleep. Rocked by the rhythm of the train Matt closed his eyes somewhere beyond Bromley. With luck he'd grab an extra 10 minutes of dreams before facing London and the short walk to his office off The Strand.

A mobile chirped. Damn it. He thought he'd set *Meeting*. Sod it. Where is it? Coat zip stuck. Eyes open, and some scowl. Which pocket? Found it. Thank Christ. Everyone listens. Everyone pretends not to. Another mobile goes off. And another. Those at home are up and about or those in the office are wondering where you are.

"The gas boiler seems broken," Jane said. "There's no hot water for a bath and the house is freezing."

"Oh," was Matt's minimal response to minimise disturbing passengers.

"We only had it repaired in summer. He said he couldn't keep fixing it and we'd need a new one. Matt, are you listening? He said it wouldn't cope with another winter."

"Right."

"Where are you?"

"Battersea."

"I thought you'd be in the office by now."

"Delayed."

"I'll have to call the gas people again. Whatever it costs we'll have to get it fixed, my parents are coming at the weekend."

No response, unless silence is a response.

"I know we're overdrawn Matt. But it has to be done. We can't live in an ice cube."

"Sure. Look, I have to go. We're just pulling into Charing Cross."

"OK. I'll call them before I get off to school."

"Fine."

"See you tonight Matt. Love you."

"And you."

Chapter Three

Scientist tell us it's safe...

Cancer was only a "theoretical risk" with this process, according to the Senior Vice President for Public Affairs and Communications from Chicago. Jenni Tallow's revelation did not cause concern for the experienced spin-doctors in the London office of public relations giant Henderson-Strutt. They had handled hundreds of incidents and crisis situations on behalf of the world's biggest companies. They had "re-modelled" and "made-over" military dictatorships and corrupt governments to enhance their image on the world stage. They call it Reputation Management. And Henderson-Strutt claimed in its glossy brochure to be the leading practitioner of this art. To the three agency staff in the windowless basement meeting room, Ms Tallow simply represented another corporation desperate to downplay the danger, real or theoretical, in a new product and enhance her company's image.

"A child would need to eat over a thousand apples or pears a day to reach the toxic levels considered even potentially dangerous by the Food and Drug Administration," she stressed. "So 22XP is safe, because nobody's going to consume anything like that amount. Even the FDA accepts that."

Henderson-Strutt's business in the alchemy of corporate spin was to turn black to white, white to black. They wrote press releases stressing the good and omitting the bad. If they couldn't avoid the bad, they'd camouflage it with wishy-washy words in the middle of a long paragraph. They coached corporate and government spokespeople on what to say to journalists during media interviews, at press conferences, or on TV and radio. They even counselled kings and queens, princes and princesses from the ranks of Europe's royal families to make them more media-friendly.

Peter Jones, Henderson-Strutt's Director of Issues and Crisis Management, tried to see Jenni's eyes to detect the real truth. Regrettably, for him, they were all but hidden behind thick black square frames. Unflattering, he thought, deliberately so, as if she wanted to hide the soft shape of her face. But he knew. Tiger-tough Wall Street glasses to hide a pussy-cat from the Mid-West. Peter would have preferred a closer view of his client's hazel eyes.

While the American was speaking, Peter asked himself did she really believe her own company's propaganda? Perhaps corporate blinkers do come automatically with the job of company spokesperson.

His thoughts were not expressed. She was the client after all. Peter said, "Jenni, this chemical 22XP, if the media found out that a known carcinogen was being used to extend the shelf life of fruit and salad vegetables - however small the theoretical risk - they'd have a field day, wouldn't they."

It was a statement more than a question.

"Well," she hesitated only for a moment, "that's why we need you guys at Henderson-Strutt to be ready to reassure reporters if the information were to leak out."

"But under US law and the Freedom of Information Act won't the FDA have to disclose this chemical has been used in fruit processing and storage depots?" asked Peter, although he knew the answer.

"You're right," Jenni said. "Sure, the minutes of the FDA's Advisory Panel on Pesticides are published on their website. A lot of the documentation is lodged in their library and in Congress. Some of the papers may raise concern, to people who don't fully understand the science, because the chemical compounds have been listed as genotoxic carcinogens."

"The cancer cells kill the body's healthy cells," Peter suggested.

"You got it in one."

"That's worrying."

"Only to people who don't understand the science Peter."

"Most people don't understand science Jenni."

As always in advance of any meeting Peter had thoroughly researched his client. And he always knew more than he disclosed. His relaxed, friendly, almost casual approach often deceived clients unaware of his detailed knowledge, meticulous planning and network of influential contacts. Peter's main objective today was to get Jenni Tallow's signature on the contract before she flies back stateside. The deal was worth at least £500,000 in fees to the agency. That excludes out-of-pocket expenses required to conduct the business, such as working lunches and dinners, taxis, flights and accommodation in five-star hotels that would be charged back to the client - with a ten per cent administration surcharge.

The work also meant at least two trips to Chicago before Christmas. A good time for Peter to top-up his drinks cabinet with tax-free whisky and buy cut-price cigarettes for his cigarette-sucking friends who ignored the health warnings.

Matt made this early breakfast meeting on time despite the late arrival of his train. As Peter's deputy he would be the workhorse handling this issue and account for AestChem Inc of Chicago. Penny Taylor, 25, Cambridge graduate, two years into the job and already considered a PR veteran, was the senior account executive in Peter's department, reporting to Matt.

They both stayed silent, focussing all their attention onto Peter. At the pre-meeting meeting on Friday they had discussed how they would demonstrate to AestChem's Senior Vice President that the Henderson-Strutt agency was the best for the job. Peter would make the half-million fee sound like a great bargain for the American corporation. It would be if they pulled it off. And her signature on the contract would come just in time for their Christmas bonus. A bonus that would help pay off Matt's growing debt.

"Jenni, I must say thank you very much indeed for a clear explanation of your company's position and the US food regulatory process." Peter was an old hand. He knew how to press-the-flesh and ego-massage without appearing an oily-smooth public relations lizard.

"In Britain, Jenni, as I'm sure you know, as long as your US food and safety authorities have accepted and registered the chemical for use on food products, the UK's Food Standards Authority generally accept its use on imports. It normally goes through on a nod and a wink," he said, before he paused. Everyone around the table, now littered with used coffee cups and half-eaten croissant, knew a "but" was coming, including Jenni.

"But, as we experienced with genetically modified food and BST - you remember the growth hormone in milk of course – and irradiated food, Europeans get much more worried about these things than you Americans…."

"I know," Jenni interrupted, "in the US we just can't understand you guys over here."

"Our research Jenni shows that Americans, generally speaking of course, trust authority more. You actually believe what your scientists tell you. You're not scared of science. And you Americans are really into what's new. In Europe we hold on to the old more. I'm not saying this is right. I'm not saying this is wrong. But we have to accept the reality of transatlantic differences in mass psyche. Even when your Presidents lie under oath to Congress and the people of America, you still vote for them," said Peter sitting back in the black leather seat. "We only need one consumer pressure group, some scare-mongering scientist out to make a name for himself, to whip up the media and wham, mam, there's a ban."

"Look Peter," said Jenni, whispering to stress her point, "this chemical is worth $billions to us. It's our patented product and process. We're years ahead of the competition. The US fruit and vegetable growers and all their associations are fully behind us on this. The scientists tell us it's safe. The FDA accept it's safe..."

"At very low levels," intercepted Peter.

"The FDA accepts a 'theoretical risk'," Jenni emphasised, "but in reality it cannot happen. No one person can consume several tons of fruit and vegetables a day. Even a starving elephant would only eat a fraction of the amount we're talking about that just might be slightly toxic. Peter, Matt, Penny, we're talking about miniscule levels of residue here, below 15ppb, parts per billion. It's the equivalent of... oh...I guess...something like a raindrop in a swimming pool. Less. Much less."

"But that won't stop the headlines," said Matt, making a greater impact for having been silent for several minutes.

After a brief pause in the meeting, while everyone gathered their thoughts, Jenni asked, "So, where do we go from here?" She breathed in heavily and awaited the draft plan from London's top PR outfit. They charge big bucks, so they better have big ideas. The directors in Chicago think Europe is like the USA: just pay the money and you get what you want. They don't understand. It doesn't work that way this side of the Atlantic.

"Jenni, I've asked Matt and Penny to make a brief presentation of our initial ideas based on the information you sent last week," said Peter.

Matt adjusted his tie, the one he grabbed from the wardrobe and stuffed into his pocket three hours earlier while Jane slept. It was not one of his best. The knot tended to slip loose. Jenni was a client who would notice details. The data projector droned into life and Henderson-Strutt's global logo appeared on screen. The room lights automatically dimmed. Lower light helped clients focus on the company's PowerPoint presentation of its issues management strategy. Peter and Matt also knew, from experience, the lower the room lights, the fewer difficult questions they received from potentially awkward clients. As Matt held the computer mouse his first thought was not, surprisingly, about the strategy he was about to present. It was not about this new blockbuster chemical process that would make $billions for AestChem Inc of Chicago. It certainly wasn't about the theoretical health risk to millions of people in Europe. He knew of far more dangerous things being consumed by consumers everywhere. It wasn't, at this moment anyway, about Penny's well-shaped body tucked into her well-cut suit that Daddy and Mummy clearly subsidised. It was the bill. Another bill. How much a new gas boiler? And what next? Jane's car probably, it didn't sound too good and the clutch is definitely going. That's what Matt had in mind, even during this presentation to one of the largest chemical companies in the world. Despite the domestic distraction, Matt's presentation went well.

"In conclusion Jenni, we have a three part plan," Matt said. "First, we work on the WII scenario, the Without Incident Introduction phase for 22XP. We assume, and hope, there will be no adverse publicity. We assume, and continue to hope, the food faddists don't hear about it and therefore cannot get concerned. We're pretty sure that once 22XP has been on the market for several months, and certainly after a year or two, the public won't be too concerned even if the media or the so-called natural food lobby kick up a fuss. Of course we will, as I outlined, be talking to our contacts in Whitehall, Westminster and in Brussels to make sure it is registered and given the license for use over here in Britain and across Europe."

"That's clear, that's fine," said Jenni, nodding. "But I'm more concerned about part two of the work, the crisis preparation plan. Can you just run that past me again?" The low light treatment for client silence hadn't work with Ms Tallow. But she was a smart operator. She knew what she wanted and she'd get it. No standard PR ploy would keep her quiet.

"No problem Jenni," continued Matt. And it wasn't. Handling problems was his specialty. The bigger the crisis, the better Matt performed. He had been the spin doctor on behalf of clients for many "special situations" in his six years at the agency: kidnapping, deaths on oil rigs and in factories, product contamination, accidents at work, blackmail, corruption, mass redundancy announcements, explosions, strikes, hostile takeovers, chief executive dismissals and more. Much more. Another month, another crisis, he would say. And when business was brisk, it was almost another day, another crisis.

These special situations could not be spoken about, even to work colleagues outside the crisis handling team. It was a strict rule. Certainly say nothing to friends. And Matt rarely said anything about these difficulties to Jane, with her teacher's bag of ethics. A need to know basis you understand, as Peter explained to Matt when he was recruited to this elite club of crisis management within the PR world. This group wasn't the place for the cow-eyed PR bimbos pushing press releases out to the media. This wasn't for the sweet-talkers. This wasn't for the naïve graduates recruited to promote everything from stately homes to washing powder.

Penny, like Matt, was an exception. Six years earlier, aged 23, when Matt joined Henderson-Strutt global public relations agency at Number Twenty Bloomsbury Chambers in Villiers Street near Charing Cross, he wasn't trusted to handle crises. No raw recruit was. As with all fresh faces, until Peter and the key directors checked out his suitability and proved he could be trusted, Matt was left in the ranks of ordinary public relations executives. After a few months it became clear here was a young man, as Peter told the board of directors, who was suitable crisis work.

He kept calm under fire, handled pressure, and was discreet. MI5 and 6, Mossad and the CIA, could use some of the skills and techniques of this agency's crisis handling team. After all, it was reciprocal, the agency used current and former security services personnel and facilities to help in special circumstances.

Matt explained part two of the crisis preparation plan to Jenni: "So if the use of 22XP is leaked to the media or the food faddists cut up rough, we go pro-active. We will then have to have a dialogue with the public in Europe. We set the pace, not the media or the activists," Matt said assuredly. "It is a key principle of ours never to let news headlines dictate our business. We can't wait for the bad news to grow and fester. That was the big public relations disaster your rivals Monsanto encountered in Europe with their genetically modified soya. We need to avoid that. Your corporate silence will be interpreted by the public as your guilt," Matt added, confident his strategy was been lapped up by the client word for word.

"Over the next few days we will draft a questions and answer document based on the information you've provided. You'll need to check our responses for accuracy with your experts at the science laboratory in Chicago. Your directors need to approve them too. We need everybody on the board to be on board," Jenni nodded approvingly and smiled at his play on words.

Matt continued, "Then we will have many of the counter-arguments in place if the critics kick up a fuss. We can also compile the key messages we need to promote and push out to the public. We should select and train up your key spokespeople at your London office so they look good in front of the media and stay on message when they're talking.

"Finally, we'll recruit a couple of independent scientists to support 22XP. They'll speak approvingly on its behalf. We'll ensure journalists contact these academics for an independent quote in their stories. But remember Jenni, as I said in my presentation, any research funding for these scientists would have to be given after a gap of at least a year. We have to put *distance* between AestChem, them, and their universities. Their academic independence and scientific respectability must be retained."

"Sure, we understand that," said Jenni. "But you'll approach them, brief them, make sure they sing along?"

"Of course. Many academics, especially here in Britain, are now starved of blue-sky research funds. Knowing a contribution from AestChem is in the pipeline will be, shall we say, extremely welcome."

"He who pays the piper calls the tune," Peter chipped in. "He who pays the piper…"

"*She* who pays, in this case Peter," quipped Jenni.

A bit prickly for someone approaching 40, thought Peter, well aware of the sensitivity to the political correctness of US companies. He remembered some of his dealings with the likes of Enron, Anderson, World Com and other American companies. There they were, worrying about whether an employee kissed a colleague on the cheek, having big debates about the use of *spokesperson* and *spokeswoman* or *spokesman*, while fiddling the books big time, shredding evidence, depriving thousands of employees their pensions. Misplaced priorities, he thought.

"Absolutely right Jenni," responded Peter, smiling and wondering if 22XP really could poison people and cause cancer. After all, he only had the company's word that it doesn't.

"I think part three of the plan is fine," Jenni said, gathering her papers together and opening her briefcase. "People in the trade, the importers, the supermarkets, the distributors, understand the science. So I think informing our potential business partners about the fantastic benefits of 22XP will be fine. Business to business communication won't be a problem. Incidentally, remember publicly in the market place we don't call 22XP 22XP. We call it FFresherFood. We use two 'fs' to stress the 'f' for fresher. Clever, eh? And we use the three FFF logo, see." She held up a sheet with the sign.

"How did people react to this concept in your focus group testing and consumer research?" Matt asked.

"Very positive. And it's certainly taken off in the USA. So let's hope European consumers react likewise."

"We certainly hope so too Jenni," said Peter.

Standing, dropping her papers into her brief case, Jenni continued, "All our business customers need to know is that FFresherFood will give them a great deal of flexibility in harvesting and distribution, marketing and selling. Their profit margins on these commodities should improve too with our innovation."

Looking down at her airline ticket, Jenni added, "All the general consumer needs to remember is that 22XP, sorry, FFresherFood, just keeps the product fresher a good deal longer. Consumers feel, when they eat food treated by our process, that the product was picked off the tree or plucked out of the soil yesterday. People don't need to be scared off buying treated product by a load of sensational stories and lurid headlines written by reporters who don't understand the first principles of science, do they?"

Peter, Matt and Penny could not disagree. The lights came back up to full power in the basement meeting room after the presentation was over and the projector switched off. Jenni had read the agency contract in detail on the flight over. She was generally happy with the terms and conditions apart from a couple of points on the out-of-pocket expenses. The company had a policy of not using first class on flights, she explained courteously but firmly. Only the President and Executive Board members could use first, if the executive jets were busy. Business class seats would have to do for air travel for Peter and Henderson-Strutt staff. Peter accepted the condition, made the change and initialled it. Jenni's Mont Blanc signed both copies on the dotted line in black ink for and on behalf of AestChem Inc of Chicago, Illinois, USA. Peter signed for the agency. They shook hands to seal the deal. Matt and Penny smiled at each other. Objective achieved.

In line with the issues and crisis department's policy, the project was allocated a codeword. From now all the documents marked, "confidential, not for distribution and privileged" would be known to the team as Project 66.

As Henderson-Strutt's driver opened the boot of the Mercedes to receive Jenni's luggage – he'd remembered to call it "trunk" and impressed Jenni with his knowledge of American - Peter, Matt and

Penny waved goodbye from the front door of Bloomsbury House. Bert opened the rear door for Jenni to slide her tall thin frame onto the leather upholstery. As she did Jenni accidentally dropped her flight ticket. Bert, always friendly and helpful, picked it up from the pavement and handed it back. "Must be nice travelling in first class miss," he said.

Before the car drove away Peter asked Penny to go and clean the meeting room. She would have to take the presentation disc from the computer, check the hard drive, gather all the papers from the desk, tear away any flip chart paper with notes or plans. No trace of the client or of the meeting should remain in the room. Then, and only then, the catering staff would be allowed to clear the cups and coffee flasks, glasses, empty water bottles, used plates and crumpled napkins. The tape recording of the meeting would also be filed away under Project 66.

Matt turned to Peter as the Mercedes took a left into The Strand on its way to Heathrow and asked, "If, unexpectedly and unfortunately, a leak occurred in the media, and we had to implement plan two, how much more would that cost AestChem over the current budget?"

"Rough estimate?" quizzed Peter, rubbing his chin.

"Rough estimate," Matt confirmed.

"Another £500,000 with all that lobbying we'd have to do, especially the facilitation work needed in Brussels."

"That's even more than I guessed."

Bert had put on his chauffeur's hat to please the client. Jenni was satisfied with the meeting and impressed by Henderson-Strutt's team. She sat back and enjoyed looking at Nelson's Column. Bert pointed out the National Gallery at the top of Trafalgar Square. He drove down The Mall to show her Buckingham Palace. And he'd take her past the Royal Albert Hall in Knightsbridge on the way to Terminal 4. After that, he wouldn't speak unless he was spoken to. She'd probably want to do some paperwork and make calls. Americans always did.

Jenni didn't disclose she knew London well. She didn't want to dampen her driver's enthusiasm for pointing out the sights. He was a friendly man on the edge of retirement. She took a perfume out of her bag and liberally sprayed her wrists and neck. It helped her relax. But it made Bert want to sneeze, although he prevented the reaction by squeezing his nose. Jenni sank into the car's soft leather and enjoyed the ride. The Executive Board would accept Henderson-Strutt's proposal, because they had done what she wanted them to do. Her plan would work. It had to.

Chapter Four

Kids are getting restless...

Jane phoned the gas people before leaving for school.

"We can't get anyone round your place until four this afternoon at the earliest I'm afraid. Friday you see. It's always busy on Fridays," the customer service woman said.

"Actually that's fine," said Jane knowing her last class was at 3pm with level 7, the 11 and 12-year-olds. Her boss, the Head of English at The Oaks, Gerry Tinkler, allowed members of his team to slip off early if he could. He was a gentle-giant of a man who commanded respect, even from the kids. And this was an emergency. No heating and no hot water is no joke in the middle of winter.

"Now you're sure the gas isn't leaking Mrs Collins?"

"No," replied Mrs Collins. "It just won't light up. Your engineer told us a few months ago once the fan or whatever it is broke down again the whole boiler would need replacing. Of course it would pack up as soon as the cold weather starts."

"Always the way dear, isn't it? So, he'll be on your doorstep at four and he will have the new boiler with him to fit. It will probably take a couple of hours to do you know. He'll have to drain the whole system."

"That's fine. Thanks."

The Oaks took 10 minutes in the car. But this morning it took virtually 10 minutes to get it started - *again*. When Jane eventually turned into the staff car park she saw that Claire Thomas and her sidekick Jessie McAleavy smoking. Or rather she saw their faces trying to look innocent as a plume of smoke emerged from behind their backs. She would have words with these girls after assembly. They know the rules. Another detention. Stupid things. Teenage smokers never think about the death and disease cigarettes cause. They know the risks. How big do the health warnings have to be on the packs? But they think it will always be someone else who catches the cancer, never them.

"Oh, Mrs Collins," said Sarah at reception, formal as always when the children were within earshot. "Your husband called a few minutes ago. He doesn't do that very often, does he? PCB he says."

"Sorry?"

"PCB – please call back."

"Of course. WDS."

"Sorry?"

"Will do soon," Jane smiled. They were good friends and Sarah appreciated the repartee. "By the way, have you seen Mr Tinkler?"

Jane deposited last night's batch of pupil reports with Sarah for the deputy head and searched her bag for the mobile. Matt must have called while she was driving to school. Jane hadn't turned it on this morning. We should say *pressed* it on, she suddenly thought, because there's nothing to *turn*. She found an empty classroom for privacy.

"Come on Matt. Come on. I've got a class to teach any minute. Answer…."

He did.

"What's wrong Matt? Sarah told me you called. You never call school, well, only when it's urgent…."

"Yes. I'm sorry. It's nothing really. Just phoning to see how you are."

"I'm okay, of course. And I do have some good news. Someone's coming this afternoon to fit a new gas boiler. So thank God we'll be able to have hot water and warm radiators this weekend."

"Are my outlaws still coming tonight?" asked Matt using his

standard joke.

"No. They're coming in the morning. Dad wants to buy us lunch at The Old Cock. Is that all right?"

Matt enjoyed the company of Jane's parents. Bob Straw ran his own successful building business in Chislehurst. Maggie was the highly efficient office manager at the local health authority, a vocation more than a job, because they didn't need the money. They had been faithful partners for 30 years. On a good day, if the roads were reasonably clear, it took about half an hour to drive from Chislehurst to Sevenoaks. They'd either criss-cross the congested road network of London's southerly suburbs or risk a jam on Greater London's infamous M25. It was about the right distance for parents and in-laws to be: close enough for visits, far enough not to cramp the style of, to the Straws, newlyweds. Jane was the eldest of their three girls. "She was born exactly a year to the day after we were married," Bob had often declared proudly over the years, as if he had precise control over the event.

Sarah's observation on reception was accurate; Matt rarely called Jane at school. And she'd only called him at the office once or twice since they'd known each other. After three years of marriage they remained good friends, smiling and laughing together. It was obvious to all who saw them: their body language spoke the language of love. But at work they concentrated fully on their professional lives. Work was for working. They split home from work, the professional from the personal. So Matt's call bothered Jane. He never phoned, "*just to see how you are*". Never. He was being vague. That puzzled Jane. Something was on his mind. And, this time, it was something he wasn't sharing with her.

"Matt, haven't you got anything to be getting on with, because I have," she asked.

"Sure. Loads. We won the business. The client signed the contract and is on her way to Heathrow as we speak as happy as a frog in mud."

"So why *have* you called?"

"I was just wondering exactly how much this new boiler was going to…"

"Oh for God's sake Matt," Jane cut in. "We need a new one. We can't live in the cold and wash in ice-water."

"I know, but with the mortgage and then the extension to pay for…

"Look, Dad has already said he'll only charge us costs. He's not making any profit out of us. He's in no hurry for the money. He didn't want the money in the first place if you remember. It was you who insisted we pay our own way in the world."

"I know. But it's still going to cost at least £50,000. Maybe we should put it off for a few months, perhaps a year or two."

"We can't. It's too late. His men are due to start this Monday. That's one reason why Dad's coming this weekend to help us get everything ready for when they start knocking walls down and digging foundation trenches and all that stuff. Anyway we need the…"

Jane stopped. She changed tack.

"Look, we'll manage. I'll ask Dad if he can hang on for the money. He won't mind."

"No," Matt said firmly. "We've already sponged off your folks too much. It's time we stood on our own two feet."

"Four."

"What?"

"You have two feet. I have two feet. That makes four. Even an English teacher knows that."

"Jane, this is serious. We're going to be left really short. Do you know how much we owe on the credit cards? The interest alone is crippling. We'll have to forget about any holiday next year."

"Matt, it will be all right. Look darling, I've got to go. The kids are getting restless in the corridor."

"Okay. I'll try and get back early. I won't go for the usual Friday-night drink with the team."

"Go. You deserve it after a hard week. I'll see you later." Jane blew a kiss into the phone.

Jane ended the call as Gerry Tinkler walked into the classroom. His large frame filled the door. "Jane, good morning, I didn't know you were in here first period."

"No, I'm not Gerry. I just popped in to make a quick call in the quiet. Our gas boiler decided to pack up and break down on the first frosty day we've had in ages and the car wouldn't start again and...." Tinkler patiently listened to the tale of Jane's domestic difficulties. The departmental head insisted she leaves in good time to ensure the gas engineer gained entry to fit the replacement boiler. During school assembly Jane listened dutifully to the Head Teacher's *Thought for the Day* as he called it, openly admitting to copying the idea from a BBC radio programme. Mr Morrison based his *thought* on this morning's tragic news that several people had died last night in a hospital fire. They were all very old and seriously ill people by all accounts.

"Imagine, children, you had to put a value on a person's life," he said. "Would it have been a greater tragedy if, instead of these elderly people perishing, children would have died? Is an old person more valuable than a young child because they have more life experience? Or is a young person to be valued at a higher price because they have the potential to achieve more in the future? Should we price people the same as cars? Should we pay more for a nice new model with all the latest gizmos from the school showroom like you? Or should we pay just scrap metal value for an old one that's written off? A bit like me, some would say.

"Of course not," Mr Morrison answered. "Because in the generation game of life, the elderly provide experience and sound advice. They've been there, done it, got the t-shirt. And most, but sadly not all, have learnt from their experiences. Your parents have brought you into the world and are bringing you up..."

The Head suddenly stopped. His eyes picked out one boy four or five rows from the front. "Peter Novak, stop talking." He did.

"Chatting with your parents at the last parents' evening, I know your Mum started to have doubts about bringing you into the world and I can see why..." The Head Teacher smiled. It was a cue for the assembly to laugh. It did. And young Peter's face went red.

"As I was saying...you children here today will provide eventually, in turn, another generation so that life's cycle keeps turning. Even you Master Novak could be a father one day," the Head said.

"He doesn't know how to do it Sir..." a pupil, hard to see which one, called out to another burst of laughter and another benign smile from the Head.

"Give him time Packard, give him time. He's only a second year, as you were once." So the wily old Head had identified the wit from the 500 faces in front of him. It impressed Jane.

Mr Morrison then delivered his punch-lines to the silent assembly: "So, whether you're a first year coming to the end of your first term at The Oaks, or you from six-two with A-levels looming next year, whatever someone's age or experience or intelligence or wealth or position, treat them courteously and well. Now some of you will think this is old fashioned. Indeed, it was around 1370 when a churchman called William of Wykeham coined the phrase 'manners maketh man'. But it's just as true today nearly 600 years later. And remember 'man' is used in the species of mankind sense, so don't think you girls can get away without having manners."

The Oaks was a friendly school and the Head was popular. Most mornings he raised a smile among the pupils. "To smile *early* in the day will help you smile *throughout* the day," he often told staff and pupils. His final comment about girls not being exempt from good manners had provoked a few seconds of banter between boys and girls before the teachers shushed them back to silence.

The Head went on to housekeeping matters. Next week is the last before the Christmas break. Cheers from the pupils. Next Friday, last day of term, would be a non-uniform day and money would be raised for one of the school's favourite charities.

"Finally, a serious note, about a potential early death among us," said Mr Morrison. He paused to gain maximum attention. It worked. Total silence. Even the teachers sat up, unaware of what terrible announcement he had to make. "Smoking causes premature death and very painful diseases before death occurs. It has been noted that some pupils, especially the girls, persist in thinking it's cool to smoke. It's not. It's stupid. So stop it. Because the longer you go on, the harder it is to quit."

Morrison closed assembly by announcing that next week there would be an "amnesty" for all pupils who admitted to smoking. A specialist nurse from the health authority would be running a confidential Quit Smoking Clinic in classroom S8 all day Friday, the last day of term. "I strongly recommend those of you who smoke attend to get some help and advice. It's probably the best Christmas present the school could ever give you," he said.

Two girls were caught in the eye-line of Mrs Collins across a sea of pupils as everyone departed the assembly hall. Clinic or detention, now that's the offer she'll put to the pair.

Chapter Five

Wild dogs ripped them apart...

Throwing himself into Project 66 didn't reduce Matt's anxiety about his debt – his debt and Jane's. But she seemed unconcerned about the growing pile of unpaid bills. She'd experienced the cotton-wool security of a comfortable family life: a mum, dad, siblings. No messy divorce, no great tragedy, no painful trauma. Nothing had shaken her confidence in life. Knowing her parents owned a thriving business, a large house in one of London's richest districts and a villa in a few acres of France generated a self-confidence Matt didn't have. He'd have to make it alone. Achieve success and financial security his way. Earn it, not inherit it. Jane lived life knowing a safety net would catch any downfall: the warmth of a close-knit family, the confidence of a bank-balance well in credit. But Matt felt all there would be if he fell off life's tightrope was a deep dark pit.

Matt started to concentrate harder on the strategic public relations plan for Project 66. Even before Jenni Tallow had checked in at London Heathrow for Chicago O'Hare, he'd mapped out the key moves and who would do what. Penny would assist Matt and act as his researcher. The benefits of 22XP would be stressed in the report. Key decision-makers in the regulatory process, and members of various approval committees throughout Europe, would be approached. They need to be fully informed about FFresherFood. This will enable them to approve the chemical process as soon as possible. They must be persuaded it would be wrong to delay and right to approve. In his strategic briefing paper for selected politicians and civil servants in Brussels, Strasbourg and London, Matt wrote: *"The regulatory and licensing authorities throughout Europe should determine that the use of FFresherFood will bring enormous benefits in four areas – medical, environmental, social and commercial. Henderson-Strutt shares the view of specialist scientists that this process should be approved without delay. The extensive research conducted in the USA by the highly reputable AestChem Inc of Chicago, Illinois – celebrating it 150th year of service to industry this year - should provide the confidence to allow FFresherFood-enhanced food into the European Union. The company has completely satisfied the rigorous and comprehensive health and safety requirements of the US Food and Drug Administration and other regulatory bodies."*

In the confidential plan for his client, Matt outlined how Henderson-Strutt would lobby to convince relevant parties in the European Commission that 22XP was necessary. Appropriate British civil servants and key politicians in Westminster would be approached first. If one country within the European Union approved a new food ingredient or process, other countries would often follow without too many questions asked. So the strategy was to strike at home first where the best contacts were close at hand. Whitehall and Westminster are a few minutes walk from Henderson-Strutt's office, with plenty of clubs, pubs and restaurants in between in which to talk.

Business leaders in the food sector, politicians with close connections or family ties to the food business, were also named in Matt's proposed strategy. They would be contacted and encouraged to endorse 22XP. Matt recommended that Henderson-Strutt's Political and Parliamentary Department set up meetings with AestChem's President & CEO and senior directors on a visit to Britain. A handful of politicians and civil servants should also be encouraged, and might appreciate, a "strictly business" visit to Chicago. This would allow them to gain a first-hand scientific review and in-depth insight into the advantages of FFresherFood, as Matt put it. Open tickets would allow them flexibility on their return flights. If *they* decided to take the opportunity to extend the visit and enjoy a short break while in Illinois, that would be *their* decision.

VIP visitations from Europe would go down well with AestChem's hierarchy. You can have all the emails, telephone calls and video conferencing in the world. But as every senior executive knows, nothing works better in building business relationships than meeting face-to-face, talking-the-talk, pressing-the-flesh. Matt's recommended "relationship exchange" would also include a visit by AestChem's senior directors to the Palace of Westminster to meet key Members of Parliament. Henderson-Strutt would naturally facilitate this.

American business executives continue to live in awe of the pomp and ceremony, tradition and history of Parliament. They adore shaking the hand of a Lord or Lady and often become visibly obsequious. For them, to meet an Earl, Viscount or Baron - although they have no idea of their rank in British nobility – impresses. Even an MBE is good enough for most of them. They'll tell all their friends back home at the next dinner party. It was good PR. And a real bonus if you could photograph the hand shake with a presidential-style back slap. "Is that Lord with the booming voice a relative of Her Majesty the Queen?" one New York businessman asked Matt at a Parliamentary cocktail party last year. The pompous peer had been ranting about "the terrible television one sees in America". No, he was not a relative of Her Majesty, Matt pointed out. "He's what we call a New Peer," Matt said helpfully. "He's been recently appointed to the reconstituted House of Lords in Tony Blair's attempt to make it a 'House of the People'."

Henderson-Strutt enjoyed close connections with several members of royal families. A prince or princess could pick up fees of a few thousand for attending a reception – more if they had to make a small presentation or cut a ribbon. As one complained to

Matt, "Maintaining an old stately pile and a few hundred acres in the country cost money you know. Her Majesty isn't as generous as one may think."

Matt's strategy document made clear there was no case for publicity prior to approval of 22XP. Pre-launch media stories about FFresherFood would simply cause unnecessary public concern. Reporters and feature writers, Matt knew, would concentrate on the theoretical risk instead of writing about the tangible benefits. There would be no balanced reporting. The public relations business is not always about promoting products or personalities. Only the naïve believe that. Much of Peter and Matt's work in issues and crisis management was keeping corporations and people *out* of the limelight. Strangling a story before it breathed is a vital skill in PR. Spin is as much about silence as stories. "Silence is not only golden, it's seldom misquoted," was an adage Matt often used when handling sensitive situations. The avoidance of media coverage was central to Matt's proposed PR strategy for Europe's discreet introduction of 22XP.

When someone's experiencing a problem, unless there is a need to inform the public or can't avoid the headlines, it is easier to handle without reporters blocking the phone lines and pouring over the organisation like hungry rats in a grain store. There's no point in running the risk of good publicity turning bad. Matt didn't want AestChem's executives under pressure from a press posse.

Over the years Matt had witnessed the fear induced by the stress of reporters and photographers door-stepping clients' homes. You go to a back room in the hope of finding calm to talk and think. And what do you see? More hacks scaling the garden wall. Curtains have to be drawn because the odd snapper puts his lens on your window and the flash scares the kids and sets the dog off barking. The police try to keep the press pack back. But reporters have far more experience at getting round the cops than the cops have of stopping them. Once, when Matt was working with a TV personality under siege after his tragic story broke, he witnessed a £20 note slipped into a cop's hand to allow an envelope to be dropped through the letterbox. It contained a bid to buy the story from the person under siege.

"We want to tell your side of the story," was a popular opening gambit from the papers, and not only from the tabloids. Broadsheets and magazines enter the story auction too. *"At least £25,000 cash for your exclusive. You can say whatever you want. We'll help you get the rest of the press off your back. Phone my mobile soonest on 1234567 to discuss the offer. Ivor Story, The Daily Hogwash."*

Sometimes clients fell for it, despite Matt's advice. They soon discovered the myth perpetuated by Calvin Coolidge that "all publicity is good publicity". The former US President was wrong. Peter and Matt knew victims of bad press. One committed suicide. Several thought about it. Careers had been ruined. Relationships shattered. Families split. Confidence lost.

Henderson-Strutt would also spread stories for many of its clients. "They want ink," Peter would say. When promoting new drugs in Europe on behalf of pharmaceutical companies, Henderson-Strutt's PR strategy was to create advance media stories about a possible new medicine. They would raise awareness in the media about the medical problem. In his early days at the company Matt had worked on cholesterol and heart disease, asthma, diabetes, impotence and migraine. Then, surprise surprise, this new medicine mentioned in the articles offered cure or relief. Matt called it Problem-Solution Publicity. Someone or some organisation had a problem, then Henderson-Strutt's client offered the solution. Bring the two together and you win the PR game.

Matt once explained to Penny, "The way it works in the drugs industry is simple: create demand. Sufferers and the medical community at large read the story in a magazine or hear about the new treatment on radio or TV. They ask their doctors for it. Demand. The doctors question the pharmacists and their professional bodies about the drug's availability. Demand. They all quiz the department

45

of health in each country. Demand. They ask the various medicines agencies where is this new drug and why the delay for approval. Demand. Then the agencies get bounced into giving the medicine their seal of approval so the patients can be prescribed the medicine. Demand met. Everyone is happy, especially the shareholders in pharmaceutical stock."

"But sometimes the authorities delay a drug's approval," said Penny.

"They do that to flex their muscles, play hard to get."

"Then what happens?"

"One of two routes, depending on the whispers in the corridors of power. Some companies rest up and give the medicine approval agency breathing space. Others pile on the publicity pressure and strangle them. The companies usually win. Big companies have big influence. Jobs and money, or the promise of jobs and money, equals votes."

Matt worked through lunch on the proposal. He and Peter would fly to Chicago, probably next week, and present the plan for approval by AestChem's bosses. He added two additional themes to his report: the HMG principle and the now fashionable CRM – cause related marketing. It is important to seek the High Moral Ground in gaining speedy acceptance of FFresherFood, 22XP, in Europe. The moral grounds were laid out. Food wastage would be dramatically cut. And if poor people in developed countries would have greater access to cheaper fruit and vegetables, their diets would be improved. With one in four Americans and one in five Western Europeans defined by doctors as clinically obese, surely fresher-tasting fruit and vegetables would help save lives by lowering cholesterol and curbing the death rate from heart attacks.

Matt knew every major company in the world now claims a commitment to corporate social responsibility. Their annual reports routinely have a page or two telling everyone how the company cares for its workforce and contributes to the communities in which they operate. They publish codes of conduct and business principles to reinforce their commitment. Try finding a Fortune 250 or FTSE 100 company that does not "care for the environment" or desire "sustainable development" to "minimise the environmental impact of our operations".

As Matt often said to Penny and others, "Corporate caring is big business".

Firms that vacuum fish leaving the sea barren of cod say it. Mining monopolies that leave craters in the earth say it. Drug companies that claim they want to fight disease and stop pain say it – and they will, providing the patient can pay the price of their pills. Supermarkets say it while selling over-packaged products and reject the smallest imperfections on perfectly edible fruit and vegetables. The European Union and the US Government say it while subsidising farmers to grow surpluses keeping farmers in the Third World in poverty. Chemical companies say it while releasing emissions into the atmosphere and rivers. Food companies say it while filling their products with fat and sugar and salt. And every day and night above our heads thousands of aircraft criss-cross the skies gushing out fuel moving mange tout from Kenya to Iceland, strawberries in June from California to London, apples in September from New Zealand to "The Garden of England" in Kent.

Matt's thoughts were broken by the phone.

"How's it going?"

"It's fine Peter," Matt said.

"Good. Chicago Wednesday. Back red-eye Friday morning. Jenni called from Heathrow just before she took off. Said Wednesday's okay for her directors and the lawyers."

"No problem."

"She's quite a looker, eh?"

"Jenni? Yes, I suppose so."

"Probably a bit ripe for you Matt. But wait until you're approaching 50."

"She's not even in her forties."

"No, but I am. How old would you say she is? 35?"

"Plus a year or two, Peter."

"That would be my guess too. Anyway, where you at with the proposal?"

"I'm just gathering my thoughts on the moral ground argumentation," Matt reported. "I thought I'd make the case for some cause related marketing too."

"What did you have in mind?"

"Well, the moral ground stuff is pretty obvious. Food wastage would be dramatically cut. Good fresh fruit and vegetables would be more affordable for poorer people. Even the overweight rich might be persuaded to eat more fresh fruit and vegetables instead of all that saturated fat."

"Sounds great Matt," enthused Peter. "FFresherFood kills cholesterol and saves lives and helps the poor. Marvellous!"

"We should also point out that fresh fruit and vegetables is the natural way of getting essential vitamins and minerals into people rather than devouring artificial supplements."

"Well that's great too, as long as our pharmaceutical clients don't find out we're recommending flushing their vitamin pills down the metaphorical drain."

"We need to check AestChem's scientific data to see if the treated product retains more vitamins and minerals compared with conventional treatment and storage methods," said Matt.

"Yes. Good idea. Email Jenni and ask her. She's the type who'll go directly to the office when she touches down, so you'll have a reply by the morning."

"I think we can also suggest that FFresherFood will allow people in the Third World better access to fresh produce. What do you think?"

"Good one Matt. Don't see why not. It will make everyone's conscience feel better. Wow. So we're helping reduce Third World starvation too. This just gets better!"

"And I was thinking of developing this line into our cause related marketing recommendation. You know, get fast-track approval for 22XP's use in one of the African countries to feed refugees or something along these lines."

"Good job Matt. Get it all down and see you at six in The Long Yard for a drink."

"Not tonight Peter I'm afraid. Promised Jane I'd be home early. Domestic trouble."

"What? What's wrong? Had a row? You always look really happy together..."

"No. No, Peter. Not that sort of trouble. Gas boiler. Bloody thing broke down this morning. Costs a packet to replace."

"Just one drink? Just a peanut or two?"

"Sorry Peter, my wife awaits."

"Well if I had a wife that looked as stunning as yours I suppose I'd be on the fast train home. Know what I mean?"

"Yes, well..."

"I'm serious Matt. You'll have to keep a close eye on her. There must be a lot of blokes out there sniffing around a woman as beautiful as Jane, you watch out."

"Don't worry Peter. She's a one man woman."

"No such thing," he quipped before he put down the phone.

Matt tapped in the finishing touches to part one of his report and recommendations for AestChem before leaving the office. Sections two and three could be sketched out at home over the weekend and completed by Monday afternoon. Unless another client crisis came along, he should also have the presentation ready by Tuesday lunchtime. He was determined to complete both the report and the presentation before travelling to America. Matt never worked while flying - too many prying eyes. Wednesday's flight to Chicago would be reserved for reading a good book, unless Peter was in the mood for talking, then he'd have to listen.

* * *

That evening Peter was in the mood to talk. Sadly Matt could not be his audience because of some silly domestic nonsense. But Peter knew where to go for company. He left the office, turned up his collar against the cold wind, and strolled around the corner to The Long Yard. He ordered one bottle of full-bodied Shiraz and one crisp dry Sauvignon Blanc. It seemed half of Henderson-Strutt's employees completed their working week in the bar - gossiping about the half who were not.

Peter took the two bottles and walked over to his colleagues bunched around several small tables. They shuffled up to make room for him. Some of his team and other staff listened to Peter the PR war-horse going on about past clients from hell, triumphs and the odd failure. Penny Taylor and the other bright young things, as Peter called them, stayed for a while before splitting to restaurants and clubs. He was invited, as always. But he declined, as usual. And they never insisted or asked a second time.

Alone among the abandoned tables and vacant chairs Peter called for a bottle of The Yard's best red, whatever it was. As one of three remaining customers Peter's order wasn't long in arriving. The couple in the corner were making the most of each other before catching the last train home. Another glance at the watch, another last kiss, another squeeze of the hand, a rush to the station. In the morning they'd both tell their spouses the pressure was really on at the office.

The Bordeaux turned out to be an excellent Pomerol, although by this time his palate had lost its usual refinement to detect the precise blend of Merlot, Cabernet Franc, Cabernet Sauvignon and Malbec the château had used in this '98. He'd celebrate the AestChem deal alone. Sod the kids. He'd drink as much as he liked. He wasn't driving or relying on public transport. Bert with the company Mercedes would know where to find him at closing time. The chauffeur would drive him into the star-lit frosty night. Bert wouldn't wear his hat. It wouldn't matter.

Peter Jones, the PR guru who saved the reputations of the disreputable, would sleep all the way home. Or try to. And tonight, in the seconds before slumber, Peter would believe he could sense the scent of Jenni Tallow on the leather seat, his temporary bed. Her perfume should evoke pleasant dreams. But would it repel his nightmares?

The boy's burnt face would appear again: one face among so many faces. Children, they were all children, the villagers said, at least thirty of them. Nobody knows if they died before they were set alight. Not all of them had gunshot wounds. But it was impossible to detect the cause of death. Not that how they died was important, but why they died, and who slaughtered them. And even the answer to those questions didn't matter now. Questions, answers, they have no use their families said. Knowledge of death doesn't return loved ones to life.

Wild dogs and vultures had ripped them apart, devouring the blackened flesh, crunching their bones, scattering the evidence. And whatever the animals abandoned, the monsoon rain washed away. Ne Win Maung's face would be there, a smiling face in a dog-eared photograph his mother's outstretched hand held in front of Peter to witness. Ne Win would feature in his nightmare if it returned tonight. For over fifteen years Ne Win had smiled at Peter. Not every night, but many. And always Ne Win's face disintegrated as flames engulfed the picture. Peter had tried all the cures to break the spell. No wine, no woman, no whisky, no work could take that burning face away.

Soldiers helicoptered Peter to the Chin Hills overlooking India. The Burmese generals insisted this atrocity was the work of communist rebels. All these inhuman acts were the work of the insurgents, they said. The rebels would be defeated. For five years Peter secretly tried to help the regime. It paid well. And the British Government had been grateful for his feedback. He'd supported the country's name change from Burma to Myanmar. A new name, a new image, he'd said. He'd advised the State Law and Order Restoration

Council to leave Aung San Sun Kyi alone. But they arrested her. They made the opposition leader a living martyr and her Nobel Peace Prize confirmed her status in the eyes of the world.

He'd counselled them not to force children to work digging trenches for the oil pipeline. But as their parents worked at gunpoint what else could the children do? In the capital, Yangon, although everyone still called it Rangoon, he'd talked about drafting a human rights policy with the Prime Minister. But the generals were in charge of everyday practice. Peter was forced to turn a blind eye, pretended to believe he was doing more good than harm. It made the work easier and his conscience lighter.

* * *

The 18.35 Charing Cross to Sevenoaks was only 15 minutes late. Not bad for Friday night in winter. Matt's eyes had suffered enough close-up work and he relaxed them by peering into the distance through the train window. The *Evening Standard* remained folded in his lap. Reading the news would remind him of his clients and their problems, and he wanted time to himself. He watched Lowry-like figures in rooms without closed curtains, the uninhibited residents of railway-track homes. Tree lights and street decorations had started to brighten journeys home as the month moved closer to Christmas. And at home tonight there would be hot water and warm radiators and a gentle Jane.

But there would be another bill waiting its turn to be paid. He needed money. More money. Money to build a better life, to give Jane everything she wanted, to give himself a safety net. Matt was paid what most people would call a good salary, above the national average. But good wasn't good enough. He didn't want to be Bill Gates. He wasn't seeking billions. But he needed to make more. And quick. He needed to get ahead and have spare cash after all the debts and costs of daily living were paid. He wanted to cut the anxiety, break the treadmill of debt and reduce the pain of poverty. Not the poverty of hunger and homelessness. Not the poverty of the Third

World. But the relative poverty of an affluent world, where a second hand car makes you a second class citizen.

An icy wind blew the sweat off Matt's face as the carriage door next to him opened and passengers departed. The next stop would be his. It would be time to end his daydreams and begin walking home.

Chapter Six

Porno movie...

They kiss. They hold each other. With those extra seconds of touch and eye contact they continue to capture the romance after three years of being together. Not yet that staleness, that boredom of familiarity, that ritual of relationship routine.

Jane and Matt part, although stay close. He places the briefcase on the breakfast bar and removes his raincoat and suit jacket. The tie had been ripped away already. She kicks off her shoes and bends down behind the door aware he's watching and her skirt is tight.

She picks up three letters, one leaflet offering half-price double-glazing, and the local free newspaper. Two of the envelopes look suspiciously like bills. They can wait until after Christmas. She slips them inside the pages of the newspaper to remove later.

"The gasman finished about five o'clock," Jane told Matt. "Everything seems to be working fine."

"It's still a bit chilly."

"Give it a chance to warm up. The house was freezing remember. When the water's hot I want to enjoy a nice long soak to get over the coldwater torture I suffered this morning. My hair needs a good wash too."

"Did he say how much it was going to cost? Did he leave the bill?"

"No, they'll put it in the post."

"Didn't he give you any idea? They must charge well over a

thousand."

"Matt, stop worrying. We'll manage. We can't boil water on the hob and live in the lounge with overcoats and woolly socks."

"Yes, I know. But…"

"But nothing. We needed a new boiler Matt," she said in her teacher's firm but friendly voice.

Two hours earlier Matt had been in central London working on a master plan for one of the world's largest chemical companies. His ideas would be accepted and acted upon. His professional confidence and experience left him in no doubt. And when his strategy succeeds almost every citizen of Europe would be exposed to 22XP. Cancer was only a theoretical risk, according to the company. In reality the risk didn't exist, or was so low it was almost impossible to detect. But Matt accepted the way it would be introduced would mean millions of people in Europe would not have the opportunity to assess the risk for themselves. Ignorance denies choice for consumers, Matt understood. But knowledge and debate would cause delay. For the greater good it was better to get 22XP approved. The gatekeepers and guardians of Brussels and Strasbourg, Westminster and Whitehall, would decide on Europe's behalf. They believe they know best. On the remote chance an eagle-eyed journalist in Brussels picks up 22XP's approval for use on certain food imports, then Matt's proactive plan will be implemented. They'll tell the story. Promote the benefits. Fight any scares. Resist negative headlines. But the odds are against such disclosure. 22XP will be introduced - quietly. The Brussels bureaucrats will note its approval. It will be on the record somewhere in a document as a testament to their openness. There will be one sentence in a long paragraph inside a complex chapter within a lengthy document published alongside several volumes of similar tedious material.

That was work. This is home, a small semi in Sevenoaks 25 miles southeast from the City of Westminster, but a world away. Matt was just another ordinary young married man worried about paying the debts we owe in life for living.

In the world of public relations issues and crisis consultancy, the few who practice this art have dramatic impact on public, government and corporate policy. But their public profile remains low. They provide the script for the chief executive to speak, the plan for the firm to follow, the message for the masses to swallow. They are the voice behind the spokespeople, the mind behind the mouth. They operate in the shadows of power because exposure would interfere with their practice: a spy exposed cannot spy.

Jane enjoyed her bath while Matt drove to the takeaway. An Indian, Mexican or Chinese had become a Friday evening tradition. Tonight was no different, although they were both at home earlier than usual. Matt had missed Friday night's drinking session with colleagues. Jane had to cancel her regular gym workout. She hadn't been for a few weeks anyway. Matt knew that by now at The Long Yard voices would be raised and slurred, the language adult and the gossip more outrageous. Inhibitions lost, affairs starting, relationships ending. Those people who on Monday vowed never to smoke again had been tempted back to the Marlboro. Matt, who'd never had to quit smoking because he'd never started, liked to remind them of Mark Twain's wit: "Smoking is easy to give up, I've done it hundreds of times."

Chinese noodles were laid out on the coffee table in the lounge. He'd emptied the large teak fruit bowl of two old apples and filled it with prawn crackers. A muscadet had been chosen from one of several bottles in the wine rack. It was still cold enough to drink, resistant to the warmth now radiating through their home. But after pouring two large glasses Matt placed the bottle in the fridge.

"That looks lovely and I'm famished," said Jane as she walked barefoot towards the table and knelt down.

"You start," shouted Matt from the kitchen.

She had. Two handfuls of crackers had already been devoured.

"What was your day like?" she asked between bites.

"Good. Peter and I met the client from Chicago – oh, I've got to go there next week for a couple of days – and I've more or less finished the plan. And yours?"

Jane realised immediately his question about her day was simply a deflection from his. Although they shared an intimate uninhibited relationship, Matt rarely talked details about his work-life with her. She respected this and so followed his cue.

"The kids are getting excited about Christmas. This time next week I'll be on holiday for over two weeks. Yippee!"

"All right for some. I'll have to work on Christmas Eve and go back after Boxing Day. In fact I might have to…"

"I thought the office was shut," she interrupted, raising her voice to make sure Matt could hear across the hallway.

"It is. But one of our clients has a little problem that might need careful handling on Christmas Day itself."

"Oh Matt, you're joking."

"I wish."

As he walked in the lounge he turned the dimmer switch. As the lights lowered Jane noticed Matt had lit two candles in front of the fireplace mirror. Each small flame cast its reassuring light across the room and into their life together.

"Are you saying you have to work over Christmas?" softening her voice to reflect the candlelight.

"It depends how big the story blows and if Peter can handle the problem alone."

Not wanting to spoil the intimacy of home with the intrusion of work, and not expecting an answer, she asked about "the problem" anyway.

"You won't believe it."

"Try me."

"It's about a porno film."

"What?" She was as surprised by Matt's willingness to talk work details as the subject matter itself.

58

"A client, by *accident* I should add straight away, has just distributed a pornographic movie. And I think the mistake will be exposed on Christmas Day when all the presents are opened."

"You're joking."

"Nope. And what's worse, they've released over 300 copies directly to media outlets as a video and DVD press release."

"You *are* joking," Jane said again, her mouth remaining open in astonishment.

"Thankfully so far, although it's early days, no journalist has bothered to view it. There have been no calls about it. Not one. In fact I believe most of the newsdesks and feature departments have dumped it in the bin."

"That's incredible," said Jane who had now started on the noodles with chopsticks. "You would think they'd love to watch a bit of naughty. So if it hasn't come out by now why do you think it's going to blow up on Christmas Day?"

"Because I'm sure some of the journalists will have given copies to their younger nieces, nephews or kid brothers and sisters."

"I don't understand, sorry. I'm not getting this. Why would they give a blue movie to kids?"

"It's not *labelled* as hard core. This movie should be about a very famous children's cartoon character. It's a promotional programme to push the character and the firm's brands. It's packaged like a movie for toddlers."

"That's not a joke," Jane said speaking with her mouth half full forgetting the manners her parents had taught her.

"The film reproduction company that duplicates from the master tape got our client's tape mixed up with... well... one of their more suspect customers."

"I don't believe it," said Jane.

"Well it's true."

"Didn't they check the duplicates?"

"Clearly not. And guess where the reproduction company's office is? Right in the middle of London's red light district - Soho."

Matt piled his plate high to compensate for skipping lunch. He'd been too busy on AestChem's plan to eat. Apart from half a croissant at the breakfast meeting he'd had nothing. As he sat back to eat he noticed Jane's dressing gown cling to the contours of her neck and breasts. The satin had absorbed the damp from her wet hair and formed a second skin. The slight scent of shampoo blended with her usual perfume. Matt relaxed as he watched his wife, sat like a cat on the rug at his feet.

"We're supposed to be going to mum and dad's for Christmas Day," she complained, softly, "Can't Peter handle it? His wife and kids have all left home, haven't they?"

"Depends how big the porno fiasco blows. You can just imagine the scene. Gran, Grandad, family and friends gathered around the telly just after the Queen gives her Commonwealth Speech. Little Johnny insists on playing the cartoon video - an unexpected present from uncle Alan, normally a tight-fisted reporter on the local paper. Then the kid presses *play* and – shock horror – the porn show starts."

"Just think."

"I am."

"What fun."

"A public relations disaster of epic proportions. Moral outrage. The *Daily Mail* malevolent. *The Telegraph* in a tantrum. The BBC gloating over another company's cock up and..."

"Literally..."

"And Jane...please stop giggling... news is often hard to find at Christmas to fill the papers. This could go front page. A top multi-million pound children's brand ruined. Imagine the red faces. A nice cuddly cartoon image tarnished by links to the hard core porn industry. And we at Henderson-Strutt have to advise and help this company under attack by the armed forces of an outraged media."

"Will it hit the headlines?" she asked, realising that Matt would have to be in London on Christmas Day missing the grand turkey lunch with Mum, Dad and her sisters and their partners, two widowed aunts and uncle Michael. "Will it be *exposed*?" she asked, giggling at her choice of word.

"You never know. But it could. We always plan for double the trouble, twice the pain in half the time. That's my job."

Jane could see Matt's mind travelling back to London - without needing a rail journey. She didn't want this relaxed moment to switch into the tense reality of his work. She didn't want this off-guard banter to transform into what Matt called a "message development workshop" for his unfortunate client. She didn't want a blinding spotlight to break the magic of this delicate candlelight. Tonight had to be special.

"Have another glass Matt," she offered her own glass before tucking into the sweet and sour. "Shall I pour it for you?"

"No. You stay down. I'll get another glass. What about you? You've hardly touched yours."

"I'll have some more later," she said, lying, because she hadn't taken a sip.

"Anyway, if Peter needs help on the porno crisis he'll call and I'll drive up to the office from the outlaws," Matt called from the kitchen while opening the fridge door. "It will only take half an hour from Chislehurst on Christmas Day. There won't be any traffic on the roads."

Matt returned and sat behind Jane with her wet shoulders held between his legs. They were looking over the empty plates towards the TV.

After a few seconds of silence, Matt asked, "Why does everyone look at a television screen even when it's switched off? It's like a magnet for the eyes, although sometimes it's more interesting off than on."

Jane offered her theory. "TV empties the mind, if some of the kids at school are anything to go by. The kids who watch telly most have the least in their heads. If you compare reading to radio to watching

TV they seem to remember more from reading than…"

Whatever she was saying, the words faded away from Matt's attention. Jane's wet hair had penetrated his suit trousers and his thighs were damp. The suit would need pressing before Chicago; Americans respected a hard crease in trousers. Jane's head stretched back into his lap and her natural blonde hair looked black, darkened by the damp. Matt's left hand moved the wine to his lips. The other held Jane's shoulder and a finger found her neck to stroke. Her legs extended forward from under her body, supple despite missing tonight's gym session. Her pink gown opened slightly at the waist as her hands reached to meet behind Matt's neck. She drew his head forward and bowed her own so his lips could find the back of her neck after making an opening in the strands of her hair.

"Matt…" she whispered.

He couldn't reply. His lips were busy moving slowly around her neck to the front, gently biting near her throat.

"Matt…"

Matt managed to mumble something while struggle to find a surface within arms length to stand his empty wine glass.

"Is this the right moment?"

Both hands now were engaged exploring softer parts of Jane's body beneath the silk. "It seems right to me."

"Hang on a minute," she said softly while gently pushing away and turning to face Matt.

"What's wrong?"

"Nothing. Nothing's wrong. Everything's right."

"Well I'd just like to keep feeling…" he said reaching down.

"I'm pregnant."

You dream. Imagine. Play the scene over and over. Devise clever lines to say. These moments in life we think about and prepare for. Then, when they really happen, real life isn't like the rehearsal. Most remember the moment, the big events: Kennedy's assassination, outbreak of war, man on moon, Concorde's crash in Paris, Lennon's death, September 11, Saddam's statue toppling, the Russian school siege. Then bigger personal events happen - like discovering your wife is pregnant - and all your visualisation turns out wrong.

Matt's mind moved rapidly in overdrive. But it went nowhere. A hundred emotions rocked his body, confused his mind. He wanted to cry out "No. Nooooo! But he had to play the role his imagination had rehearsed. His instinct was fear. But his love for Jane demanded expressions of happiness. He smiled for Jane. But inside his stomach tightened in fear.

Sliding from the sofa to the rug to meet Jane face to face on his knees, he pulled her close. She thought it was Matt's love and joy. It was. But it wasn't absolute, unconditional. Matt was buying time. By holding her so tight he could look over her shoulder away from her face. Eyes tell the truth more than the mouth. Eyes reveal the truth when the mouth lies.

He had to prevent Jane looking into his eyes when he said it was great news. And it was a great act. But Matt had other thoughts. Bad timing. Kids cost. Can't afford it. No time to spare from work. Jesus. Christ. Damn. Pressure. Why the hell didn't she tell me she'd stopped taking the pill? Why didn't she say she was trying to get pregnant? Why the secrecy? Doesn't a man have a right to know he's been used to father a child, especially from his wife? It's man abuse. But his love for Jane was – for now - stronger than his fear of fatherhood.

Jane held Matt's hands. "You must have known. You've always been so in tune with my body. I can't believe you missed the obvious fact I've not had a period for nearly 10 weeks. I was waiting for you to comment on it, to see how long you'd go before asking."

"I suppose…"

"Haven't you noticed a little swelling and tenderness in this department?" she asked looking down at her breasts. "Haven't you noticed I go for a pee more often?"

"You've not had morning sickness," he said in his defence.

"Actually I have. Not much thankfully. But it usually starts after you've left for work when I get up."

For now Matt tried to suppress his worries and share Jane's joy. He was in shock, real shock. He was genuinely pleased *for her*. He was a little proud of himself too, but not much. This news brought with it a sense of responsibility that he couldn't or didn't want to face right now. A woman can look after herself. Jane's independent. She could survive without him. A baby couldn't.

This child, his child, her child, *their* child, meant someone would be dependent on him. He'd never experienced such responsibility before. This baby had taken something away from him. A baby would be born, a new life created. But part of Matt would die, or at least lost for a long time, perhaps forever. When does your child become *not* your child? Never. When are the physical and emotional ties broken between parent and child? Never. When would Matt feel free and have his own body, flesh and blood unshared, exclusive?

This baby was a burden already, not one minute after hearing of its existence. The embryo had turned into a foetus. Ten weeks old she said. It would be nearly the size of a plum inside Jane's body and already loved, fed, warmed and protected by her. It would look *human*. It would be developing separate fingers and toes. And eyelids. Little ears too. How could something so small generate such inner turmoil in a grown man? For Jane's sake he couldn't share his anxiety with her. He would have to play Happy Father, especially tomorrow when Jane's parents arrive for the weekend. And when *it* is born Matt knows he will have to coo and smile and play Modern Man. He'll attend the birth of course and be supportive and say all the right things men in today's world are supposed to say. He'll play dad. The baby will be beautiful like its mother. He'll have to hold it and smile into its face.

They kiss. They hold each other. Matt places both hands on Jane's stomach, tenderly, more tenderly than usual.

"So, it's in there?" he whispers.

"Yes. Well, unless two tests, a scan and a doctor are wrong,"

His hands start to move slowly over Jane's soft skin, surveying the extra sensuality of her new shape and state.

"There's no need for this any more," Jane says warmly, smiling, knowing what Matt wanted. "I've already got what I want from you right here."

But Matt needed Jane. She readily gave him warmth and comfort and love, allowing Matt to share part of her inner body close to their child with tiny fingers and tiny toes.

For a while Matt found a new excitement and temporary relief in Jane's arms.

Afterwards, Jane slept like a baby, with her baby. Matt didn't.

Chapter Seven

Woodland inheritance...

Sheila Valerie Chamber was found dead in bed. The post mortem report said Miss Chamber, 89, spinster of the Parish of Maidstone, Kent, had died approximately forty-eight hours before been found. No suspicious circumstances could be detected, according to the coroner.

Neighbour Miss Campbell from Rose Cottage found Miss Chamber's body. The milkman had reported four pints of untouched milk in the porch so Miss Campbell decided to turn Miss Marple and investigate. She fetched her spare key in case Sheila had fallen and couldn't open the door. It wasn't needed. The back door was wide open and the house freezing. Miss Campbell called out as she cautiously entered the kitchen. "Sheila? Sheila, dear, are you all right? It's me, Alice." The milkman waited nervously at the door, anxious to get on with his round. Collection day, you see, cash in hand. A radio was playing classical music somewhere. Sheila didn't have a TV. Never had. She'd had a conflict with the TV Licensing people who refused to believe her. They kept sending her threatening letters demanding a license fee payment.

Sheila's body looked cold and felt like ice. Alice had long-forgotten how cold the dead feel. She was shocked - and secretly ashamed - to find her friend this way. Why hadn't she called in for a chat those last couple of days? Her cottage and Sheila's house were the only properties for two miles along the track through the woods.

But Alice was sure someone had visited Sheila two days before her body was found; a friend from town perhaps, a relative, a workman. The coroner asked Alice, very politely, if she might have been "a little confused" about the time of the "alleged" visit. And she admitted sometimes days got mixed up. "But I definitely saw a car parked outside Sheila's house *one* evening – and no alleged about it," she'd told him firmly. "I suppose it could have been a van," she added quietly. It was night. And, yes, she confirmed there are no streetlights down her country lane. The coroner made a note.

The neighbours should have relied on each other more. But Sheila had an independent streak. She also used heat sparingly and in winter the house always felt chilly. That was one reason why Alice didn't go round as often in the cold months. Her feet would turn to blocks of ice by the time she left. Sheila preferred an extra cardigan to extra on her fuel bill. It was a big house for one person, and difficult to keep warm and dry. Sheila died in bed fully clothed wearing gloves and her woolly hat. Even her cats – at least ten of them - couldn't keep her body warm. The coroner declared "death by natural causes". Heart failure. There was no point in distressing Miss Campbell or the few remaining relatives of this eccentric old lady by saying "hypothermia". Anyway, the cold was only a "possible contributory factor", according to the pathologist's report.

* * *

Jane enjoyed a refreshing sleep and woke before Matt. He'd suffered a fitful night. On Saturday's she usually went downstairs first to put the kettle on. Tea was now completely revolting to her thanks to the pregnancy. Coffee tasted even worse. The power of hormones, she'd begun to acknowledge. But she would make Matt a coffee in a minute and wake him shortly because they needed to go shopping before her parents arrived. After drinking what was described on the carton as freshly squeezed orange juice – with a sell-by date six weeks away - Jane went into the lounge and opened the curtains to the dark of early December.

A figure, heavily dressed to insulate him from the cold, started to cross the road away from Jane's house, as if her drawing the curtains had urged him to move. It looked like he'd been waiting, perhaps for a lift to the rail station. Maybe he was a local resident she didn't recognise. Most neighbours in London's home counties are strangers. Thinking no more of it Jane started clearing the debris from last night's takeaway.

She was so pleased that Matt was clearly delighted at the news she announced last night. He'll make a great dad. Jane couldn't explain it, and she struggled to find the word, but she felt...complete... wholesome...rounded...at the prospect of motherhood. As if a final piece in the jigsaw of life was about to slot into place. And last night with Matt was special. There was extra tenderness, a special sensuality, an intimate intensity she had never experienced before. The mind and the soul and the body seemed as one: two bodies, one being, and now three lives - together. The baby added another dimension to love.

Jane grabbed a pile of old magazines and newspapers to throw into the rubbish bin when two buff envelopes fell onto the carpet. "Hell, I forgot about those," she whispered. She opened them expecting bills. One was. She tucked it behind the breadbin alongside several other requests for payment. The second contained a letter from Moles & Moles Solicitors, written in that copperplate script solicitors use to add respectability to their profession. Looking at the letter she now realised it was addressed to Matt but, in her haste to open it, hadn't noticed. Anyway, it was too late to tuck back into the envelope she'd ripped open. The opening line of the solicitor's letter read: *We are acting for and on behalf of The Last Will and Testament of Sheila Valerie Chamber of Bower House, King's Wood, near Maidstone. We are obliged to inform you...*

"Wake up Matt, wake up. Quick."

He had no choice. Jane was bouncing on the bed.

"Read this. Just read this."

He did, slowly at first, until he realised the letter's importance.

"Your aunt really was mad," said Jane as Matt digested the news. "What's the point of leaving all that money to a cat sanctuary and the RSPCA?"

"Beats me. I can't understand it." Matt rubbed his hair with both hands to make sure he was fully awake.

"Well it's her money – *was* hers – to dispose of as she liked," said Jane.

Matt was bolt-upright in bed now. "I know. But how stupid. That house is going to be sold off to provide even more funds for cats. It's in a decrepit state. Last time I was up there it looked like it needed a new roof, windows, everything. It was draughty and damp. But it's a big house in a good two acres. What really annoys me is that someone will snap it up, do it up then sell it on for a fortune, you watch."

"But what's this she's left you?" Jane asked reading over his shoulder.

Matt tried again to turn legal language into understandable English. He read aloud, slowly, as if this would assist the translation of legalise: "It seems…her 260 acres of woodland… are bequeathed in trust… to me… until my death and thereafter my progeny in equal part ownership…"

"Wow, that's well timed considering little one here," Jane interrupted patting her tummy and bouncing on the bed.

He stayed serious: "…part ownership…for me and my children for 99 years."

After his third reading the solicitor's letter was clear: Matt and any of his children and their children were the new owners of 260 acres of woodland currently managed by a forestry company on a renewable three yearly contract. But he must comply with his Aunt Sheila's strict conditions. The woods were part of Kent's picturesque North Downs and no building permission could be granted. He could not sell it, whole, nor any lot or parcel of woodland – well, unless he lived that long - for 99 years.

"I knew she was reasonably well off, although she always lived as if she hadn't two pennies to rub together. But I didn't realise she was so bloody wealthy," Matt said. "And the silly woman has left nearly £200,000 - in bloody cash - in bloody cash, to cats. What's the point of doing that?"

He sounded annoyed. He was.

"She liked cats," Jane answered, not helping.

"I know. The place was infested with 'em. They stank the place out and bred like rabbits."

"Bet she didn't have any mice around the place," Jane smiled. I remember her saying she preferred cats to men. "She used to say 'they're easier than men to look after. They wash more, smell less, eat less and make less mess'."

Matt wasn't listening. "And that house will sell for a packet. But why didn't she leave the money or at least the house to her brother? Or to my mother? Or even to me as her favourite nephew?"

"You were her *only* nephew," Jane quipped.

"Same difference. She liked me. She always liked me. You witnessed that for yourself when we visited."

"Yes. But we hadn't seen her for... what... a couple of years?"

"I know, there's never time." Matt regretted not making the time.

"But isn't her brother senile in a nursing home on his last legs? And your mother always says Sheila and her haven't got on for years. Did they have a row or something?"

"Don't know to this day why they fell out with each other. They were once really close. We used to spend weeks up there every holiday. I played everywhere in those woods as a kid. I suppose that's why she left them to me. Now I think about it, Aunt Sheila would actually say go and play in *your* woods. I didn't realise how significant that was at the time."

"You wouldn't, would you?" Jane acknowledged.

Matt mulled over the family history with Jane. Aunt Shelia's

Bower House had been his grandparent's home since the 1920s. Aunt Shelia was the eldest. Then came "the boy" as he was always called. Then Matt's mother. "A late accident" Grandfather called her. The boy, George, left home, joined the Army which "made a man of him", became a Member of Lloyds, made a fortune in insurance, lost most of it, and ended up with Alzheimer's in a nursing home near Brighton. He never married. Matt's mum did marry and produced one son. "That's me," Matt said, as if to make sure Jane was following the plot. Dad died from heart disease years ago and mum lives alone in Devon in a former council flat now owned by a housing association. She seems happy enough working in the local CoOp as a shop assistant.

"Couldn't your mother contest the will?" Jane wondered. "I'm sure there are legal ways to fight for some of the money. She was her sister for God's sake. Surely she's more right to the money than a load of cats? And so have you."

"Don't know," said Matt. "But mum won't. She'll respect her sister's wishes. And she's too proud to fight for money. And I don't think nephews count contesting wills."

* * *

Shopping again cost too much. But credit cards buffer the pain of payment from the pleasure of purchase and possession. Jane was high on happiness and that meant more money was spent. They bought stuff that would sit in cupboards for months. Pregnancy really did engender the nesting instinct in Jane, Matt noticed. More loo rolls, disinfectant, cleaning materials, another brush and dust pan, long-life milk, packets *and* tins of soup, frozen peas – giant size, sweet corn – family pack, and the list went on. The house was to be made cosy for the baby. Its bedroom would be made an extension of Jane's womb, warm and welcoming, safe and secure. Jane was lining the house with items that would bring comfort to her family, like a mother blue tit lining her nest with moss before depositing her eggs.

Matt's mobile rang when they were unpacking bag after bag in the kitchen trying to find space on packed shelves and in the freezer drawers for all the additional material. Matt answered and walked into the hallway to avoid the rustling plastic bags from the supermarket.

"Who was it?" asked Jane when he returned to help in the kitchen.

"Peter."

"What did he want?" Jane asked sounding suspicious. "Surely you don't have to go in the office, Mum and Dad will be here soon and..."

"No. Stay cool. He didn't want anything really. Sounded knackered. Must have had a skin-full last night. He had a couple of ideas about my report and the presentation for Chicago, that's all."

"Did you tell him?"

"Tell him what?"

Jane sighed, placed her hands on her hips and looked at the ceiling as if it were the sky. "The baby. Didn't you tell him the news about the baby?"

"No. Of course not."

"Why not?"

"Well, I didn't know if..."

"You men! You don't talk about *important* things."

"He did tell me about the car."

"What car?"

"Despite the tax disadvantage, I've decided to have company car so that we can sell that heap of crap out there and get one that starts properly. It took *me* ages to get it going this morning. Peter had forgotten to tell me it would be ready to pick up next week."

"That's great news love," said Jane as the doorbell rang and spun into a mini panic. "That's Mum and Dad. Oh dear. Look, I'll tell them...no, we'll tell them...they'll be thrilled...but let them get their coats off first."

"Why would they be interested in our new car?"

"About the baby - idiot," said Jane quickly realising Matt was teasing. "About you becoming a father, a grown up, an adult."

The doorbell rang again. Bob and Maggie Straw arrived with more bags and boxes. More food. More things. They were always generous and Matt and Jane always grateful. And the six bottles of good-looking wine would fill their depleted rack. God knows where to find cupboard space for the rest of the pile.

Jane broke the news within two minutes. She couldn't hold back. Bob and Maggie still had their coats on. The grandparents-to-be were thrilled. Kisses, handshakes, congratulations, advice about nappies and warnings about sleepless nights followed. Champagne was ordered at The Old Cock at lunchtime and Bob put back a couple of extra pints, which he slept off in the afternoon and missed the soccer results on TV.

Hardly a sentence was spoken over the weekend without a cross-reference to the baby. Everything focussed on The Baby.

"When the baby's here you'll...."

"That will change when you've got a toddler running around...

"Jane, darling, take it easy, don't strain yourself...

"You won't have time to do that when the baby's born...

"You'll have to fix that when little hands are reaching out...

"Now when you were born we didn't have all the things they have nowadays...

"We'll buy you the cot...and a pushchair."

The new car wasn't mentioned over the weekend. It didn't mean that much to Matt really, and a new car couldn't compete with a new baby in the attention of grandparents. Jane too had her priorities right. The baby filled her heart. But over and over in Matt's head was a sense of despondency, even anger. He couldn't shake it off, however much he tried. The deception, the façade, of playing happy father had already started with Maggie and Bob and the regulars at The Old Cock. He'd said the right things. Smiled appropriately. Acted happy. But the fear grew. The impending responsibility of fatherhood, the burden of baby bills on top of everything else, dominated his thoughts.

Jane's quip had hit home hard. Matt had to become a "grown up" for the first time in his 29 years.

Chapter Eight

This was adultery...official

Since "nine-eleven" in 2001 excessive US immigration security had made life hell for visitors. Mugs and dabs – photographs and fingerprints – had become standard procedure. Security chiefs secretly suspected terrorists would still get through. The policy was designed to reassure the public and maintain the impression politicians were in charge. High priority on high security also gave security bosses high status and big budgets. Sure, officials might get lucky and pick up the lone nutcase. But al-Qaeda operatives would slip through the net. It was just a question of time. They'd link up with "sleepers" already inside the United States and plan deeds of death. Then when they hear from al-Qaeda, *the base*, they would die. They would have a date with death, a place for sacrifice. Their *jihad* suicide would be glorious knowing they would soon see Allah and his Prophet Mohammed - and the infidels' bodies blown to hell.

But Peter and his team were escorted like VIPs as they left the aircraft at Chicago airport. Immigration officers took them along a quiet corridor into a private office. They avoided the long queues they could see through large one-way mirrors. Their documents were stamped without question and the officers accompanied the three of them through luggage pick-up and customs. Matt and Penny were impressed with their unexpected green light treatment.

AestChem Inc's limousine driver held a sign for Matt Collins and Peter Jones. Penny Taylor's name was not on the driver's sign. But the youngest member of Henderson-Strutt's issues and crisis team noticed his board first. Penny was more than a bag carrier. She made sure things happened: flight tickets and transport, hotel bookings and coordinating arrangements with clients. Although a brilliant strategist, and adored by clients, Peter could be absent minded about day-to-day details. Penny covered this weak flank. Her ability to research the rules and regulatory process for chemicals, pesticides and novel food introductions throughout the European Union were invaluable. Her sophistication, intelligence, humour and burning ambition to get to the top would doubtless combine to make sure she succeeded.

"Now that's a cliché," Penny sighed as they sat in the stretched limo on their way downtown to AestChem's global headquarters.

"But a nice one," according to Peter.

Frank Sinatra was singing the Sammy Cahn and James Van Heusen song:

"It's my kind of town, Chicago is…"

"Let's hope it's *'One town that will never let you down'*," Peter sang alongside 'ol blue eyes. Sinatra was undoubtedly the better singer.

"D'ya mind the music? I always plays it fer new folks in town," said the driver through the intercom. "Or d'ya wanna talk?"

"No, thanks. You can play Mr Sinatra all day long as far as I'm concerned," Peter reassured the driver.

"Yer like him then Sir?"

"He's the greatest. No-one else can sing a song like Mr Sinatra,"

"You're sure right there Sir. Even Crosby."

Peter had a rule. His team stuck to it. They never talked business in cars or taxis. Drivers have ears, especially when consultants are in town working for a big company. Driver's feedback can save corporations big bucks. The rule applied to planes and trains. Passengers have eyes and ears. Sammy Cahn's words turned out to be right for Henderson-Strutt. AestChem's President and Chief Executive Officer, and his key directors, praised Matt and Peter's presentation.

Although Matt noticed some of them spending more time snatching glances at Penny than concentrating on the more sophisticated points in the communications strategic plan of Project 66. After 30 years in the PR business Peter knew how to deploy a pretty junior executive. He'd worked out exactly where to sit her for maximum influence with the men in suits, white shirts and red ties. "Always give older men eye candy in meetings," he once advised Matt.

Jenni Tallow was far from jealous. She was completely aware of Peter Jones' tactic and enjoyed observing its impact. She publicly thanked Penny for her "special" contribution to the meeting. Everyone nodded while trying to work out what "special" contribution Penny had made. As AestChem's communications chief she had used the eye candy ploy herself – many times. And although nearly 15 years older than Penny, Jenni retained the looks to turn heads of men, older and younger.

Jenni's glasses today were more suited to the shape of her face, Peter noted. A definite improvement on those heavy squares she wore in London last week. They'd reminded him of Mrs Thatcher's successor John Major, forgotten as a Prime Minister, but famous for his glasses. Forgotten, that is, until years later when the British public were stunned to learn he'd enjoyed an affair with one of his ministers Edwina Currie, responsible for agriculture, fisheries and food. The *grey* man of British politics overnight became *interesting*. Currie, also married, had resigned for using just *one* wrong word in a media interview. It provided another classic case in public relations, which Peter often used. Currie claimed "all" poultry was contaminated with salmonella bacteria. If she had used "most" instead, only ripples not waves would have rocked the powerful food lobby's boat. They openly called from the minister's head, and, covertly supported by their friends inside the Ministry of Agriculture, got it on a platter.

Ms Tallow didn't care about her colleagues on the board ogling the girl from England. Penny helped get what Jenni wanted: approval for the issues communication strategy and a generous budget allocation to pay for it. Her colleagues liked the plan and the Henderson-Strutt team from London who devised and presented it. They approved the idea of travelling to Europe and meeting top politicians, even royalty, although at this stage promises could not be made. Likewise, if senior people from Europe in the decision making process wished to visit the laboratories here in Chicago to learn how wonderful the process works, then AestChem's board members would be delighted to welcome them. Ms Tallow's future and influence at AestChem had been consolidated because of Henderson-Strutt's strategy. One or two directors had recently expressed doubts about her ability to handle this issue surrounding the launch of 22XP in Europe. She'd been tipped off about the rumours, of course. Jenni had the ability to network upwards from the most junior secretary in the company. And while she had the support of the President and CEO, she was untouchable. Jenni was street-smart enough to know that ending her year-long affair with AestChem's marketing president left her vulnerable at board level, especially as his wife was now suing him for $5 million. Thankfully she was citing other woman in the torrid affairs of her husband.

Peter decided his team should skip the overnight red-eye flight landing 07.15 at Heathrow. A night in Chicago would give them time to incorporate additional information into AestChem's strategy documentation – and enjoy a night in America's third largest city. Peter said he was going to crash out early, watch TV, eat a burger delivered by room service and wash it down with some wine - and a tot of whisky. But when Penny called his room early evening to confirm the morning's rescheduled flight time, Peter didn't answer. She left the message on the hotel's voice mail.

Matt and Penny dined in the skyscraper restaurant of their five-star hotel with its impressive panoramic views. Their waiter pointed to the Sears Tower, the city's tallest building, as Penny surveyed the magnificent skyline. "And down there's where the White Sox play," he said. Looking at Penny's expression, he added, "That's the baseball team ma'am. The Bulls play basketball, the Bears football and the Black Hawks ice hockey." They lingered over their dinner and ordered a second bottle of wine. "Well," Matt said, "Peter told us to relax and enjoy ourselves." Penny tipped her head to one side and smiled. "We're only doing what the boss has told us to do," she added. They talked about work, the infamy of Chicago's Al Capone and his notorious gangsters of the 1920s during prohibition, the mystery of why Peter hadn't come to dinner or answered his phone, and many other things.

Then it happened. It shouldn't have done. It was a mistake. It was stupid. It was wrong, especially for a dad-to-be. But jet lag, wine, stress, then a successful day and a couple of whiskies from Penny's room bar landed them in bed together.

Matt played the scene over and over again in his mind on the flight back to Heathrow. The storyline didn't change. They intended to watch a film on TV. They did. But somehow the whole thing got out of hand, as he confessed to her later. At first he remembered just a light touch when squeezing past Penny. It was his hand on her arm, like the casual contact you make in a crowded room when walking by someone. Nothing serious.

Penny had spilt coke down her blouse. She needed to sponge it to prevent a permanent stain, or so she said, and was rushing to the bathroom. Then, perhaps a minute later, their heads clashed while simultaneously peering into the minibar fridge searching for another drink. It wasn't a heavy blow. In fun Penny feigned the injury and exaggerated the hurt. Matt rubbed her forehead to sooth the bruise. He can't remember the next move, nor who made it. Did he pull her to him, or did she pull him to her? And how did their heads clash? He was certain she was the other side of the room when he opened the minibar. Who took the condoms from the bathroom dispenser? He thought hard but couldn't remember doing that. They did enjoy each other. That was very clear. It was great fun, Penny said. It must have been. Matt picked up three spent condoms on the carpet in the morning - after stepping on one of them going to the bathroom.

Matt felt guilty. Penny was the first fling since marrying Jane. This was adultery. Official. Groping in dark corners at company Christmas parties doesn't count. But guilt is not strong enough to stop a man when aroused by a beautiful woman allowing him access. He enjoyed Penny's body. Any man would, especially AestChem's overweight marketing director. Matt had watched him watching every move she'd made out of the corner of his eyes at the meeting. He'd have paid $1 million to have being in Matt's shoes later that night.

Matt felt good and guilty in equal measure. It wasn't hypocrisy. He simply couldn't deny he had enjoyed the excitement with Penny while remaining very much in love with Jane. Making love with one was not denigrating love with another, whatever magazine agony aunts write. Spending the night with Penny only served to reinforce his special relationship with Jane. When with Penny he surprised himself how much he thought of Jane, and even the baby, even though it was the baby, the pregnancy, he was trying to forget.

Reflecting last night on the plane home, Matt concluded it was his reaction to the news of the baby that drove him into the arms of another woman. He now believed it was the stress and burden of responsibility that created the conditions pushing him into physical relief and mental distraction. Matt was not looking for an excuse but an explanation for his behaviour.

Like all affairs, did the couple create the circumstances or did the circumstances create the coupling? Penny just happened to be there at the right time in a convenient place for Matt. She relieved his anxiety, exhausted his stress. Did she seduce him or did he allow himself to be seduced? He couldn't find the answer. But if Peter had not delayed the flight, if Penny had stayed in Britain, if Peter had dined with them, if they'd have gone to the bar, if they hadn't drank so much, if the day had gone badly, if they hadn't wanted to, if...

For Penny, looking across the blanket of clouds through the Boeing 747's window, what happened, happened. Matt was another man, a pretty attractive one, but a man. She fancied him and he fancied her. Simple. The only slight complication was that he was her boss. But by sleeping with him she'd reduced the hierarchy, levelled the relationship. She now felt more power, more control. Matt had been a good one-night stand, a nice man. Married. No complications. Better than single blokes. She might have him again one day.

Chapter Nine

He kicked her legs apart...

"Who's that?" Jane asked as she got out of bed reaching the phone on the dressing table. Matt wouldn't call so early in the morning - unless it was urgent.

"Hello."

She knew someone was there. She could hear breathing.

"Hello. Matt?"

The breathing grew louder, faster, difficult. Struggling as if suffering an asthma attack. An injury? Accident?

"Matt. What's wrong? Are you okay?"

And then he spoke, quickly, nervously. "They must not do it. They must say 'No'. They must not accept the contract."

Jane couldn't recognise the accent. It wasn't British. "Sorry, I think you've got the wrong number. This is a private house in England. What number were you trying to....?"

The line died. And Jane started to dress for school wondering from where that call came.

An hour later the builders arrived on time at exactly 8am Monday. When Dad's the boss of the firm you expect that level of service at least. Ray Sykes and builder's apprentice Paul Potts had been parked outside in the van for half an hour. Before the day's work, Ray read *The Sun* and tucked into a ham sandwich his wife had made last night. Potty, as the lads inevitably called him, preferred a sausage roll and crisps from the garage. After looking over Ray's shoulder to view the day's Page Three, the lad watched the routine early morning activities of the suburban street, a collection of late Victorian detached, 1930's semis and 1960's terraced housing.

Ray, who had worked for Jane's father for most of his working life after "emigrating south" from Yorkshire aged fifteen, would probably retire next year. Sixty-two is about right after a lifetime in the building game. They had the cottage in Somerset. He'd go down there with Doris. He remembered Bob bringing Jane as a schoolgirl on some jobs. He'd seen all Bob's daughters grow up. Of the three, Jane was the one who liked to come on the sites with her dad.

That was in the good old days before all these health and safety regulations stopped youngsters growing up properly. Before schools banned conker fights unless kids wore safety goggles, gloves and hard hats. Before homemade jams and cakes were banned from church fetes because some jumped up official warned it could pose a risk to public health. In the old days you could take your boys to work, let them give you a hand, learn what proper work was all about. When you could take a pee and not be told *Please Wash Your Hands* - a building site's for builders for Christ's sake, not bloody hospital surgeons. Bob Straw had worked real hard in the early days to build up the business. Ray continued to recount those days to Paul. But he was more interested in a shapely woman still in her flimsy nightdress opening curtains in an upstairs room.

"Aye, Bob worked every hour God sent. He's just a pen-pusher now," Ray joked. "But he gets the contracts. He keeps 50-odd of us all busy most of the year, so don't knock it lad."

The lad stayed silent. Or he may have mumbled "Yeh". Ray's hearing wasn't as good as it was. Nearly 48 years of pneumatic drills, chains saws and hundreds of decibel-generating machines had taken their toll. And it was time for work and the doorbell chimed.

"Hello Ray. Dad said yesterday you'd be here in charge of our extension," Jane said greeting him with a hug and peck on the cheek. "Dad promised me you're the best brick layer and carpenter he's ever had."

"Now you know he tells all the girls that love. Told 'em for years. But aye, suppose it's true."

"Unfortunately I've got to get off to school in a minute. Make yourself at home though. Take the spare key home with you to let yourself in if we're out. It's in the kitchen, next to the kettle, because I know you'll be using that a lot to make your tea. Do you still like it strong, piping hot with three sugars?"

"Aye lass, thou still remembers." Ray was pleased she remembered.

"How could I forget? I spent half my holidays making you, Dad, and all the other blokes cuppas all day long."

"Aye. Good days them," Ray said.

Jane said a quick "Hello Goodbye" to Paul, a tall skinny youth, as he was bringing tools from the van.

Strangely - and thankfully - the car started perfectly as soon as the key turned. This was the first time for over a week it started without causing trouble. Did this car know it was soon to be sold when Matt's company car arrived? Had it started behaving itself to save itself from the scrap heap? Did it hear us talking about a brand new BMW on its way to replace it and was jealous? It's odd how inanimate machines pick up animal instincts, Jane thought as she drove to face 500 kids in their final week before breaking up for Christmas. Jane met her English department head Mr Tinkler before assembly and told him the great news. He was pleased for her, and for the father who had "done his bit" of course, and gave her a gentle reassuring hug with his bear-like frame and kissed her on both cheeks. She said she'd tell the Head, but not yet as it was still early days.

At the Collins' home Ray and Paul cleared the back garden, started excavating the foundations for the extension with a small digger, and left at four as the dark set in. They'd be back tomorrow and every day until Christmas Eve, except weekends. But the whole job wouldn't be finished until late January, depending on the weather.

* * *

Term ended Thursday and, apart from Gerry Tinkler, the only other person Jane swore to secrecy about the pregnancy was her friend Sarah. In reception, after glancing round to make certain no ears were listening, she told her that after Christmas she'd be over 12 weeks. "It will be safe to start telling everyone at school then."

Matt returned from Chicago a day later than expected and Jane noticed his euphoria of becoming a father had died down. She blamed jet lag. He looked tired and needed a break. Christmas would give them a few days together. But on Sunday Matt had to catch up on work. Henderson-Strutt had become involved on a new project in Russia. Peter had dashed to Moscow for a few days – leaving most of the AestChem work to Matt and Penny. So Jane went shopping alone for a few things. They didn't need much because they were spending Christmas in Chislehurst with Gran and Grandad, as she now teased them. And, knowing Mum, there would be enough food to feed an army.

* * *

The week before Christmas, heavy rain prevented some of the foundation work. But Ray said they'd get on with other jobs before Christmas. Ray and the lad fixed up a large blue tarpaulin to shelter the ground from the worst of the downpour and keep the rain off their backs.

"I've got to get a load of two-bi-four to sure up footings," Ray told Jane as he stood drinking his mug of strong sweet tea. "I'll only be gone about an hour." The lad was enjoying a roll up outside. Ray had quit smoking years ago. Felt better for it. And he'd told the lad never to smoke in a customer's house. "They'll always smell it when they get in, even if you just have one," he said.

Jane also had a visit to make, but not to the timber merchants. They left within a minute of each other: Ray for wood, Jane for her doctor's appointment.

"Everything seems to be making good progress Mrs Collins," Dr

Shah said. "And do continue with the folic acid tablets because they may help prevent any nerve problems as the baby develops. Is your husband pleased?"

"He's in shock, I think," said Jane. "But yes, he's really happy about it."

"That's good," the doctor said as she helped Jane off the examination table. "And you have your maternity appointment?"

"Yes, that's all arranged."

"And make sure your husband goes to the pre natal classes too."

"I doubt if he'll do that doctor. Anyway he's busy and usually gets back too late from London."

"Men need to know as much about the birth and child care as the mums, you know," said Dr Shah. "He probably thinks he knows it all already. Then when he's with you in the delivery room – he will be there of course – he'll wonder what's going on and panic."

"Oh, he'll be there all right doctor. He can't wait. But Matt's not the panicking type. He'll be calm and in control, I'm certain of that."

When Jane returned from her appointment she went up to the bedroom for a change of clothes. For a split second she thought Matt had come back from work early. She actually called out his name to check, certain that someone was there. But he wasn't in the bathroom or the spare bedroom, which they used as the home office. The house itself was empty, although Ray and the lanky lad were mixing concrete out the back and she could hear them talking.

Jane looked in the wardrobe mirror. Was she really three months pregnant? Sure, her breasts had grown slightly, and would definitely need a couple of new bras when next in the high street. But her waist appeared as slim as ever. She slipped the skirt down and pulled the jeans up. Perhaps they were just a little tighter than usual.

Ray's white van drove away as it routinely did for lunch at 12.30. Like clockwork, unless he had building materials to pick up, he would return at 1.30 to start the afternoon's work. His wife always made sandwiches for lunch, if 40 years of marriage qualified as "always". But it became Ray's habit to eat them for breakfast or with his mid-morning cuppa at the latest. Every working day for nearly 40 years his wife also packed an apple. And in 40 years Ray had not once, ever, eaten it. The apple saga was probably the biggest secret between them. Pie and chips, fish and chips, burger and chips or a pub lunch had become his proper lunch. Now that was no secret to Doris. She had witnessed over the years her husband's growing girth and portly paunch.

After tidying the bedroom Jane went downstairs to make herself a light lunch before shopping. She still needed presents for her two sisters. A cold draft suddenly swept through the house. She noticed Ray or the lad had left the back door ajar before driving off for their lunch, so she closed it. She finished off the salad that was left in the bowl from the weekend with a couple of bread rolls. She poured herself a glass of milk. Even the smell of tea or coffee made her queasy now, so Jane was happy Ray had Paul to make his "builders' tea".

He grabbed her from behind. The glass of milk dropped to the floor smashing into fragments. He pushed her hard against the worktop. Her first thought – my baby. Mother's instinct fully developed in three months. She tried to relieve the pressure on her stomach by pushing backwards into him. One large hard hand gripped both her wrists and held them in her back. The other had already ripped open the front of her jeans. She could feel his fingers trying to violate her.

Scream? Scratch? Fight? Talk? Run? Resist? Poke eyes? Stamp foot? Kick his balls? Jane had read the magazines. What use now? That was theory. This is fact.

"I won't hurt you if you let me, right," he breathed in her ear. She could smell stale tobacco on his breath. Jane shocked herself at finding the time to think that it wasn't a very original line, just like in the movies.

"Okay. Okay," Jane said. Keep calm. Buy time. Get free. Avoid hurt. Stay alive. Protect my baby.

"Look," he said quickly, " I'm going to let you go but promise you'll let me."

"Okay. Okay." Then I'll fight.

"If you mess me about you'll get it bad misses, know what I mean?"

"Okay. Okay."

"You like it really, don't yer?"

He pushed and gripped harder.

"Don't yer? Don't yer? Yer really want it, don't yer?"

"Okay. Okay."

"Not good enough misses. Say yeh. Say yer wan' it."

"Yes. Okay."

He kicked her legs apart with his foot. His force had the desired impact and made her plead, "Yes. Yes. I want you to."

"Go on, say it again," and his fingers pressed inside. "Say you want me to fuck you real hard."

"I want you to..." she cried and hesitated. He kicked her ankles and smashed her against the worktop again. Jane knew what she had to say, "... yes I want you to fuck me..." another blow, "...fuck me really hard."

His grip eased. But her arms remained locked in his hand vice. His body forced hers forward over the worktop. His fingernail tore her thigh as he pushed her pants and jeans down to her knees.

It was over in seconds. He moved back and zipped himself up. Jane didn't turn around. Trembling, she slowly pulled her clothes up. She stood there, looking at the bread bin, and reading over and over again "Bread", "Bread", "Bread".

"If yer tell anyone I'll be back with me mates and we'll all 'ave yer, got it? Then we'll fucking burn this place down with you in it, know what I mean," he said.

"Bread. Bread. Bread..." whispering.

"And that's a warning. Tell your fucking husband to keep his fucking nose out or this'll be just the fucking start."

"Bread. Bread…"

"Anyways, you said you wanted it, and that's what I'd tell 'em," he said before walking through the back door into what was once Jane's lovely little garden transformed into a building site.

Jane heard his words despite her dizziness. His strange threats echoed in her spinning head. She couldn't understand. What he said didn't make sense. Her head rocked forward and backward as she read "Bread" and "Bread". She was in shock. She knew it. Jane realised she retained the ability to be *rational* about what had just happened. But was it seconds, or several minutes, before she staggered slowly up each stair to sit on the edge of her bed?

A thousand thoughts and a hundred voices raced through her mind. But one voice was heard downstairs.

"What's been going on 'ere then?" she heard Ray call to his apprentice in the garden.

Jane heard the friendly voice of Ray ensuring her safety and bringing relief, at least for now. It was a voice from childhood and she recalled slow, sunny, warm reassuring days with Dad and all his men on a building site, full of daisies and dandelions and other weeds that had found a home on derelict building rubble.

"Potty, a glass of milk has spilt all over this kitchen floor."

"Mrs Collins must 'ave dropped it 'cos I didn't." Jane heard the teenager's voice shout back to Ray.

One idea contradicted another. I should do…I must do…I need to…I will do… I mustn't do… I, I can't… Do I phone the police? Shall I go round the station? Do I put up and shut up? I'm still in once piece. Tell Mum? Phone Dad? No way. Matt. What will he think? Can't tell him, he won't be able to handle it. Tell Ray. Tell Ray downstairs now. What did I do wrong? Why didn't I…? Maybe I'll….

Jane did nothing. But it wasn't a decision. It's just what happened. She sat in silence, listening to the turn of the concrete in the mixer and the chatter of workmen. It was as if nothing happened. Did it happen? Was this some nightmare? Had she really been…? She stopped. She didn't want to even think the word.

She jammed the dressing table stool behind the door to prevent anyone entering. She removed her jumper over her head and noticed her bra was undone, the fastener broken. Walking back towards the wardrobe Jane saw blood across the carpet and a red stain was next to the bed. In fear she glanced down fast. But it wasn't the source of the blood. The baby was safe. Broken glass had gashed the ball of her foot.

This focussed her mind on cleaning the carpet, cleaning the carpet with a bucket of water and cleaning materials from the bathroom next door. She rubbed and scrubbed until all traces of blood vanished. To make sure, she cleaned the carpet again, a third time rubbing harder, and perhaps again. Toilet tissue and handkerchiefs curbed further blood loss from her foot. Dr Shah would have advised a couple of stitches in that wound. But Jane packed tissue into her shoe.

It must now be 3pm. It was beginning to get dark, darker than the dismal day had already been. It was time for afternoon tea for Ray. It was always at 3pm, had been for years, except on some jobs where the foreman was fussy.

"Are you up there Jane?" Ray called, knowing she was. He had heard scrubbing noises. The toilet had flushed a few times and he saw water running away through the open wastage pipe he'd been inspecting earlier outside. He'd have to move that piping outlet to the back of the garden after Christmas because it can't go under the new extension. Building regulations.

"We're having a quick break Jane. Did you want a cuppa?" he tried again for a response.

She waited. Hesitated. "I'm not feeling well Ray…got a bit of a headache…I'm just resting on the bed," she called, hoping he could hear through the bedroom door.

"Can I bring thee an aspirin or something? I'll take me shoes off before I come upstairs," he said.

"No, Ray. I'll be okay soon and Matt will be back early," she lied.

"Look, why don't you both knock off early? The place will be quieter then. I won't tell Dad, promise," she shouted downstairs trying to sound light-hearted.

Jane didn't think Ray would bite the bait. He was an old-fashioned dedicated worker set in his ways. To her surprise he did. He must be feeling his age. They swilled out the mixer of old concrete with the hose, scraped their tools clean, tidied up a bit and were gone within 20 minutes. Jane looked through the net curtain as the van's engine started and Ray drove away.

Jane walked downstairs and locked the back door. She chained the front. Looked in every room. Downstairs. Upstairs. Then she showered. That way the dirt went away. She watched the soapy water work its way down her body and out, away from her, far away from her. A trace of blood from her cut foot stained the water as it swirled away. She then soaked in a hot bath, not for cleansing, but for consoling.

Matt arrived late, around nine. Must act normal, Jane thought. Can't show anything's changed. Nothing has. She didn't want anything altered, apart from a daytime nightmare to be forgotten, like a scene from a bad movie to rewind. The mind is harder to clean than the body. She didn't know how to greet her husband tonight. Should she kiss him and hold him? Did she usually do that on Monday night? Was it Monday? Should she just say "Hello love," as usual, if that's what she normally said? Or is that too casual? Will she give anything away? What will he think? She must behave the same as she always behaves, but she couldn't remember how she always behaves. What was normal now?

Matt's mind was on work. He had talked with the minister's assistant today and arranged the meeting for AestChem. Penny told him people in Brussels were interested in the new technology and would be willing to review the scientific research in Chicago. Peter had talked with people who understand the complex EU regulations. They told him how best to word and present the data *"for maximum processing efficiency"*. Word oil would calm any unwanted political or bureaucratic waves. Unless some paranoid pressure group heard about 22XP, at this stage it looked as if the American chemical giant would get its way in Europe. Henderson-Strutt was doing a good job. Matt was really pleased with Penny too. She carried on totally professionally. She behaved just the same as before their night together in Chicago. He recalled every touch and move he made with her, refreshing and updating his memory. It wasn't his fault. He was a victim of circumstances. What he did with her was simple, primitive biological instinct.

Confusion reigned in Jane's head. Matt had come home with a takeaway, but it wasn't Friday. Or was it? Doesn't matter. They sat together on the sofa watching telly. Something was on. Norman Mailer was right, tonight at least. "Television," he wrote, "is chewing gum for the eyes." Matt couldn't remember who'd switched it on. Jane couldn't remember who'd switched it on. It was on, that's what mattered. It provided a distraction, a focus from real life, something to look at and not think about. TVs are good at preventing talk.

But Jane did think, Matt had his thoughts too. She was fuming about how that thug had been where only Matt should go. She was furious because that bastard had touched where only Matt should touch. She vowed when they married to be faithful, unlike one or two of her girlfriends who said fidelity didn't matter. It did to Jane. Her body was now for one man, and one man only, despite the fashion. Her promise to Matt had been broken. That…that…*animal*…had forced her to break her vow.

Matt tried turning off the day, but failed. On AestChem, despite today's success there could be problems tomorrow. On Peter, he was drinking too much and heading for the rocks again. His speech was slurred on the call from Moscow. And it looked as if Henderson-Strutt would be dragged into some Russian project. More work when they were already at full stretch. On the car, delivery delayed until after Christmas, according to the HR department. Very frustrating.

Then there was Penny. Will he, *should* he, take her to Chicago for January's meeting? And why were all those bills scattered around the bread bin in the kitchen? More bills he hadn't known about – with a baby on its way.

Matt had really wanted to rid himself of all this mental clutter. He wanted time to himself. Since learning of his aunt's gift, he had tried to work on his plans for their 260 acres of woodland. He'd managed a list on the train home: first, draw up a good map, second task, a land and tree survey, third, short, medium and long term woodland plans. But that's as far as he'd got.

Jane was tired and went upstairs early to bed before Matt. She had noticed a long red-raw scratch on her thigh, bruises on her arms and a gash in her foot. Her nightdress, the duvet and darkness would hide them and stop questions, at least for tonight. It would give her time to think.

As she turned off the bedside lamp, Jane realised she hadn't seen his face. Someone had forced his way inside her body, and she hadn't seen him. There was no face to hate. No eyes to despise. But she recalled his hands were rough, his breath stale, his voice strange in some way. Her attacker was half identified, half anonymous. But she tried to sleep.

One thought made her feel better, or at least less sad. Her baby, Matt's baby, remained pure and uncontaminated from anything that faceless animal did to her. Their child remained immune from his attack. In the stillness, Jane could feel a slight small movement inside. The pleasure from this little life reduced her pain - more than the tears she now released.

Chapter Ten

_____

AFTER CHRISTMAS

Secrecy makes you strong...

They walked in the woodland, Jane's hand in Matt's. Their woods now, thanks to Aunt Sheila. Apart from evergreen holly, some bursting with bright red berries, the trees were bare, dull grey or mud brown. Hazel and hornbeam shrubs under the large oaks retained their dead, brittle leaves. But fallen oak and chestnut leaves crunched under their feet as they trod deeper into the woods.

Until they approached the area Jane had not realised Matt's "mystery tour" was to King's Wood. On their last visit to Aunt Sheila the garden was an untidy patch of mixed cottage flowers, broad beans here, tomatoes there and neglected lawns everywhere. "Cats like long grass," Aunt Sheila had said.

The Bower House displayed its For Sale sign at the front gate. As so few people travelled this narrow country road Matt couldn't see the point. The locals who owned their homes wouldn't buy it, and farm workers and young couples couldn't afford this *"substantial property set in 2.25 acres surrounded by ancient woodland"*, according to the estate agent's blurb. Peering through the windows, the house had been cleared of all its contents and the garden tidied. The agents would doubtless charge thousands extra for short grass.

Time seemed in limbo on this cloudy damp day in late December. With a sunless sky there were no strong shadows, no indication of the hour. Christmas was over but just too early to think about New Year. As always Christmas had the usual build up with high expectations of joy and happiness. It had been a good break for Matt and Jane. As always, Bob and Maggie made everyone welcome at their spacious home in Chislehurst. They were constantly offering food and topping up the drink. Back in the heart of her family, Jane felt secure. She smiled, with others. She laughed, with others. She carried on, happy in her pregnancy, even when alone. There had been no more tears. Her secret had not been shared.

Jane and Matt had arrived the day before Christmas Eve and entered into the party spirit immediately with Uncle Michael, Maggie's older brother, and her two aunts. Pregnancy and babies were, of course, the main talking point. And Jane, the mum-to-be, was at the centre of attention. Names? A boy? Girl? Jane's sisters Ann and Heather arrived separately on Christmas Eve. Unfortunately, Heather's long-standing boyfriend, a hospital registrar, had been asked by his consultant at the last minute to work over Christmas Day.

Even in the midst of happy chatter, Jane remembered much of the dreaded moment she most wanted to forget. She tried, but she couldn't hide the memory. She knew she never would. Time will heal the wounds. But the scars will stay. She had rationally and carefully gone over her options. Cry rape or stay silent? What would it be? She knew all about how well the police now treat "alleged rape victims" and how abused women support groups functioned. She knew strangers would be supportive, provide a shoulder to cry on, listen to all she had to say. But Jane, with her own free will, decided there would be no police, no investigation, no therapy, no rape counselling, no exposure. There would be no shoulder to cry on - because there were going to be no more tears.

Secrecy would be Jane's strength. Silence, not speaking, would be her support, her therapy. She didn't believe a burden shared is a burden halved. In her case disclosure would double the trouble. Talking would not provide healing. For her today's counselling culture was not the answer. Speaking out would compound the crime and her suffering.

And where would they find that bastard? How could she identify a man whose face she never saw? How could she begin to describe him? A man who stank of cigarettes with a strange voice? Not much to go on. And even if he were found guilty after months and months of legal wrangling, what would he get? Three years? Five? She read the papers. She'd seen all those cases where criminals were locked up for just a year or two and the victims left with a lifetime sentence of fear, disability and nightmares. The justice was not worth the disclosure. Anyway, she knew it was now too late. She'd washed the evidence away and destroyed the clothes he'd contaminated. Without DNA there's not a hope, the police would surely say.

Jane surprised herself how she had recovered in a little over a week. It was mind over matter: her mind over his body, determination over brutality. She knew she would never forget. She could live with the memory because there was no alternative. She was pleased with her progress.

Her trauma locked away in her mind was, on balance, better than everyone knowing - even though she was convinced the attack was totally unprovoked and certainly not her fault. How could it have been? But if Mum and Dad, colleagues and kids at school - my God the kids - heard about this, just think of the gossip in every classroom corner. Everyone looking. Pointing. Knowing. Thinking what happened. Embarrassed. Avoiding. Not knowing what to say apart from a stumbling "Sorry to hear about..."

And Matt. She'd thought long and hard about his reaction, his thoughts and feelings. Would he move closer or step back? Emotionally? Physically? She didn't know. Or wasn't sure. Anyway, he would never know, because she would never say. Why should he suffer? He didn't *need* to know. He couldn't *help.*

Their hands parted as Matt walked ahead forging the trail for Jane to follow through a patch of dead bracken. For some reason Jane trailed behind appreciating the landscape in her own private way. Matt instinctively knew when to provide space for Jane to think, and she appreciated that quality in him.

"Over here Jane. It's over here."

Matt found the tall beech. He walked around its substantial girth. One hand brushed the smooth grey bark and his eyes searched for something.

"These woods are fantastic," said Jane, slightly out of breath as she caught up with Matt. "How old is that oak?

Matt smiled. "At least 300 years I would guess."

He took Jane's hand as she approached and asked her to close her eyes.

"Why?"

"Go on, close them."

Jane stepped back. "Oh, hold on, I remember what happened last time I trusted you Matt Collins in these woods when I closed my eyes," she teased.

"Really?"

"Are you saying you forgot?"

"Of course not. How could I? But it's too cold for that today."

"Exactly. You were a very naughty boy and it was a very warm summer's day. I'd had something to drink so you took advantage. And I wasn't a respectable married woman then..."

"Jane, shut up a minute and close your eyes."

She obeyed, smiled and relaxed. Holding a wrist, Matt helped her fingers find a groove in the smooth bark.

"Keep your eyes closed…"

It did not take Jane's fingers long to trace the outline. "It's M… C… your initials. You carved these in the tree," she said opening her eyes to confirm Matt's childhood handiwork.

"I must have been seven, maybe eight," he said, "And even then, 20-odd years ago, I promised I would bring my wife and my children here to this spot. And here we are, all three of us."

It was the very first time Matt had spontaneously mentioned the baby since she'd broken the news. He'd never initiated a conversation about their child. He often joined in the discussions when Jane or others raised the subject. But this was, to Jane, a turning point for Matt.

"You know what's strange?" Matt said looking skywards through the bare branches. Jane knew he wasn't really seeking a response, so stayed silent to allow him to continue. "Legend and custom is that this tree – incidentally darling it's a beech not an oak – is considered as 'The Mother of the Woods'."

"Why?"

"Because it gives shade and shelter to many baby trees, I suppose. And it provides food that can be eaten raw. You know, beechnuts. Mother's milk in symbolic terms."

Jane loved sharing these moments with her best friend. She wanted him to keep speaking, even if he said nothing of importance, even if she forgot what he was saying, like words written in sand washed away by waves.

"The beech is known as 'The Queen of the Forest' because she often stands next to her 'Oak King' in the ancient woodland that once covered most of Britain."

After a moment's thought, Jane said, "That's nice."

"I shouldn't have done that you know," said Matt, half seriously.

"I'll forgive you," Jane said fully joking. "You weren't a respectable married man then…"

"No, not that you idiot. My initials. The carving. It's a stupid thing to do because the tree can get diseased, especially beech."

"What's special about them then? Apart from they are forest queens."

"They've got thin skin – like you."

"Oh yes?"

"The cambium layer that transports the nutrients up and down the tree is near the surface, just under the bark. One little scratch, and it bleeds and gets infected..."

"HIV. Sod it. Jesus, I need a test." The thought struck Jane hard as if hit by the tree itself.

"Jane. Jane? What's the matter? What's wrong?"

"It's okay. It's okay Matt."

"Obviously not. Let's get you back to the car. Quick. You've gone as white as a ghost."

Jane held her abdomen. It fooled Matt. Pregnancy provided easy deception.

"It was great you didn't have to work over Christmas," she told Matt as they drove back home, feeling better now the "twinge" in her tummy had stopped hurting. "So that promotional porno video situation never got out?" The question deflected Matt from his concern over her health.

"No. We put out a recall notice with a pre-paid reply envelope. Phoned round all the newsrooms it had been sent to. Got most of them back. The ones we didn't get back had already been thrown away, as I suspected. And if any were given away, and watched, perhaps they were too embarrassed to tell anyone."

"The woods are really nice," Jane said as they reached the outskirts of Sevenoaks. "Thanks for taking me. It was a pleasant surprise. And it's incredible to think that when you were just a little boy you carved your initials in a tree..."

"Loads of lads do that..."

"Yes," continued Jane pretending to be upset at the interruption, "but they don't think about bringing their wife and kids to the spot years later. It's shows that deep down you're a real softy."

When Matt spent his holidays in those woods alone as a boy, they represented freedom, a wild world without adult control or parental discipline. Woods were the place of adventure, excitement and activity. They were full of fascinating animals to watch and study - ants, badgers, birds, squirrels, snakes, rabbits, hares, foxes and deer. England didn't have the big animals of Africa, he regretted, but who wants to be eaten by a lion? And with a bit of bindweed and lots of sticks you could easily make a shelter to keep off the rain. Today, with Jane, Matt recalled those childhood thoughts.

Now, King's Wood was his, his private patch of freedom. It was his turn, his duty, to care for the ancient wood. Matt accepted he was simply the transient caretaker, never the permanent owner, whatever the legal paperwork drafted by Mole and Mole Solicitors said and the documentation from the Land Registry. He vowed to plant more trees knowing he would never see them mature. He would plant acorns believing that someone, three, four or five hundred years from now, would do exactly the same. Trees outlive men but give oxygen for man to breathe.

"Are you feeling okay now?" asked Matt opening the car door for Jane at home.

"Sure, as I said, it was just a twinge."

"It's too early isn't it for the baby to be kicking?"

"Well if it's not kicking, it's shuffling around and definitely growing."

Matt never told Jane he had made up the story about his initials in the beech. When MC was carved with his penknife - swapped for a bicycle tyre pump and four chews with a schoolmate - Matt was simply making his mark. It had been one of those hot, still, summer days when, even in the woods of adventure, a small boy became bored. Why should a small lad think about girls, women, babies and stuff like that when you've got cowboys and 'injuns' roaming around, enemy soldiers with guns, buffalo to find, shelters to make, tigers to watch out for and trees to climb?

It was a nice story about returning to the spot years later with a wife and family to see his boyhood tree carving. But it was a lie. A white lie. Jane had appreciated the romance. It would be a shame to spoil its effect, especially as she had been acting oddly recently, going into her own, insular world.

And Matt *might* have been thinking about the future when he cut into the bark of the beech with his blade.

Chapter Eleven

Success measured by silence and secrecy...

The white van of Ray Sykes turned into Jane's drive. It must be eight o'clock. She confirmed the time with her watch. Perhaps he'd perfectly judged the traffic. Or, as she had seen through the window some days, he had parked nearby reading his favourite tabloid and eating his lunchtime sandwiches for breakfast.

It had been good having a break from the building work over the holiday. But things had to get back to normal. The drains would be moved this week and the brickwork would start. Dad had explained the next steps to them over Christmas. It was the first day back for Matt too. He left even earlier than usual because the trains were always bad just after a holiday. His American colleagues and clients would have been working over the holiday firing off emails building up the workload. They don't take Christmas as seriously as the British, he explained to Jane.

The short holiday had taken away the outward signs of stress from Matt. Jane had watched him relax over the break and enjoyed the return of her husband's casual wit and humour. Thankfully the porno video story didn't hit the headlines or he'd have been in the office with Peter sweet-talking the press on behalf of their client. Matt worked too hard and too long. She knew today, first day back, he wouldn't be home before 8pm. And his treadmill started at 5.30am when Jane heard the shower in the bathroom. But she turned her back to the door, cuddled the duvet and tried for two more hours of sleep, however fitful.

She could hear Ray whistling, as builders do, going through the side gate to the back garden to assess the day's work.

"Jane love, are you in?" she heard Ray call.

"Happy New Year Ray. I'll be down in a minute." And she was.

"Bob said you'd spent Christmas at their place," he said to Jane as she unbolted the kitchen door.

"Did you have a good one?"

"Quiet, you know. But everyone came round Boxing Day."

"No helper today?" she asked looking around.

"No, by hell. That lad, you know, my apprentice, that Paul, he's packed it up."

"Really."

"His mum called over Christmas, your dad said. Left a message on the firm's answer-phone thing, saying he were packing up building trade. Kids nowadays, eh? They won't stick at anything unless it puts lots of money in their pocket. They never think about what they'll earn in future if they get a good trade. A half-decent chippy or a sparky or plumber will never be short of work, not if he's willing to move 'bout a bit. No, lass, these kids today just want to get rich quick. Now in my day...."

Jane stopped listening. She'd heard Ray's views before. She just kept nodding.

"...was it then?"

She retuned to Ray's wavelength.

"What? Sorry?"

"Christmas," Ray continued looking puzzled. "You know, Christmas. Holly. Ivy. Cards and presents...was it a good one?"

"Oh, sorry, it was fantastic Ray. We had a really relaxing time."

"By the way, I hear congratulations are in order. Are you hoping for a boy or a girl?"

"Oh, thanks."

"Has your dad let the cat out of the bag too early?"

"No, that's fine. I haven't told school officially yet. But all the family know now, so that's fine. And you're practically family Ray!"

Ray had met Bob Straw at the depot in Chistlehurst that morning before driving to Sevenoaks. They often recalled the first time they met forty-four years earlier. It was Bob's very first day on a building site. The lads sent the youngster to fetch a glass hammer from the foreman – a traditional trick played on all fresh-faced apprentices. Ray of course had seemed very experienced. After all, he'd already been in the building game two or three years – a *long* time when you're a teenager, when hours seem days, days seem months, and years are a lifetime. He'd taken young Bob under his wing and helped him settle in the world of work. Bob was now taking care of his old mate, a skilled all-rounder, a Jack-of-all-trades *and* a master of all of them. He could do it all. Carpentry. Bricklaying. Electrics. Plumbing. The lot. A perfectionist. Although Bob realised a year or two back Ray was becoming too slow for many jobs.

Some of the contracts didn't require a perfectionist. And some of the companies didn't want perfection, just the job done quick. But this was his daughter and son-in-law's house, where there was no rush. And Ray was the best. Bob also remembered those days when his eldest daughter made tea for the builders in the era before accountants and lawyers and local officials dominated his business day.

"Well Jane, a boy or a girl, what do you want?"

"The usual. As everyone always says, I don't care as long as the baby's healthy."

"You know your dad wants a boy."

"Really?"

"Well he only managed three girls. They're no good in the building trade, are they?"

"Ray," she chided with her best teacher's voice as Matt called it, "you know that's a very sexist thing to say."

"But I'm right, aren't I? All this political correctness stuff's gone too far, that's what I say. It's not safe for a lass to be on a building site with all those blokes, is it? And most of 'em wouldn't be able to lift more than a couple of bricks."

"Rubbish."

"It's not good for the lads' blood pressure having all those lasses around either. They get distracted."

"Men should learn to control themselves then, shouldn't they?"

"Aye, they should. But when you're young and your hormones are high… Anyway, Bob will want someone to leave the business to. I bet he wants *Bob Straw and Grandson Ltd* above the depot gates and on all the vehicles."

"He could have *'and Granddaughter Ltd'* on his business letterheads you know. It might be good for business."

Jane smiled. She knew her dad would love any grandchild, boy or girl. Ray knew too.

* * *

Despite the constant criticism of the National Health Service, Jane arranged for an appointment immediately at the clinic. She left Ray to his strong tea and biscuits and went to be tested for sexually transmitted diseases including HIV-AIDS. The nurse reassured her the test would be totally confidential and the results would be back within a few days.

"You don't have to say why you need the test," said the nurse as she pulled up a chair next to Jane. "But it might help to know about the circumstances. It might also help you to talk about it."

Jane kept quiet.

The nurse probed, gently. "Do you think your husband has been unfaithful and caught something perhaps?"

"No, nothing like that. He wouldn't do that."

"Husbands do, you know. You can't always tell. Most women think their partners are faithful, believe me."

Jane told her story. "It was just before Christmas. You know, an end of term party in the teachers' common room. We'd all had too much to drink. It was just a fling. I'd almost forgotten about it, really. I know that's a terrible thing to say. But it was almost like a dream, not real. It was as if it happened to someone else and I'd heard the gossip. Then over Christmas someone said something – my husband actually – that made me think I should have a check."

"So you've *told* your husband?" the nurse asked trying to disguise her surprise.

"My God, no! What, just after I'd announced I was pregnant? He'd be devastated. He's just managed to get over the shock of becoming a father."

"Mrs Collins," the nurse asked while reaching for Jane's hand, "if you would not have been in the early stages of pregnancy, do you think you would have told your husband?"

That question had already plagued Jane. Had the baby forced her into submission and silence and secretiveness? Would she have been stronger, less vulnerable? Or had the life inside provided the strength for survival, for silence, for a secret solitary fight? *Bread. Bread. Bread....* She didn't know the answer.

"No. Definitely not," Jane told the nurse firmly. "Especially now I'm pregnant. I don't think I'd have told him anyway. It's never happened before. And it definitely won't happen again. My quick-fling days are over. But now I'm pregnant it's worse. Well, we're supposed to grow up, become mothers, responsibility and all that. This...this...quicky meant absolutely nothing. It was over in two minutes. If that. Honestly, we teachers are sometimes worse than the kids round the back of the proverbial bike shed. Look, you must get hundreds of women in here saying the same thing."

The nurse refused to confirm or deny. She allowed Jane to talk on.

"Matt - that's my husband not the teacher - and I were walking in the woods after Christmas and he said something about trees been infected and, all of a sudden, I thought I'd better get tested. I'm pretty sure this teacher's been around a bit. I bet I'm not the first fling he's ever had. And he was in South Africa recently where AIDS is rife. Who knows what he got up to?"

"He didn't...*you* didn't use protection then?"

"I know. It was stupid, really stupid. But you know what it's like. It starts as a quick kiss, a bit of a touch up and then before you know it..."

The nurse knew exactly what it was like. "But you know Mrs Collins it's also not good to drink alcohol when you're pregnant. It could damage the baby."

"Yes. Drinking was stupid too." Jane ate humble pie.

She'd not touched alcohol for weeks.

* * *

He never thought the list would end. Delete. Delete. Why do people add all these attachments? Delete. Matt was always highly selective in the emails he read. Delete. He wasn't usually interested in notes from Administration, although this one said his new BMW will be delivered Friday January 10 and "sorry for the delay". There was an interesting message about a woman's earring found in the cleaner's basement cupboard. But how did it get there? He was sure she wouldn't own up for it would fuel gossip and give the game away. He'd find out later what really went on. The cleaner's room was a notorious location at Henderson-Strutt for "private functions", as Dave the porter described it.

If Matt was copied alongside many others on a note to the chief executive officer his instinct was to delete. Most of the senders were over-estimating the value of a prospective new business client. Or, worse, they were full of self-praise seeking more praise from the bosses. They were showing off around the company network. The good guys in business simply do the business, generated the money, and didn't write notes telling everyone. In crisis and issues management, confidentiality was crucial. Success was measured by silence and secrecy.

Within Henderson-Strutt's worldwide agency network of around 2,000 staff, there were several time-wasting colleagues. They were high maintenance colleagues who talked about talks, held meetings about meetings, wrote memos about memos. They read books on management methodology. Their offices were full of slogans on teamwork. They wrote reports - long reports naturally - on "client-centred strategic alliances" and "global infra-structural change". They spent long hours in the office and never left - or were never seen to leave - before their boss. They talked about getting results without achieving any. They should join the United Nations or work for the European Commission, Peter had said of them. Matt agreed. He deleted their emails without reading them. If it's that important, they'll phone. And they did occasionally phone. But they couldn't talk up their scheme any better than write it. Matt's response was always helpful and encouraging: "That sounds great. I'm really too busy to help because of this time-consuming situation at the moment. Try contacting…"

* * *

Peter experienced a Christmas without his wife and children, although he didn't say much to Matt at their first meeting of the day to review client work. Peter had been with them every Christmas Day, apart from a couple of years when they were babies and he had to work on a crisis. Peter's family were at *her* parents in the country, perhaps with *her* new lover-boy. He wouldn't ask. Didn't want to know about *her*. He phoned to wish the kids Happy Christmas. But his mother-in-law said they had gone for a walk. Peter was sure he could hear the kids in the background, despite the generous double whisky he allowed himself for Christmas breakfast.

Maybe the sound of laughter was something on the telly. He wished his wife's mother Merry Christmas and she said thank you and the line cut. He had another drink. There was no bread or milk and the freezer was empty. When he called later in the afternoon his father-in-law muttered something about the children being happy with their presents but currently involved in some game or other and they'd call later. Who knows what tales she'd been telling her parents about him? He was no longer the favourite son-in-law, if he'd ever been, that's for sure. Peter started to call a third time, but after tapping 0121... he noticed *Only Fools and Horses* on the TV and the kids loved Del Boy and Rodders. He put the phone down somewhere. It didn't matter. It wouldn't ring. Their mother was making him suffer. It was the reward for putting his work and a high income first. Anyway, the telly was always more fun than daddy.

Peter returned to work Boxing Day. He had office keys and knew the code to switch off the security alarm. He liked working when everyone else wasn't, although some junior executives and one or two managers did appear mid morning to catch up on some project or business proposal. Thanks to Christmas-quiet roads, his drive took half the usual time, and he always drove faster than Bert. Peter spent the quiet time in the office planning his next moves for several clients, who to see and when. Like home, there was no fresh milk in Peter's office either. But at least the drinks machine could produce white coffee.

Over the next few days, between Christmas and New Year, Peter wined and dined in quiet clubs and restaurants with key influencers, as PR jargon describes people with power. Whitehall's civil servants were enjoying the absence of Westminster's politicians. It allowed them to get things done and not be distracted by politics. For many years, from Harold Wilson's government onwards, MPs had tried to curb the influence of the civil service. They generally failed. The civil servants let the politicians have their own way for a time, make a few concessions, allow them the delusion of power, but then emerge triumphant as the government's majority in the Commons inevitably decreased.

Even Margaret Thatcher couldn't handbag them out of power. The reason is simple: politicians come, politicians go. As one TV interviewer famously challenged a transient Secretary of State for Defence, "...you're a here today gone tomorrow politician". The politician walked out of the studio. The country voted against the party. Another government came and went. But the civil servants Peter talked with were there then - and now. Whitehall's changes are structured, ordered, planned. Politicians change with the mark of a humble X on a ballot paper.

Peter's first contact in Whitehall was confident that, in Britain at least, AestChem Inc's 22XP or FFresherFood, as they preferred to call it with non-scientists, would gain approval. Brussels was different.

"They stick their nose into virtually all our business nowadays," said Peter's long-time friend from DEFRA, the Department of Environment, Food and Rural Affairs. "But there are indirect routes to circumnavigate their resistance. And direct ones of course. We should take the more complex but certainly less expensive indirect route I think." Peter agreed while topping up their glasses with fine claret. Waiters at this gentlemen's club realise distance and discretion is an essential skill.

"If the French would have fought Hitler as strongly as they now resist common sense reforms of agricultural policy, the panzers would never have rumbled into Paris," he chuckled later over the excellent port, a fine vintage from '85. Peter nodded and laughed. He'd better call Bert to drive him home.

The next day Peter contacted another old chum, now a key policy advisor to the European Commission. A phone call to his home in the Scottish Highlands to arrange a meeting in Brussels could not have been better timed.

"Bloody damn pleased you called Peter," he blasted down the phone. "Now look old thing, a gun's dropped out, so if you can get your arse up here PDQ for New Year you can join us up in the heather to bag a few."

Peter snapped the invitation to pot a few partridge. There's nothing better than a few days upland game shooting. He immediately booked the flight to Inverness. He'd hire a car and drive to the estate of his childhood friend. In the small castle, with nearly 20 bedrooms, he knew there would be a warm welcome, a roaring log fire, the finest malts, and a cold bed in a musty room with an old-fashioned hot water bottle. Even highly paid Commission staff, with their lavish expenses, can't afford to keep every room warm in a highland castle. "But it's a bloody sight warmer than Balmoral," the owner told new guests.

At home that night Peter opened the gun cabinet to choose his weapon. He would take a shotgun suitable for a day's walking high on the heather moors. From his six guns Peter reached for his lightest side-by-side 12 bore with double triggers, hand-crafted by Holland & Holland. His insurers had valued the gun at about £30,000, thanks to it quality hand-engraved game scenes and its bold foliate decoration. It weighed about 6½ lbs, suitable for fast shooting and carrying all day, probably in driving rain or snow. He'd take his reliable Beretta over-and-under too. One of the beaters could carry this heavier gun to the high land. He checked with British Airways if the carrying rules had tightened following another spate of terrorist hijacks. But as the guns would be partially disassembled, cased, and placed in the hold, there would be no problem. The castle had a cellar room full of ammunition and several spare guns, so he'd leave his cartridges at home.

* * *

At their meeting on Matt's first day back, Peter finished briefing Matt about the progress he'd achieve over the break, although he didn't tell him exactly how, or who had helped him. Matt didn't ask. He didn't need to know, although he wanted to know. But Peter would not have told him. "A 'need to know' policy is the best policy," he'd often say.

Back in his own office Matt phoned Chicago and updated Jenni Tallow at AestChem Inc that everything, to date, seemed to be going well for the European acceptance of 22XP. With "so far, so good then" the Senior Vice President of Corporate Communications said goodbye to Matt. After one or two urgent personal calls, Ms Tallow informed her President and CEO of Henderson-Strutt's update. Over the next few days AestChem's stock experienced high volume trading, probably because traders had returned to work after the holiday. Its price on New York's Stock Exchange started to rise, nice and slowly. Perhaps the reason for the stock price movement was because of the increased costs of base chemicals from Eastern Europe and China. One or two analysts predicted that several giant US chemical and pharmaceutical firms may reconsider placing future raw material orders with AestChem now the price differential had decreased. Specialist fund managers followed each other like sheep in the meadow. When one recommended "buy" others chewed the hay too. The US President had also recently talked about *"Americans supporting American business and American business supporting Americans"* in his latest nationwide broadcast.

Peter invited Matt for an after-work drink. The bar was quiet, apart from several Japanese tourists who'd clearly taken a wrong turning off Trafalgar Square. Holidaymakers didn't usually find this side-alley haunt of politicians and mandarins. And MPs were not yet back in town. Some were in their constituencies. Others were on official trips, especially to the Southern Hemisphere or somewhere near the Equator at this time of year. Several were on fact-finding missions to help them find the right solutions and make the correct recommendations in their general Parliamentary work or in their select committees. A number of Whitehall's middle management were taking a break in the bar, while others extended their holiday as the kids were off school. And in early January, as all publicans know, many people still maintained their New Year's resolution to stop smoking and ban booze from their bodies. The bars would be buzzing again next week.

Matt caught a late train home. He shared a litter-strewn carriage of graffiti and knife-slashed seats with a nervous young woman. She pretended not to hear the lewd remarks from the gang of yobs. Matt, uncomfortably, also kept peering through the window, but looking at nothing. He heard the abuse. But what can you do? Oblivious to the abuse, a balding red-faced guy in a crumbled pinstripe sat across the aisle snoring. The burger and beer guaranteed his sleep to Sevenoaks or beyond. Tomorrow morning he'd notice the ketchup stain on his loosened yellow tie. It would have to be thrown out. Several greasy chips had slithered down his trousers, through his lap, and rested around his black brogues. Matt didn't wake him at the station. Experienced late night commuters pin a note to themselves naming the station they wished to be shaken awake. No notice, no shake.

As Matt slammed the train door another crashed closed. One of the gang, the tall skinny one, walked several paces ahead. He didn't look tough now. Away from his mates his demeanour was of a shy coward of a kid. Remembering the vile bile towards the young woman, and the anger induced from his own fear of the gang, Matt resisted the urge to pin him against the wall and beat the shit out of him.

The lad turned left and Matt right when leaving the dismal empty station. Walking home he noticed frost crystals beginning to form on the rivulets of rainwater in the gutter after the day's downpour. It was rubbish collection day tomorrow and the first opportunity after Christmas citizens of Sevenoaks had to throw out excess packaging and unwanted presents. Next to many bins were the sad skeletal remains of Christmas trees. Their scented pine needles fallen and the festivities already a memory. Matt turned into his short driveway and passed their troublesome old car. This old heap could be sold and the cash would bring a little relief to their growing overdraft. Soon a brand new BMW would sit in its place.

Jane, alongside her neighbours, had put their bin out for rubbish collection. Having been away for Christmas, their bin should have been almost empty. But Matt noticed the top wasn't quite closed. To stop the local gang of foxes tipping the bin over, Matt lifted the lid to squash the rubbish down harder than Jane could manage. For some reason she'd thrown away the wooden bread bin, although it looked in perfect condition. So he rescued it, opened the front door as quietly as possible, and returned it to its rightful place in the kitchen. He hadn't noticed the new bread container at the other end of the worktop.

After a long drink of water to counter the effects of Peter's hospitality – at least six large glasses of red and three shorts - Matt crept upstairs. He hoped Jane would be sleeping, so he could sleep too.

Chapter Twelve

Insider dealing makes business sense...

Peter closed his office door.

"Sit down," he told Matt. It was not a polite request.

At Henderson-Strutt a closed door meant Do Not Disturb.

"Have you seen AestChem's share price Matt?"

"No."

"Well you should. Always watch a client's share price. It's crept up significantly in recent weeks. Why do you think that's happened?"

"Demand for their products? Growing economy? Shortage of chemicals?"

"Bollocks. Someone's tipped them off that 22XP is going to get European approval, that's what."

"Well it will, won't it?"

"We can't say that. We don't know for certain. I've still to get to a couple of key people. The deal's not done until the deal's done."

"But it will get the go-ahead. Surely it's just a question of time."

"It will, unless some disaster or someone gets in our way. Even so we don't want to be talking it up. Not now. It's too early. Someone's leaking optimistic news on Wall Street and bucking AestChem's price. That's not good Matt, not good."

"Why?"

"Where's your fucking brain today Matt?"

Peter went to his cabinet and took out two tumblers and, from the freezer compartment, the vodka. He splashed in a little tonic and handed Matt his drink. "Here, this will loosen you up."

"It's a bit early for me..." Matt stopped. Peter was not to be refused, not today. Matt found the glass in his hand.

"Two reasons why it's not good Matt. First, we don't want clients thinking their ride will be a smooth one. As I always say, we've got to make it look hard, even if it's not. 22XP's approval isn't fete accompli. These gravy-train jockeys in Europe may need serious persuasion. They're screwing us too remember for all they can get."

"You mean they're taking..."

Peter ignored the interruption. "Second, it now makes buying AestChem stock expensive."

The vodka on Matt's empty stomach had already made his head spin. "What's that to do with us?"

"Jesus Matt. It really isn't your best day. Aren't you listening or haven't you understood? Some people are going to make a fortune on AestChem stock when 22XP gets approved. And we're talking millions, not peanuts. The shares will go through the roof when the paperwork's completed."

"I see," Matt said. But he didn't, not clearly.

"Why don't you buy some stock?"

At first Matt thought he'd misheard. He momentarily closed his eyes hard, as if it would make his hearing clearer. Peter, conveniently, repeated the question. Matt had heard the words correctly. But he found them hard to believe. "Eh?" was all he could utter.

"I've got three simple words of advice for you Matt, *buy AestChem stock*."

"Where am I going to get..."

"Make yourself some proper money - instead of fiddling your expenses for pathetic amounts."

Matt's stomach turned as if he'd been thumped. He stuttered, "Peter, what you talking about..."

"Matt, I've known for weeks. Don't deny it. And don't insult me by trying. You've been putting in inflated mileage claims, false or doctored receipts. How specific would you like me to be? For example, you claimed a British Airways business class flight to Geneva last month when you actually took some cheap bucket flight. Are you that desperate for a few quid?"

Denial was clearly a dead end. Matt struggled to save his job. "Look, I'll give it all back. I'll..."

"I don't want it back. It's not my money. And Henderson-Strutt doesn't deserve it back. The client pays in the end. And we can't tell them about your fiddling. Just wise up Matt."

"I'm sorry, I'll..."

"Don't fucking apologise either. I don't want it. Just get smart Matt. Think about making some real money."

Had he heard correctly? If so, Peter was not going to sack him and, furthermore, he was tempting him to a greater crime. "You mean I should..."

"Yes, exactly. Get a loan and buy some AestChem stock. Or tip someone off. Someone you can trust. Someone who'll share the proceeds when they sell for a good price. Someone who won't rip you off. But don't go over the top. Buy some other safe stock at the same time to hide your hand."

"I couldn't."

"You could. Buy as much as you can, perhaps £500,000, something like that. They'll be worth at least £700,000 immediately after EU approval. 22XP is a revolutionary product. £200,000 clear profit in a few months is good money. And clear-cut chances like this don't often come along. But any rise in price now cuts your profit margin later."

"Peter, I don't know anyone with that kind of money. It's a totally different league to..."

"What about your father in law? He's got that building firm, if I remember correctly. He must have a broker. Four or five hundred thousand would be a snip to him. Both of you could make a lot of money fast. He'd be grateful."

"But it's illegal. Insider dealing. It's…"

Peter kicked hard. "It's no worse than fiddling expenses, just a lot more profitable. Get real Matt. Half the City's at it – the smart half. And Wall Street. The sin is getting caught. The regulatory authorities like to make a public token gesture every now and then and prosecute. Then the police struggle to get a guilty verdict anyway, unless the case is handed on a plate to them. Coppers don't understand what the hell's going on in business. City boys' brains against PC Plods' is no contest. You've got to be pretty careless to screw up. Stock markets couldn't function without rumours, tip offs, loose talk, innuendo, inside knowledge, informed guesswork. It's fucking better than your petty theft. What's the point of a few quid here and there? Matt, let me give you some advice. If you're going to become a thief rob a bank not a bakery. Otherwise you're going to spend all your life working your pants off for sweet FA."

Matt was confused with the cocktail of vodka, guilt and conspiracy. He hadn't noticed Peter topping up his glass again, or that he'd swallowed the contents in one gulp, as if in shock. Matt had come to realise over the years Peter had a dark side, chapters of life best unread. But insider-dealing? Bribing officials? Covering up expenses fraud?

Matt started to explain. "It's just that we're up to our limit on all the cards. Jane gets all sorts of expensive stuff. She's been used to the best money can buy. She'll pay five times more than me for a pair of shoes just for work. She bought a handbag for a few hundred a couple of weeks ago. We've got an extension being built…"

"Save it. I don't give a toss. It doesn't matter. We'll say no more about it. But you know what the accounts department is like here. Get smart before you get caught. You're lucky. I sorted things out before I signed your expenses off. You're a good operator Matt. I don't want to lose you. We'll get round this money problem. Okay?"

Peter snatched the vodka bottle from the ice bucket and topped up his own glass. Matt shook his head at Peter's offer of another refill. But again – was it the third or fourth time - the tumbler got filled despite the refusal. It was a while before Peter continued, in a calmer, friendlier voice. "I need to trust you Matt," he said. "And you've got to trust me."

Peter's raised eyebrows and fixed eyes encouraged a pledge from Matt. Can you be trusted at a deeper, personal level than the contractual obligations of Henderson-Strutt? As co-conspirator, and because of the cover-up, Matt felt obliged to nod his head confirming his allegiance. But to what? He'd stepped into unknown territory, mainly out of guilt, unsteadily because of the drink, and intrigued by the mystery. A contract had been entered into. But no words were spoken, and no papers signed.

Satisfied with Matt's promise, or at least a mutual understanding, Peter revealed, "I have a new commission. It's sensitive, highly sensitive. May involve working with other agencies. Government agencies. Foreign agencies."

Matt put his tumbler on Peter's desk. He needed to clear his head, ask questions, get things sorted, discover what he was getting into. But Matt knew questions at this time would demonstrate a lack of trust. His boss had things to say and questions would be perceived as a challenge. Peter stepped away from the drinks cabinet to sit behind his desk. He leaned forward and pointed his finger, first at Matt's chest, then at his own. "This is between you and me Matt, you and me. Nobody else *needs* to know. Nobody else *should* know. You will not discuss this project anywhere with anyone. Understood?"

Matt nodded again, less hesitantly this time. A contract of silence as well as compliance, he thought.

"And when I say *nobody*, that includes pillow talk at home with Jane - and at work with Penny."

Matt shook his head. But he hadn't misheard. "How the hell did you know about...did she say..."

Peter showed Matt the palms of both hands to silence him. "Don't worry. Your secret's safe with me. We'll talk later. Go. Take the rest of the day off. Have a think about what I've said."

Matt staggered back to the sanctuary of his own office fully aware he was drunk trying to act sober. On route he deliberately kept his head down avoiding all eye contact with colleagues as he walked through the corridors and across the open plan office with junior staff working at their desks. It's easier to think clearly staring at a bland floor than at someone's animated face. As he passed Penny's desk he was however aware she was watching. Her head remained still although he could sense her eyes following him. He didn't want to talk to anyone at this moment. Even her. Especially her. Matt had to clear his head from the vodka and dissect everything they'd discussed. As instructed, he focussed long and hard on what Peter had said. But the more he recalled Peter's words, the less he understood their meaning.

He had made a promise to be loyal. He had taken a vow of silence. He had accepted a cover up over his own petty crime. He had even discussed insider dealing. He had committed himself to work on some new commission. But what was the project? When would he start? Who with? And what would he do? Matt had no idea. No idea at all.

Chapter Thirteen

Massacre in Chechnya...

It took only 20 minutes in the speedy BMW along the M20 eastbound for Matt to reach his woodland. The final mile-long dirt track took him to where Aunt Sheila lived and died alone. He didn't see anyone apart from the old face at the window of his aunt's only friend and neighbour, Alice Campbell. They had met briefly at the funeral. But he didn't wish to stop and talk so he drove on past Rose Cottage. He would pop in and say hello another day.

Sheila Chamber's dilapidated Bower House at King's Wood near Maidstone in Kent, "The Garden of England", had been sold, or so the estate agent's sign said. Matt parked outside on the verge. It was clear nobody had yet moved in. Matt always believed a builder would snatch the house, renovate it and sell it quick for a tidy profit. Jane's dad should have bought it, but he never thought to tell him about this opportunity. Matt had other matters on his mind.

He locked the car and the bleep indicated an active burglar alarm. With crime rife in the countryside even this remote track could be part of a crook's patch, however unlikely it seemed this bitter winter's afternoon. Thanks to the potholes the car's pristine bodywork and wheels were already splattered with mud. What would Jane say when she saw its filthy state? She had already fallen in love with the car's slick lines, metallic paint, comfortable seats and firm driving. A big improvement on the little third-hand car sold "as seen" earlier that morning for a few hundred, in cash, to someone who responded to

125

Jane's advertisement in the local newspaper.

Matt walked into the woods on a narrow overgrown footpath that started from the side of Bower House. He passed the tall beech with his carved initials where he had taken Jane over Christmas. But then the trail became indistinct, swallowed by dead bracken and bramble. Few people ever came into the woods anymore, so the track was almost impossible to follow. Plants had reclaimed the pathways pioneered by generations of woodsmen and walkers.

Although the track was lost, Matt found his childhood memories. He knew exactly where he was and where he was going. He'd explored these acres as a boy in those long weeks of hot summer holidays at Aunt Sheila's. Woods change appearance as often as chameleons, although the key landmarks of King's Wood remained whatever the time of year, time of day, or type of weather. The main valley, the streams, the kidney-shaped pond, trenches and banks – dug in medieval times to protect young trees and coppice from deer and straying animals – remained as remembered.

Many of the old oaks still stood proud in Matt's acres. Most had resisted The Great Storm of October 1987 when an estimated 15 million trees were uprooted, most of them in Sussex and Kent. The Oak King maintained his woodland throne. Yet many mature shallow-rooted beech toppled. They were unable to fight the might of the wind.

The great elms had already perished. Matt, as a boy, watched them die their slow death ravished by a disease spread during the '70s and '80s by the small ambrosia beetle burrowing into the bark and depriving limb and leaf of life-giving sap. Fast-growing willow and silver birch had filled the clearings cleared by the deadly Dutch elm disease, although some of the elms had resisted the disease and were growing again.

Years ago timber contractors had planted two ten-acre plots of dark Sitka spruce in King's Wood. Governments since 1946 allowed tree planting grants and tax relief to encourage farmers and landowners to replenish wartime timber felling. But Aunt Sheila instructed them to stop planting Sitka because she, like Matt, preferred native tree species. Commercial conifer planting created dark dead forest floors. They were not much fun to play in for Matt either. Upright trunks were hard to climb. There were not many animals within these columns of conifers. And birds don't sing bright songs in dark woods.

Matt's geography teacher at school, Mr Webster, had told the class five hundred kinds of bugs, beetles, butterflies and moths could live in a single oak. He'd never forgotten that fact. It stuck like the spelling of "Mississippi" – M I double S I double S I double P I – from English. Like school kids everywhere also remember the birthplace of Abraham, the father of the Jews, from religious education class - because teachers worldwide crack the same joke. When asked where Abraham was born, and the child hesitates with "Ur", the kid is right. Mr Webster had also said there were around 1,700 types of lichen in Britain, although Matt could only find ten species for his first-year geography project.

But he had discovered more than thirty species of mushrooms, toadstools and fungi. At the beginning of autumn term Matt took an old shoebox to school to show off loads of great samples of *Amanita phalloides*. He couldn't understand why his teacher made such a fuss, until he explained the scientific name in English. It was understandable that Mr Webster did not want children in his care to eat Death Caps. And they do look similar to many perfectly safe mushrooms. "You only need a sweet-sized bite to poison you to death," he told the class. "You can also get very bad stomach pains if you don't wash your hands after touching them and then lick your finger."

"Grassy" Green, the tallest boy in the class, suggested using them to rid the school of some 'orrible teachers. But the killer mushrooms were confiscated. The teachers had clearly second-guessed the treachery. A year later Green's life ended, killed by a hit-and-run, aged 12. School assembly the next day was sad. Even some of the boys cried in front of the girls. John Green had been the best joke-teller and funniest kid in the class. He'd have been the first to make a joke out of his own death. "I wasn't running fast enough," or "The car swerved to miss me" or some such nonsense he would have spouted. But dwelling on the past didn't stop Matt worrying about the future.

Matt reached a clearing covered in long dead grass near the centre of the woods. This was it. This was the place. His childhood fantasy could now become his adult reality. Of course there would be no Robin Hood, Little John, Friar Tuck or merry men to join him anymore. There was no King John either to impose terrible taxes on the poor, although taxes live on.

Here Matt's camp would be set up. There would be a campfire surrounded by logs to sit on. In this spot he would site his woodland base. He'd build a shelter – the straight trunks of felled Sitka spruce would be useful for that. This would be perfect for the enclosure. It had water, from a stream in a gully about six feet deep and twelve feet from bank to bank looped around the clearing. Today the water was shoulder deep and even in the driest summer the brown trout, perch and stickleback survived. He drank its water as a lad and came to no harm, although he'd probably boil it before drinking now. The spread of grassland was surrounded by mature stands of oak and ash to provide shelter. A tall Scots pine stood alone, its lower dead branches broken under the canopy of bluish green needles and grey cones. Clumps of holly provided a winter wind barrier for Matt's camp. An outcrop of rowan held clusters of ripe scarlet berries on their branches to help songbirds survive the winter.

This place would become Matt's spiritual sanctuary. This was nature, natural and real, not artificial, constructed and deceitful. This enclave would enclose his life from the world outside, a ring-fence from the 21st century. Here, at least for a few hours at the weekend or on holiday, there would be no bills to pay, no debt mountain, no pressure to perform, no deadlines. Matt would use these woods as his private nature reserve away from real life. Time could take its time.

It was getting dark. It was time to get practical, get real and go home. Matt could normally follow his own track out of the woods as he did as a child. But as dusk descended the signs were harder to detect.

It should have taken 15 minutes or so to get back to the car. But 45 minutes after leaving the clearing Matt was struggling for a geographical signpost to lead him out of the forest. Clouds stopped any moonlight giving depth and form to his surroundings. He stumbled across a block of pine planting. The treetops swayed in harmony as the wind increased. But which conifer plot, the block to the north, or the ten acres nearer to Bower House? Matt walked around the pines to find a clue to his location. He assumed this was the plot near to his Aunt's former home, and his car, and strode in what he believed the right direction.

The woods became thicker, and it was getting darker. But he enjoyed the freezing rain stinging his face. Brambles ripped his trousers and tore into his legs like barbed wire. He stumbled when a branch struck his face. Matt held his cheek to ease the pain and saw the blood on his fingers before the rain washed it into the earth. Matt was invigorated, alone, alive.

Short sharp barks cracked in front of him as animals the size of large dogs leapt from the dense undergrowth. Matt was startled but not scared. He'd disturbed several muntjac deer, descendants of escapees from Woburn Park in Bedfordshire and now naturalised all over central and southern Britain. Further on he alarmed a pheasant that fluttered and screeched as it escaped to find roosting on a higher bow.

Through the storm Matt was relieved to see a dim yellow light in the distance, its beam broken occasionally be swaying trees. He followed like a boat at sea sets its line to the harbour lighthouse. Fighting through the final thickets at the wood's edge, Matt reached the white picket fence around the back garden of his former Aunt's neighbour Alice Campbell.

"Hello," he heard her elderly voice on the wind.

"Hello, Mrs Campbell?"

"Oh there you are," she said as Matt opened the gate into the rear garden. "I wondered where you were. I was beginning to get worried. I knew you were still out there. It's been dark for some time now and it's a dreadful night."

"You can say that again."

"Come in. Come in," she fussed. "Here's a towel to dry your hair and…my heavens, you've cut your cheek. Best sit down. I'll get a dressing. Now, where's my first aid tin? I know, it's in the bathroom. I'll just pop and get it."

"There's really no need, I'll be all right," Matt called as she went to find the kit. "I must be getting home. My wife was expecting me ages ago."

"There you are. Now just hold that to your face while I find the sticky tape. Oh, where's that?" She left the room again to search.

Matt stood and looked in the gilt-edged mirror above the fireplace in which coal burned. Odd, he thought, when the cottage was surrounded by wood. The heat caused steam to rise from his wet mud-stained trousers. The cut was superficial, nothing more than a scratch, and it had stopped bleeding by the time Alice returned with sticking plaster.

"I put the light on in the back garden deliberately you know," she explained. "Those woods can be as thick as the rain forest in Borneo. Sometimes your Aunt Sheila went walking in those woods at night and she'd get lost occasionally. It's very easy to do, especially at night when you can't see the nose on your face."

"I'm very grateful, thanks, I really must be…"

"I told Sheila many times not to go gallivanting for stray cats and whatnot at night. What's the point, you can't see in the dark anyway?"

"Thanks Mrs Campbell but…"

"The kettle's boiled so I'm sure you'd like a cup of tea." She scurried into the kitchen.

"I'd better phone Jane to let her know I'll be home soon," raising the volume to carry into the kitchen.

"I don't have a phone, you know," the frail voice spoke from the back of the house. "No need. Nobody to talk to. The woman from the council drops in sometimes, when she remembers that is. Most of my family have gone you see. There's a few relatives in New Zealand and a cousin in Scotland somewhere..." Her words trailed away.

"Don't worry Mrs Campbell, I'll use my mobile, it's in the car."

Matt went to the front door but turned back. What's the point phoning now? He won't get back any quicker and he'd get wet again. The car was parked well up the lane. He enjoyed hot tea with Alice and listened to how she found Aunt Sheila in bed, cold and dead, while the milkman stood "scared as a mouse" in the doorway. "I've no-one now," she said as Matt said thanks and goodbye as he ran through the rain to the car. He promised to drop in again soon to see how she was. Alice would look forward to that. "Make it soon," she said as the car's lights disappeared.

* * *

"I'm *so* sorry Jane," he said crashing through the front door soaked and steaming. He'd had the car's heater set maximum.

"Where have you been? What on earth have you be doing? Have you seen the state of your clothes? There's mud everywhere. Do you know you've got a bruise on your face? Have you messed up the inside of the car? You said you were only going for an hour."

Jane stopped the inquisition. She breathed deeply to hide her anxiety at being home alone as dark descended. Hugged him. Kissed him.

Her behaviour surprised Matt. Since before Christmas Jane had been avoiding most advances, sensitive to touch, quiet, moody. She wanted to be held but not squeezed, needed love but not passion, desired psychological warmth without physical heat. Pregnancy affected some women in this way. He would give her time and space to recover. Her coolness had, frankly, helped him. He'd been tired, under pressure. He needed time and space too to think through his plans for King's Wood. And work on Peter's plan to help President Alik Vadimov of Russia "rebuild his global public image" – a near impossible task after the massacre in Chechnya.

Chapter Fourteen

The bureaucrats in Brussels...

"Thank you very much Peter for that kind introduction," beamed Claude Perlemuter from Henderson-Strutt's office in Brussels. "I'm delighted to be invited here to London and address our esteemed clients from Chicago about the complicated workings of politics in Europe. I hope you're enjoying London gentlemen – and, of course, Ms Tallow?" He bowed towards her and she smiled at the special recognition.

AestChem's directors nodded agreement at Claude as he stood tall and elegant at the front of the main conference room in Bloomsbury Chambers. Jenni Tallow had experienced no trouble persuading AestChem's President and three fellow board directors to accompany her to Europe. The stock was rising. Analysts were optimistic. Their pensions were secure. They would be meeting many influential people for the good of their chemical corporation. They would reassure Europe that 22XP was a marvellous product to preserve fruit and vegetables. They would visit London, Brussels, Strasbourg, Paris and perhaps other cities. Two wives accompanied their husbands. Two personal assistants accompanied their directors. Ms Tallow had booked a modest double room at The Dorchester in Park Lane. They were today a little jet-lagged as they made themselves comfortable in the black leather chairs at Henderson-Strutt's London headquarters. But they would soon get over the time difference.

"Jenni, gentlemen, before we facilitate your visit to the shrines of decision-making in Europe, Peter wisely suggested we give you a short briefing on who does what over here. To start, I can tell you most people in Europe don't understand how Europe is governed. Actually the bureaucrats and politicians like it that way. They do nothing to help our understanding. In *our* confusion and ignorance rests *their* power."

He paused for laughter, or at least a smile. He received neither. Then he remembered these were Americans *working*. Work is serious, because work is about money. And money is serious business to Americans. Stick to the facts Claude, forget the subtleties, he told himself. Peter, Matt and Penny did smile, mainly at their clients' inability to do so. They were sat at the far end of the board table offering support to their colleague from Brussels. They knew exactly what was going through Claude's mind. They also knew he was a very experienced presenter and smooth operator, fluent in seven languages, a PhD in Food Science, an INSEAD MBA, and trained by the European Commission itself.

Claude continued undeterred. "Before I outline Europe's political structure, I know you wanted more information about the so-called Common Agricultural Policy. As in your country, the rich countries of Europe wish to protect their agriculture by erecting tariff barriers against imports of food. To make it more difficult for importers, protectionist countries pay their farmers cash subsidies directly or subsidise food prices. Believe it or not nearly one-third of all the rich-world farmer's income now comes from subsidies and support. The average family in the European Union pays at least $25 every week in taxes and higher food prices to pay these farmers. Some reforms were proposed during 2003 but the politicians pulled a lot of wool over a lot of eyes. Subsidies will remain for many years. Jenni, gentlemen, think on this fact: each day your average cow in the European Union receives more in subsidies than half the world's population has to live on. Incidentally, that's still only one third the subsidy Japanese cows receive."

"What about agrochemicals Claude?" asked Jenni, seemingly more interested in corporate income than global poverty.

"There is a new EU Chemicals Agency. Around 100,000 older substances have not been tested and probably won't be. A new system called REACH, Registration, Evaluation and Authorisation of Chemicals, is being phased in as we speak. This will be applied to all new imported chemical introductions, including your 22XP."

"What if we were to manufacture 22XP in Europe instead of importing?"

"For all substances manufactured in amounts of one tonne per year or more, then you would require registration. Basic information about the chemical's properties and a brief assessment of likely impacts on health and the environment would be recorded. Substances produced in quantities of 100 tonnes per year or more would be fully evaluated. The registration data would be examined by the competent authority of the member state."

"So if we made the raw stuff in France, the French would do the examination, right?"

"Right."

"Are some countries easier to get approval than others?"

"Right again. And we can, Jenni, talk about that in detail over lunch," Claude said before taking a sip of water and continuing.

"Now, in the few minutes before what I know will be an excellent lunch, perhaps I should complete the outline of the European way of working. This will just take two minutes and it will help you put into context all the people we will meet, and the places we will be visiting, over the next few days. Europe is ruled by three elements, the European Union, the European Commission and the European Parliament. They are not the same thing. And it's easy to get them confused."

"What about the EEC and the European Community?" chirped one of the dark-suited directors.

"Well, sir, the European Community came into existence in 1967 through a merger of several organisation including the European Economic Community. The EEC was established in March 1957 by Treaties of Rome, sometimes incorrectly called the Treaty of Rome. But thankfully we can forget about these because, in 1993, the European Union was formed following the Treaty of Maastricht, signed one year earlier."

"You were right Mr Perlemuter. It's as confusing as hell," admitted another AestChem director.

"In short, my friends, all you need to remember for your visits are salient facts. We have, of course, prepared a briefing paper for you all with the key facts on who does what. Simply remember the European Union replaced the European Community and all its institutions. We have outlined its responsibilities in the briefing paper. Now, let's turn to the European Commission. This is one of the principal institutions of the EU. It is responsible for planning EU policies. Its loyalties are to the Union as a whole rather than to its individual states. The Commission heads a large Secretariat in Brussels. This submits proposals for consideration by the Council of Ministers. It is also the Commission that is charged with the implementation of decisions taken by the Council. The Commission also acts as the mediator between the different EU members."

"My God," the President declared. "No wonder you Brits object to all your taxes going to fund these talk shops across Europe."

"Actually, sir, I'm half French half Belgium from Lithuanian grandparents on my mother's side," smiled Claude. "And the taxes are worse in Belgium."

"No offence Mr Perlemuter."

"And none taken. You are certainly correct to highlight its complexity. It is growing into a bureaucratic nightmare. Currently, in Brussels alone, the Commission uses over 70 different buildings with over 25,000 staff. The Commission also has 145 delegations elsewhere in Europe and around the world. And these figures *exclude* Parliament and the Council of Ministers and their respective support staff. But we at Henderson-Strutt turn this complex adversity to our simple advantage – on your behalf."

Peter, Matt and Penny admired Claude's charm and knowledge of European affairs. As with all clients, AestChem's bosses were clearly impressed by the PR agency's European expert. Soon it would be time for lunch, in a private room at a Covent Garden restaurant. Peter had arranged for a Special Advisor to one of the key European Commissioners to address the party. A fee had been agreed following an excellent day's shoot and several fine malts. The cheque would be made out to his wife for "hospitality services and consultancy". Peter did, after all, remember discussing with her the possibility of bringing clients to Scotland for a "corporate party shoot with catering". This would also help reduce the advisor's tax burden and he wouldn't have to declare this "small speaking engagement" to the Commission. His £2,000 fee wasn't considered significant. And a discussion about a possible conflict of interest would indicate a probable conflict of interest. Best avoided. Peter understood. The Special Advisor would simply consolidate the information provided by Claude and answer questions from AestChem board members. It was, as he explained, his way of helping the business community understand the Commission and demonstrate its willingness to be "open and transparent".

On AestChem Inc's schedule for 16.00 hours was a visit to The Palace of Westminster. Peter and Matt would escort their clients in their chauffeur driven cars from the restaurant in Covent Garden. Several Members of Parliament had agreed to meet the giant US chemical company's senior team at Portcullis House, the office accommodation for MPs who can't find rooms in the House of Commons itself. But Peter wanted to impress his clients with the history, dignity and grandeur of the Palace of Westminster. Visitors whisper in the lobby; they talk at Portcullis House. An unused committee room had been booked for the meeting in the historic heart of Great Britain, right under Big Ben.

"So in conclusion," Claude continued, "the final piece in the jigsaw of European politics is the European Parliament. This meets in Luxembourg and Strasbourg."

"Where in Germany is that?" asked the marketing director.

"It certainly sounds German and, my good friend, many people in Britain are also fooled by its name," smiled Claude. "But it is actually in France. Now although the Parliament has the theoretical power to dismiss the Commission by a vote of censure, its actual powers are restricted. Its role has traditionally been advisory rather than legislative. There are 626 seats filled by Members of the European Parliament from all the member states. You will be meeting several of them tomorrow in Luxembourg over dinner at this small country's finest restaurant. So thank you for listening so attentively. Any questions before we depart for lunch?"

Matt was in awe at Claude's diplomatic skills. He had clearly fine-tuned them when he worked at the Commission before head-hunted by Henderson-Strutt.

The next five days were busy for everyone with meetings and movement across Europe. On Friday afternoon in Paris, as the visitation came to an end, AestChem's President and three other directors, wives and personal assistants went their separate ways. The President and his wife flew direct from Paris back home to Chicago. One director and his wife returned to London. Peter had secured tickets for two West End shows most people waited months to see. Two other directors had factories and suppliers to visit elsewhere in Europe early next week. They stayed on to work over the weekend in Paris with their assistants. After five days constantly together on business the directors could not wait to part for leisure and pleasure, despite their handshakes, backslaps and smiles.

Jenni Tallow returned to London too. She took Eurostar from Paris Gare du Nord to Waterloo International. Peter had recommended the train in preference to the plane. But none of her colleagues could recall her saying where exactly she was going, what she was doing, or whom she would see.

Chapter Fifteen

She left confused and upset...

Jane's appointment was at 3pm. She was fortunate the Head had any free time at all. First day of term is always hectic. But her long-standing friend Sarah, the receptionist at The Oaks, made sure the Head's secretary found a slot in his diary. In any case Mr Morrison would have made time for Jane Collins, even at the end of a tiring day. He regarded her bubbly personality alongside her teaching skills highly. She was an asset to the school.

"Please do sit down my dear," he said, aware of but not inhibited by the political incorrectness of "my dear". He was of the old school where manners maketh man, a specimen of bygone generations in attitude to ladies, gentlemen and children. He never used the word "kid" although accepted it had become everyday parlance. "A 'kid' is a young goat," he argued until the 1970s then gave up trying to turn the tide of its usage. He accepted rapid radical change in today's world while struggling to maintain the sense of community he remembered as a small child in war-torn 1940s Britain. His computer skills were as sharp and speedy as any child under his care. But he longed for the soft-focus slower pace of the 1950s without the bleeps, buzzes and flashing lights of now. He desired discretion, instead of today's wall-to-wall innuendo and crudity.

"Thank you." Jane accepted his invitation to be seated. The Head's office resembled an old library packed with leather-bound books on dark wood shelves with the aroma of bee's wax polish. It represented tradition, learning, integrity.

"Now Jane, please don't tell me you are leaving The Oaks. I do so hate resignations. We have here such a good team spirit."

"No, nothing like that Mr Morrison."

"Something troubling you?"

"I'm going to have a baby, that's all."

"That's all," he beamed before walking around his desk to plant a kiss on Jane's cheek. "That's wonderful news. Congratulations."

"Thanks."

"Good for our little business too. Remember today's babies are tomorrow's school children. Is Matt happy?"

Jane was impressed. Did this man ever forget anything? It must be over a year ago since he met Matt, at the school's Christmas play. She was certain his name had not been mentioned since. He showed the same attention to detail when a teacher mentions a child. He always had instant recall of their family circumstances and the child's progress across the curriculum. He would know if the child's history needed improving or their maths was going well.

"Matt's delighted now, thank you. But it did come as a bit of a shock at first."

"Yes, I too remember suffering from new-father shock syndrome," he said before lowering his voice and looking over both shoulders as if plotting a conspiracy. "Now Jane, tell me to mind my own business if you like, but is everything all right?

She looked at him.

"You know, do you need a little time off for anything? Is everything all right in the morning? I remember my wife suffered terribly with morning sickness for months, with all three of our tribe."

"Thankfully I've had very little of that. I've just gone right off tea and coffee. But I love chocolate even more."

"Good. Good. And when's the baby due?"

"The middle of June."

"June. Excellent. Jane my dear, if I may say so, your timing is excellent. It's so much better to have a little one in summer so you can enjoy the fresh air together and not be stuck indoors."

"I know you're very busy Mr Morrison so I should leave you to get on." Jane started to stand, but the Head's hand gesture suggested she stayed seated.

"There's no rush. I have a little announcement too," adopting his conspirator's voice again. "Tomorrow I shall officially announce to the school my retirement at the end of summer term. I gather most of the teaching staff think I'm passed it and speculating this would be the year of my going."

He waited for a response. Jane obliged.

"Well, yes, there had been a rumour or two, that's true. But I can honestly say every teacher in this school thinks very highly of you. Nobody could possibly think you're 'passed it'. You're as sharp as a butcher's knife. None of us wishes you to go. The Oaks won't be the same without you, although you deserve your retirement more than anyone."

"Very nice of you to say so, very nice. Now Jane, is the world to know about your condition, or do you wish it to remain confidential until the bump becomes too big to keep a secret in a school like this?"

"Now you know, I don't mind anyone knowing."

"Including the children?"

"Knowing how nosey some of them are, quite frankly, I'd be surprised if they didn't know already."

"You're probably right my dear. You're probably right," he said walking towards the door.

Before opening it, with his hand on the brass handle, Mr Morrison looked deep into Jane's eyes and added, "It's very hard to keep a secret anywhere, especially in a school. So many people hear so many things from so many people in the neighbourhood. And children have such big ears and they can't wait to gossip."

It was the way he looked at her. Sympathetically. It was the way he spoke. Slowly. Deliberately. As if he knew. As if he could read the mind, feel the pain, recognise guilt and shame. What could he have heard? Nothing. Nobody knew about what happened. She'd said nothing to anyone. But Jane sensed he sensed something. She felt uneasy and ashamed. Was it paranoia? Or a simple coincidence he made a remark like this in the way he did?

She left Mr Morrison's office confused and upset. The corridor was seething with excited children searching for their next classroom for the final lesson of the day. In the chaos Jane couldn't recognize any face of any child.

Bread. Bread. Bread.

Chapter Sixteen

Tears merged as their faces touched...

Penny Taylor never mentioned the night before Christmas when she tempted Matt into her bed in a luxury Chicago hotel. Well, not to him, although it was discussed casually in conversation to a few friends and colleagues. Since then Henderson-Strutt's graduate trainee in the crisis public relations department had behaved as if nothing had happened between them.

Matt had also failed to detect any difference in her behaviour towards him, in what she said, how she said it, or in her body language and attitude. She acted normally because, to her, the occasional one-night stand was normal. Not that she slept with every Tom, Dick or Harry. She was a highly selective man predator. She needed to know something of her target's background. She didn't like scoring with a stranger. The physical man had to have emotional depth. Intelligence, imagination, humour and sophistication were prerequisites in the men she wanted. "Dull talkers make dull fuckers," was a line she'd used since she was sixteen at the expensive boarding school for girls in rural Sussex. Penny was of that genre of educated young women who wanted fun before work, life before marriage, men before husbands. Her thrice-married barrister father provided financial security, verbal dexterity and razor-sharp intelligence. Her mother, his first wife, provided beauty, flair and emotional instinct. At fifty the former

Mrs Taylor's face and figure were extensively used in catalogues and magazines to promote products "for the older woman market segment", as the model agency's profile gushed.

Penny enjoyed going out with her mother and watching the men decide which, of the two of them, they fancied most. Penny was fascinated by the dynamics: Mummy fancied the younger ones, she the more mature type. Either way, the men didn't complain. Penny had become a friend as much as a daughter. She was proud to have raised Penny knowing how to handle men and get the best out of them, physically, emotionally – and financially. In the world today "manploitation", as she dubbed it, was an essential life-skill.

The night with Matt meant more to him than her. To Penny it was no big deal. It was what it was, one night of fun and frolics with a reasonably handsome bloke. It seemed right at the time. It didn't seem wrong later. Matt was another man on another night. Not quite. They did work together and he was her immediate boss. That added a dimension she was not familiar with, although she had handled a similar situation with her tutor at Cambridge.

Matt had called Penny into his office, the glass box he called it. A year earlier this human aquarium became the source of office leaks. Every senior manager who sat behind a glass panel at Henderson-Strutt seemed to be suffering from lapses in confidentiality. Peter, using logic, deduction and a little trap that Sherlock Holmes and Hercule Poirot would have admired, discovered that a secretary could lip-read. She could "hear" what was going on and consequently became the leading office gossip – until Peter ordered the caretakers to stick fuzzy plastic on all important office windows. You can now see shadows, but you can't read lips.

Penny walked from her desk in the open plan area she shared with around 30 other junior executives, personal assistants and secretaries on the first floor of Bloomsbury Chambers. Matt needed an update on the budget for several clients, including AestChem. The finance director had asked him to bill the expenditure and out of

144

pocket expenses for the company's recent top-level delegation visit to Europe. Peter had been right. The finance department were tightening their procedures.

As Matt started to go over the figures, Penny suddenly asked, "Could this chemical process really cause cancer?" Matt looked up. "Do you think we should be helping to promote this product if it could end up giving cancer to millions of people?"

Surprised, Matt replied, "I hardly think it's as bad as that. 22XP has been used in the US for some time and people aren't dropping dead like flies in winter."

"Sure, but nobody knows for certain."

"What's brought on this concern Penny?"

"Oh nothing, I'm just curious to know what you really think."

"Well, on that basis, do we know anything is 'safe'? Scientists still don't know the real cause of most cancers and many diseases. And if they know a general cause, they don't know the specific cause in a particular person. There are several reputable scientists who are still not certain mad cow disease really caused Creutzfeldt-Jakob disease through infected meat. Some of those scare-mongering scientists predicted a plague of dementia. It didn't happen. They talk about 'contributory factors' and 'confounding factors' and 'genetic make up' and 'pre-disposition' and 'trigger mechanisms'. But nobody really knows why one person gets a disease and another doesn't."

Penny looked unconvinced. It compelled Matt to continue. "Why do some people who never smoked get lung cancer? Why do some people who sunbathe their skin to elephant leather never get malignant melanoma? In the end, if you chose the wrong parents, you're in trouble. Could lettuce be the cause of cancer? I don't know. There isn't a scientist in the world that can say a product is totally safe. Even a paperclip can spring up and hit you in the eye."

Matt tried harder. "When I was at junior school a boy was walking across the classroom and fell over. The pencil he was carrying went through his eye into his brain. Dead. Just like that. Should all pens and pencils be banned in schools? My grandfather was a gamekeeper for over 60 years. He used rifles and 12-bores virtually every day of his life and never once had an accident with a gun. 'The most dangerous thing in the woods,' he'd say, 'was your own carelessness.' Penny, do you know, statistically speaking, the most dangerous place in the world? A bed. More people die in bed than anywhere else."

Mentioning *bed* in Penny's presence temporarily distracted Matt. As he lost his flow, Penny persisted. "But how can we trust AestChem? How do *we* know they are telling us all *they* know?" When asking questions Penny modelled herself on her father in court. She had watched him several times from the public gallery dressed impressively in wig and gown at the Old Bailey, and once at the Court of Appeal.

Matt's mind remained locked on images of Penny naked in the Chicago hotel bedroom. But he managed an almost automatic response. "Should we trust clients? Doubt it. That might be a quick route to commercial suicide. We certainly don't know if AestChem are telling us all they know. We have no way of finding out either. Think of your father, Penny. Does he believe everyone he has successfully prosecuted was truly guilty? Or those he defended innocent? No, of course not. But we all have to do our jobs and live with the consequences."

"If 22XP turns out to be a killer chemical, are we legally liable? Could we be prosecuted helping to promote a product that kills people?"

"Ask your Dad. He'd know better than most."

"I will and I'll ask him about…"

Matt interrupted, "Penny, forget about work for a minute, what happened….in Chicago….before Christmas…when we…"

"What about it? It was fun, wasn't it?"

He hesitated, "Yes but…"

"You had a good time didn't you?"

"Sure. It was fantastic. But…"

146

"I had a good time too. It was great. Your wife's lucky to have you."

"So is that it?" His mouth stayed open.

"What do you mean 'is that it'?"

"Where does it go from here?"

"Where do you want *it* to go Matt?"

"I don't know."

"Does *it* have to go anywhere?"

"You've not said anything about what happened. You've behaved as if nothing happened."

"Did you want me to? Did you want me to be...to be...different? What is there to say? Matt, what is there to be *different* about?"

"I don't know."

"It's not like you Matt not to know."

"I know I don't know..."

They laughed at the impasse. It eased the mounting tension and left them smiling and comfortable again in each other's company.

"Look, Matt," sighed Penny measuring her words. "We'd had a drink. We were excited. We were high on a fantastically successful day. We were in a luxurious hotel suite at someone else's expense. You fancied me. I fancied you. We had the opportunity. We took it. We spent a few hours together. Had a laugh in the Jacuzzi – and later in the shower I remember with a whole bottle of shampoo. What's the problem?"

"There isn't a problem. But is that it?"

Penny moved towards Matt and kissed him, slowly, deeply, with her hands holding his head tight against hers. She couldn't resist that little boy lost look. But they were both aware that tales could be told through shadows on glass office walls. So they pulled back, hoping filing cabinets obscured the image or distorted the action.

On his release she asked, "Is that what you wanted?"

Catching his breath he responded, "Yes.... No.... Oh God, I don't know Penny. We shouldn't."

"Would you like me to make this easier for you?"

"What do you mean?"

"If you want to, say so. If you don't, that's okay. If we find ourselves together sometime and the opportunity arises, let's go for it. If it doesn't arise, then no hard feelings – forgive the pun."

"Jesus Penny. That's to the point. Doesn't it matter to you?"

"Look Matt. You're a nice bloke. My boss. Married. But you're a man. If a woman offers it on a plate you're going to lick it up. You can't help it. It's animal instinct. So why not enjoy yourself? If both adults agree, what's the harm? A fuck is just a fuck not a relationship – and not necessarily the start of one. It doesn't always mean anything more than an animal act. You don't want anything long-term. Neither do I. Not now. I can live with that if you can."

Matt still doesn't know why he responded to all this with, "Jane's pregnant".

Penny's bouncy tone immediately softened. She responded cautiously, "That's great news...isn't it?" The question came instinctually from her emotional intelligence. *"Isn't it?"* invited Matt to be honest.

He swivelled his seat to face the window and the world outside, "No. It's lousy news. It's selfish. I know it's selfish. But I can't cope with a kid just now."

Penny continued softly after pausing a respectful few seconds, "You must have known Jane wasn't taking the pill or whatever."

"Well, no, not really. We wanted kids at some point but..."

"But the timing's bad. You didn't think it would all happen so quick," she said.

"Right. Exactly. I wasn't ready. I'm not ready. I hate playing the happy expectant father. It's not me. I don't want the responsibility. It's changed me Penny. It's definitely changed Jane. She's more edgy, more tense, more serious, more cautious."

"Give it time."

"I don't want to. It's not fair. A man can't have an abortion if he's

148

not ready. He's forced to be a father but the woman has the choice of motherhood."

"Would Jane...would she have an abortion?"

"Absolutely not. Totally out of the question. Wouldn't hear of it."

"Have you asked her?"

"No way!"

Matt turned to face Penny, and he found her next question amazingly perceptive. "Matt, in Chicago, did you know about Jane being pregnant?"

"Yes. Why? Does it make any difference? Does it have some significance for us?"

"No, none whatsoever - as far as I'm concerned. But perhaps knowing Jane was pregnant affected you."

It did. But that would be a confession too far. Penny that drunken night offered relief, distraction, escape from responsibility, adventure from routine, memory loss until morning. The child, his child in Jane, had created the first barrier between them in over three years. Supposedly babies bring couples together. Yet for Matt it made him feel rejected, used, abused, unwanted, unneeded. In Jane's life Matt was now relegated to second place - and would be forever. He would never be Number One again in her heart. No man could be. The child always replaces the man who helped create it.

* * *

They sat Jane down on one of six red plastic seats outside the Head's office and gave her a glass of water. Echoing voices spoke disjointed words: *"What's wrong? Can someone drive her home? Is she all right? Sir, what's happened to her? Don't know if we're insured to drive their new car. She's fainted. He can come and pick it up tonight. Gates will be locked. She's had a heart attack. What's wrong with Mrs Collins, Miss? She was fine a few minutes ago. Move back. Give her air. She's coming round. Should we call a doctor? No.*

Yes. No."

Mr Tinkler's authoritative voice provided order and direction. His strong arm steadied her shoulder. "I'll take you home Jane," she heard him say calmly above the fuss. "Mrs Jay can take my class. You were on a free period anyway."

"It's fine. It's fine. I'll be okay in a few minutes. I'll drive…"

"Don't be silly. We're not taking any chances. I'm taking you home Jane and that decision is not open to debate."

The Head of English drove Jane home with Sarah sat in the back seat with a reassuring arm around her friend's shoulder. The receptionist called Matt at work.

"Yes, what?" Matt answered aggressively. It had interrupted his dialogue with Penny.

"Matt, it's Jane," said Sarah. "She fainted at school. She's all right. There's nothing to worry about. I'm with Mr Tinkler in the car. He's driving us to your place. I can stay with her until you get home."

"Oh, thanks," said Matt quickly compensating for his aggression by being overly contrite. "I'll finish off here and get home as soon as I can."

"What's wrong?" asked Penny and he switched off the phone.

"Jane's ill. They're bringing her home."

"Is she losing the baby?"

"I hope… I don't know. I didn't ask. She just fainted."

"You'd better get home quickly," said Penny, genuinely concerned for Matt and his wife. "I'll finish off the figures. Have I got all your expenses and receipts for AestChem's visit?"

"Everything's in the folder," he said struggling into his coat. "The visit's financial file is up on my screen, so just fill in the gaps and send it to accounts copied to Peter. See you in the morning. Let Peter know I've had to leave early. Thanks."

Matt took the short walk up Villiers Street to Charing Cross. His pace was slower than usual. Mid afternoon was too early to adopt

150

the urgency of a commuter. The need to get home fast seemed to evaporate, and a delay of half an hour for the next train helped slow the pace.

Waiting on the station concourse gave Matt the opportunity to think over the Russian file Peter had given him. It made disturbing reading. Intelligence reports disclosed Russian troops had killed far more than even the most exaggerated media coverage reported. President Vadimov's army had wiped out nearly five hundred thousand Chechens. Nine out of ten victims were Muslim, according to MI6's *"best estimate"*. In twelve months a reign of terror had massacred nearly half the republic's population. Grozny, the capital, lay in ruins. The world suspected. But it didn't know for certain the extent of the extermination. Journalists and cameras had been kept out of the country by Russian forces and the secret police. The handful of brave but foolish reporters who did infiltrate the country had been *"accidentally killed in crossfire between rebel terrorists"*. Even in today's world the Russians proved you can still ring-fence parts of the world from prying media eyes. But US and UK satellites detected the tanks and convoys. This was ethnic cleansing, according to the US Central Intelligence Agency, *"but it was justified as all other methods of reconciliation had failed"*. The oil had to be protected. Vadimov had promised Europe and the US continuity of supply as the Middle East collapsed. Islam had declared a "War on Oil" as President Bush had declared a "War on Terrorism" after September 11. Fundamentalists, according to US and UK intelligence networks, wanted to return the world to the *"medieval dark age"*.

Peter's task – with Matt's assistance – was to draft a public relations communications plan on a grand scale. Its aim was clear: to persuade the Western World that Russia had acted responsibly. There had been *no* violation of human rights, *no* ethnic cleansing. Peter's job was to lie or deny and tell untruths for the greater good. This would appease the conscience of non-Muslim westerners. "You will tell the world only what it really wants to hear," Vadimov told Peter at their first meeting at the Kremlin in Moscow.

Diplomatic contacts in London and Washington had informed the Russian leader Henderson-Strutt's Peter Jones was the right man for the job. He had a successful track record "re-imaging" Chile, Argentina, Indonesia and, more recently, Myanmar, although this was considered "work in progress". Peter would report directly and exclusively to Vadimov. Matt's role was to – discreetly - commission research and develop key messages to address key public concerns on Chechnya. He had started to draft the communications strategy document for Peter. It included a "charm offensive" on important media proprietors and organisations. Vadimov at first reacted angrily to this suggestion. "Journalists are lizards," he declared. But Peter persuaded him to eventually start a string of "exclusive" interviews with key print reporters and major TV channels. But only after Vadimov received intensive media training to ensure a slick interview performance. Matt had also suggested a re-branding of Russian in addition to the re-image of Vadimov himself. They would make him a warmer, friendlier person to Western eyes. The "shop front" of Russia, its embassies, hotels and airports, would become "user-friendly". Complicated visa requirements would be stopped for most Americans and Europeans, and simplified for other visitors.

Until recently Matt had always managed to isolate work from home. But the dividing line had become unclear. At work he thought about the baby and bills and how Jane had changed in some way. At home the pressure of work prevented him from relaxing. The shame of his petty expenses fraud constantly haunted him. He felt uncomfortable about abusing public relations techniques to hide the truth about Chechnya. Yet he was excited to be at the heart of this high-powered project – even though he was sworn to secrecy.

He also owed a debt to Peter for not exposing the fraud and sacking him – or worse, reporting it to the police. Then there was Penny and their relationship - if that's what it was. Her questions too about AestChem and 22XP causing widespread cancer deaths

152

bothered him. She had simply voiced the questions he had thought about but not dared to ask?

As Matt approached home doubts grew stronger and his confidence weaker. He asked those questions everyone asks from time to time. Was he in the right job? What else could he do? Is this all there is in life? Wife. Kids. Semi, perhaps detached one day. Mortgage. Bigger mortgage. Insurance. Overdraft. Bigger overdraft. Monday to Friday work. Saturday recuperate from the past week. Sunday prepare for the next.

Nothing emerged from the mess in his mind. But as Matt approached his front door, the simplest of objects returned simplicity to life, if only for a few moments. A box of chocolates was propped against the doorstep. Attached, a scrap of paper with an unpunctuated message: *To dear Mrs Collins hope you are better from everybody at school we miss you lots come back soon.*

Mr Morrison had slipped away to the corner shop to buy the biggest box on sale. He had asked Peter Novak from 2A to write the note and deliver it to Jane's doorstep. The pupil lived two minutes away from his teacher's house. A phone call from the Head to Mr Novak confirmed a safe delivery. "Thanks very much. And thank Peter again. He's doing really well now at school. Is Mrs Novak keeping well? Is she still working for the council? Good. And remind Peter not to tell a soul. It's our little secret. Mrs Collins should never get to know who exactly the chocolates are from."

Matt was tempted to remove the note and present the chocolates as his gift. Jane had always liked chocolates, but the pregnancy had turned them into a craving. Why had he not thought to bring a box home, or a bunch of flowers from the stall outside the station? He felt a pang of guilt for thinking more about his work than his wife as he opened to door to see her.

Sarah left Matt to care for Jane. She would walk the 10-minutes home. Matt couldn't drive her anyway. The car was locked in the teachers' parking area at The Oaks overnight.

Later, alone together, Jane cried. Matt cried. Their tears merged as their faces touched. They both gave a reason for their crying. But he didn't know why she cried. She didn't know why he cried.

Chapter Seventeen

Tons of solid muscle charged...

The gun was placed carefully in the boot. New possessions are treated with respect. In a few weeks it will probably be chucked in the back like old boots. He didn't need the weapon now. He simply wanted it. Fun. Escapism. Adventure. A boy thing. An ambition of childhood realised in adulthood. Something a lad craves for but can only be satisfied with hard-earned cash as an adult. The .22 cost a few hundred. With the fitted silencer he believed he'd bought a bargain. At under a hundred, the telescopic sight was cheap. But the gun and sight were well-made basic tools that would do what he wanted. The sheath knife too would complete the job. He ticked the items off his shopping list.

Matt knew spending money at this time was stupid. Perhaps forking out extra money on 5,000 pellets was excessive. That's a lot of shooting. But the airgun wasn't an impulse buy. It would be used often, eventually, if not now. King's Wood was full of rabbits to shoot, gut, skin and turn into pie and stew, as his grandfather had taught him. Woodpigeons, "woodies" as he remembers local gamekeepers calling them, needed controlling too. Farmers don't appreciate lazy landowning neighbours who fail to keep these seed-eating crop destroying pests under control. "Rats with wings," his grandfather called them.

Matt and Jane had spent so much money recently on decoration, furniture, carpets, fridge, freezer, washing machine, dishwasher and other items since moving to their house from the rented flat, the credit card debt had got out of hand. And when you have one credit card, you might as well have two, or three. Likewise, now, a few hundred extra spent on a personal pleasure won't increase the deficit dramatically. Matt knew the interest the high street banks charged was punitive, considering the Bank of England's base rate. "Institutionalised theft", he called it. But debt is bad. They knew that. The save and pay by cash philosophy at the start of their marriage didn't last long. At first one or two agreements seemed easily affordable. But one thing leads to another. Then the car breaks down. You face a four-figure repair bill. "Sorry mate, yer see it's the cost of labour for a big end re-bore job, init," the garage man's standard script went. Car and house insurance premiums rocketed.

Close friends get married. You can't skimp on their present. Then last year's holiday in the Med. Perhaps not a good idea when you're planning to buy a house. It would have been wiser – cheaper - to stay at home, take it easy, go on day-trips.

Italy's balmy nights, swimming in warm sea, sand between toes, poolside cocktails, romance and relaxation, deceiving the poor into the lifestyle of the rich. With the mortgage deposit safely in the bank at home, the money flowed as freely as the wine in the lazy hazy herb-scented atmosphere.

Then the killer blow: the additional loan to pay for the house extension would mean no spare cash at all. No savings. No holiday abroad. Constant cost cutting and watching the pennies. It was not how Matt, or Jane, wanted to live. But pride inhibited any public admission they were broke. Matt would pay his own way through life. Then Jane's plea for more room, her frustration at not being able to buy a bigger house, her father's promise to provide the extension "at cost", her mother's encouragement "to have more kitchen space" had resulted in extending the mortgage to its maximum. The big lenders don't care how stretched you are. They can't lose. If you can't pay, they'll repossess. It's a one-way win-win situation - for them.

"Babies don't cost much," Peter had told Matt in the wine bar last week. "They get their food for free from their mum. Doting grand-parents insist on buying the cot and pushchair. Friends buy the clothes or pass stuff on from their kids who've outgrown them. Nappies are your biggest worry." Matt didn't believe him. On top of everything else, the baby would add to their burden of debt. He could see no way out of the financial gutter as he drove to the woods with his unused rifle in the boot. Matt knew he would have to seek a pay rise, or find another job. He'd talk with Peter next week. But the timing was bad. Just two months earlier Henderson-Strutt had made 25 staff redundant - nearly one in 10 of their London office - in a bid to reduce costs following a takeover by one of the world's leading advertising agencies. Matt would argue, correctly, the Crisis and Issues Management Department was highly profitable and efficient. That could not be said of several other departments.

Matt and the team made a lot of money on behalf of Henderson-Strutt. Premium rates were charged from clients in crisis. Under pressure from the press or public most companies paid up - few questions asked about the fee. Firms pay more money to keep or get out of the headlines than they do to get in them. But Matt knew Peter's counter-argument would be that profitable departments, for now, would have to support the loss-makers until they had a chance to return to profitability.

He repeated Peter's words in his mind, "*Nappies are your biggest worry.*" If only. Matt smiled at the irony - the man spearheading the biggest propaganda campaign Russian had witnessed since the Soviet days of Stalin could be talking about *nappies*. Here's the man, reporting directly to the president of the world's biggest country, talking about *nappies*. The man covering up genocide, talking about *nappies*. Nappies for Christ sake. Laugh? Cry? Matt couldn't decide. Comic? Tragic? Matt couldn't decide that either. Right or wrong, Matt's current need for cash outweighed any guilty conscience. Making moral decisions is easier when you have the money to pay for the consequences.

Matt reached his Aunt's former house at the edge of King's Wood and parked on the track leading into his acres. Miss Campbell at Rose Cottage further down the lane was nowhere to be seen. A car on this quiet country lane usually attracted her attention. But today the net curtains remained undisturbed. Saturday morning. Probably shopping. Matt unpacked the rifle, held it under his arm, grabbed a small round tin of .22 lead ammo, tucked his notepad and pen into one pocket, his flask of tea in another, and walked into the woodland through the thicket. He easily found "base camp", the clearing near the centre of his woodland with the lonely Scots pine. This time, unlike his last visit, he would not get disoriented, even if a mist or the dark descended. He'd marked the route from the road to the clearing with twig arrows and by scraping the earth. Even on the blackest night Matt would now know the fast route from the clearing to his car. He didn't want Miss Campbell acting as a woodland lighthouse keeper again.

In the bright winter sun he sat on a log, rested the gun against a stump, took out his notepad and checked his list:

Clear enclosure area

Build shelter – four corner poles, raised floor

Build tree observation/shooting platform

Construct log seating and small table

Campfire

Buy chain saw and brush cutter + fuel

Tools – hammer, saw, drill etc

Camping stove + fuel

Supplies – tea, coffee, dried milk, plate, cutlery etc

Rope and string

.22 airgun (rabbits and pigeons)

Rifle (deer) – apply for license

12-bore (pheasant, woodcock etc) – apply for license

Matt ticked off the .22 airgun and listed other ideas: a water butt would be useful to collect and store rainwater and pans for boiling water and heating food.

Then it charged. They charged. Fast. Agile. Sharp left. Acute right. Over. Through. Nothing stopped them. Matt sprung up. Instinct urged him to climb a tree. Get high. Be protected. He couldn't believe his eyes. They'd beat him to the nearest tree. Telegraph pole trunks of Scots pine can't be climbed. The beech. Can reach that. His heart thumped. Adrenalin opened his eyes wide. Fight or flight. Grab the gun.

No good. Pellets would bounce off their hide covered in wiry hair. Anyway you could only hit one. And that would be a lucky shot. The pack changed direction again. They'd gone. Vanished into the undergrowth as suddenly as they'd emerged from it.

Wild boar, seven or eight of them, dominated by a male six feet long with dagger-like tusks and tiny eyes, had been disturbed. They pounded the ground as several tons of solid muscle charged into the dark depths of King's Wood. Like bear and wolf, boar was once native to Britain hunted by kings and feared by commoners. They had returned. Alongside muntjac deer, these escapees from parks had made themselves at home in British woodlands. They were back, back in force. Hundreds, perhaps thousands, were again roaming freely England's woodlands for the first time in over 300 years.

It took a few minutes for Matt to recover from the charge. It had been exhilarating as much as frightening. As his heartbeat returned to a steady rhythm he determined to find out just how dangerous they are. Do they attack people? Would they threaten but then flee? Are they only dangerous when cornered or when you disturb their young?

Matt sat down near a broken beech tree, one that could be quickly climbed in case the wild boar returned. Although he was sure the boar were more scared of him than he was of them, better not take the risk. Most animals avoid humans, even the big cats. He poured coffee from the flask to ease his thirst and quell the excitement. As he relaxed his eyes scanned the clearing mapping in his mind the plan for his woodland retreat.

Then came a second surprise, a gentle one, not frightening like the first. Across the clearing Matt saw a gentle rural scene, a handful of rabbits bobbing around searching for the sparse green shoots of mid winter. No permanent hibernation for them anymore, thanks to global warming.

Matt slowly reached for his rifle, broke it to prime the spring piston ready for firing, inserted the lead pellet and took aim. His trigger finger squeezed. But it failed to fire. Damn it. The safety catch still engaged. He moved to release the mechanism but the rabbits sensed the danger, sat up, caught sight of their would-be killer and scurried away. No rabbit stew tonight.

To discharge the gun Matt put the epicentre of a felled log in his sights. The oak's heartwood, the annual concentric circles revealing the tree's age, created a natural target. Butt to shoulder. Eye through scope matching the cross-hairs. Trigger squeezed. The pellet struck four inches low. Matt shrugged. The sights, like life, needed adjusting to find the right direction for bull's eye.

Chapter Eighteen

Imagine where those long legs ended...

"We have a problem. Come up."

Matt went immediately to Peter's office and closed the door. He was surprised to see Jenni Tallow. This was an unscheduled visit.

"The press officer at AestChem's chemical plant in Germany has had a call about Project 66," said Peter.

Matt was shocked. "What? He used the codeword?"

"No," said Jenni, "But he asked about 22XP."

"What were the questions?"

Jenni looked at her notes. "He asked 'Are we planning to introduce FFresherFood-treated produce into Europe?' and 'If so, when?'"

"Is that all?" asked Matt.

"It's enough," Peter said.

"More importantly, what was his story?"

"What do you mean?" asked Jenni.

Matt explained to someone he thought should already know. But his impatience was disguised. He measured his words. "Well Jenni, *why* is he asking is actually more important that *what* he was asking. In short, what is he going to do with your answers? What's the story? The big picture? Where's it going?"

"We don't know."

"His approach could be innocent. As 22XP is used in the US, and you've had some coverage in the farming and food press over there, it could simply be this reporter's doing a routine pick up. Who is this journalist anyway? Who does he work for? Does your press officer in Germany know him? Did he say where or why he was picking up the story?"

"Sure. He works for a small circulation German chemical industry magazine."

"But we fear it could spread?"

"Right. And my German colleague tells me this guy sometimes sells stories to newspapers and international magazines. We need to eliminate the risk."

"Jenni, we can't do that. You know we can't," Peter intervened. "What we *can* do is to be ready to respond to any reaction."

"Can't we get this guy or his editor to kill off the story – or eliminate them?

"You are joking Jenni. We're not in..." Peter pulled back from saying *Russia*.

Matt continued to assess the situation. "Did any question suggest he knew about the theoretical cancer risk?"

"No."

"But of course he wouldn't reveal his hand at this early stage."

"Right."

"Is the press officer in Germany fully aware of the situation?"

"Of course she isn't," said Jenni. "She's only the press officer."

"What do they know? What have you told them to say?"

"They know about the benefits of FFresherFood. They know it's been a highly successful product in North America. They know it's safe. They know we have plans to import food processed by 22XP and, eventually, that we aim to introduce the process across Europe."

"Is that what she told the reporter?"

"No. She told him nothing about our plans for Europe. She played it by the book. If asked the script is to check with head office in Chicago. That's what she did."

162

"Did he ask about your plans for Europe?"

"Yes. She said she'd get back to him on that after checking with Chicago later in the day, when they arrived at the office."

"Saved by the time difference again, eh?"

"It's a marvellous mechanism, every transatlantic company uses it," said Jenni, lightening up a little with her first smile of the morning. "You guys here in Europe stall for time while we in the US sleep. Then we buy time on European issues because you guys have usually gone home by the time American journos have got their act together."

"It provides that 3 to 5pm UK time *danger zone* with our US clients," Peter said.

"It gives us loads of extra hours response time in most cases."

"It doesn't work in a crisis," said Peter. "Explosion. Fire. Bodies. Grieving relatives. Spill. Poisoned water. Hundreds ill. Town evacuated."

"Absolutely right Peter," she said. "But fortunately crises are the exception not the rule. Companies do try and avoid death, injury, disease and pollution you know, despite the propaganda from so-called environmental activists. It's in our commercial interest to care for people and the environment you know." Jenni displayed her second smile of the day, to Matt's eyes anyway.

Matt had handled potential leaks many times. He outlined a strategy built on past success. Henderson-Strutt would draft a holding statement. This brief document, after approval, would be circulated to AestChem Inc's sites and offices around the globe to people authorised to speak to the media. Jenni, and only Jenni, would be authorised to speak to any reporter anywhere if the health issue was raised. The word "cancer" would not be used by any person inside AestChem when talking about 22XP to any person outside the company. The word would not appear in any statement. All press officers around the world, and the agencies that monitor the company's press coverage, would increase their vigilance. A search would be conducted on the journalist who called the press officer in Germany. His background would be dug into, data bases scoured. Did he, for example, have a science degree? Or was he a graduate in a subject that would throw doubt on his ability to analyse highly complex scientific material, data sets, statistics in, say, meta-analysis? His articles would be checked for bias, especially if he had left-wing tendencies and sympathy with health or environmental groups. His contacts would be traced and monitored more closely during this period of high sensitivity. Claude Perlemuter would be alerted immediately in Henderson-Strutt's Brussels office. He could check if this journalist is known to have contacts or influence in Brussels. Claude would also develop a ready-made rebuff for his contacts in Brussels should any miss-informed sensational articles appear and cause a ripple of concern. There should be no delays to the approval of FFresherFood that will, after all, help Europeans eat more fresh fruit and vegetables, lower their weight and prevent heart disease and obesity. Sensational headlines should not stop the due process. European Commissioners only like good publicity, although they ignore most of the bad. But, as Claude knew, they are human. Their skin can be sensitive. Sometimes negative publicity required extra resources to calm fears and correct misunderstanding. Public perception too had to be taken into consideration.

"We don't want this story to grow legs," Matt told Penny in his office, now fitted with translucent glass to stop lip-reading gossips.

"No. We certainly don't want it running away now, do we?" she joked.

Jenni and Peter went to lunch leaving Matt, Peter's lieutenant in charge, as he often described him, to write the holding statement, make calls, spread out the safety net to catch any fall out from any unwanted story. Matt knew Peter was going to discuss increasing the budget for Henderson-Strutt's work on Project 66 for AestChem. After the president's and directors' successful European trip, several extra items of work not envisaged in the original brief had been commissioned. It was only reasonable for Henderson-Strutt to seek further fees to cover the extra tasks. Peter and Jenni clearly now had a very positive working relationship. Matt was in no doubt an extra £50,000, even £75,000, would be granted by Jenni. She had the budget. She had won the respect of her board of directors. In AestChem Inc's financial language, this amount was peanuts, loose change in the turnover. It would hardly register on the balance sheet of $billions. A raise in income from this client would also play nicely into Matt's hand for a pay rise. He was waiting for the right moment to pop the question. The right moment would arrive when Peter asked Matt for an after-work drink. Tonight could be the night. He'd have to accept, whatever promises he'd made to Jane to try and get back home early each night.

Matt gave Penny instructions for the rest of the Crisis and Issues Management Team. "Nobody," he said, "should leave for lunch until the various jobs are complete. We've got to nip this in the bud or get ready if the story bursts."

Matt was pleased with the draft holding statement and instructions. If approved, and he was certain it would be, it would be emailed to every press officer and the head of each office, laboratory and manufacturing site of AestChem Inc worldwide.

MEDIA POLICY: FFresherFood

For a general media inquiry, or whatever the questions, respond in a conversational style:

We're pleased you're calling regarding our FFresher Food process. Thanks. We at AestChem are delighted that throughout North America FFresherFood has enjoyed remarkable success. Sales have exceeded expectations. Everyone loves it. Farmers, distributors, food manufacturers, shops, supermarkets, restaurants, food chains and – most important of all - consumers who love eating fresh fruit and vegetables with all the fresh-picked goodness, taste and texture that FFresherFood brings. It's a great success story and we hope that achievement will, eventually, be repeated around the world soon.

Then refer to general Questions and Answer documentation previously supplied.

If any reporter raises any question about health, respond:

Millions and millions of people have been using FFresherFood products for many months now. They're absolutely fine. As you know the US Food and Drug Administration – with the most rigorous and respected product approval system in the world – has given FFresherFood a clean bill of health. We at AestChem and millions of Americans have every confidence in the health-giving benefits of FFresherFood. Fresh fruit and vegetable consumption has increased in America since introducing FFresherFood. Now that's got to be good news.

If any reporter raises any other issue about health, or who seems unable to accept what you have just explained, repeat sections of the above. Remember the media training you have been given and NEVER repeat a negative word or phrase the journalist may use. If you do, you could be quoted as saying it, as if you originated the word or phrase.

For persistent reporters, reassure them they WILL be called back by the company's communication's director from Chicago. Preferably do not at this stage – unless they ask – give them Jenni Tallow's name or phone number. IMMEDIATELY after you receive the call - or better still while you keep the journalist on hold - phone Ms Tallow's office to alert her to the journalist's call.

Matt emailed the document to Peter for him to see after lunch. His call to Brussels was answered immediately.

"Claude Perlemuter, how may I help you?"

"Claude, it's Matt. Possible problem." He outlined the facts and viewpoints.

Claude was not only a charming charismatic presenter. He could listen carefully too. His confidence was always reassuring.

"No problem *mon ami*. Of course I can do that. I will check with one or two friends at the Commission's press office and in the secretariat to see if they've heard of this reporter. You say he writes for a little magazine in Germany for the chemical industry?"

"That's right."

"Well, as you say Matt, it's probably nothing to be worried about. But we would be negligent to our client if we didn't prepare for this little health issue blowing up."

"We've seen it before, as you know, the smallest scare-mongering paragraph in some small specialist journal picked up by one of the big newspapers. The little nib – a news in brief – becomes the headline in bold."

"*Exactement.*"

"I'm here all afternoon Claude and I'm around all tomorrow should you discover anything, please call."

"Will do, farewell."

Matt placed down the receiver. Penny walked towards his desk and placed down a buff paper bag in front of his nose, dumped like a bale of hay in front of one of the horses at her father's estate.

"What's this?"

"Lunch."

"I thought I'd said nobody should go to lunch until..."

"Until all the tasks had been completed. Well they have been, so relax Matt. Delegation is the art of good management, you know, and I've delegated everything. So you've no excuse not to have a proper lunch break for a change. So *they* are tuna. *They* are chicken flavour. *That's* fattening. *That's* ice-cold."

Penny handed Matt sandwiches, crisps, Kit-Kat and can of diet coke. She sat on his office sofa, removed her shoes, put her feet on the coffee table and started to devour her own sandwiches, crisps, Kit-Kat and coke. But her crisps were cheese and onion.

"Missed breakfast," she mumbled, mouth half full. "Power cut during night. Knocked alarm off."

"I've not heard that excuse before," he teased.

"It's not an excuse. It's true. And you know how much I like my bed in the mornings," she teased lowering her voice and eyelids slowly.

Penny's legs attracted Matt's eyes. Indeed, they had been placed on display. Instinct. Natural. Normal. Biological response, he'd said for years - especially if a girlfriend caught him eyeing another woman. Can't be helped. Girls who wear miniskirts have their legs looked at. It's nature's law. If there were no attraction, there would be no desire, no arousal, and no survival of the species.

Legs like those supporting Penny's body get looked at more than most. They are a work of art. Even better than her mother's model legs. And Mrs Taylor's, aged 50, are still advertising tights and stockings to millions of women in catalogues and magazines produced by high street retailers. If the mother's legs are worth thousands, just imagine the price on her daughter's. And Penny's miniskirt, as they say, left little to the imagination. But Matt didn't need to imaging where those long legs ended. He'd been there, in Chicago, at the top of a skyscraper hotel.

Peter was late back from lunch. He'd said 2.30. But it was nearly 4pm when Matt's door burst open. "Great holding statement Matt. Jenni's approved it. So you can send it out. Fancy a quick drink tonight?" A hand was trembling near his lips.

"Isn't Jenni still around?"

"No, Bert's driving her to Heathrow this very moment. She's on a flight to Chicago this evening. We won't see her here for another three or four weeks, perhaps early March."

As he was leaving Peter added, "If any of the team want to join us for drink, tell them I'm buying."

Matt realised he hadn't replied to Peter's invitation. But Matt's silence with Peter always meant compliance. He wouldn't extend the invitation to the team, even Penny, although he'd like to spend more time with her, especially as the image of her sprawled out on his office sofa was playing in his head. But money, not Penny, or what she

168

could provide, was tonight's priority.

Matt wanted exclusive talking time with Peter, especially now Peter developed a lighter, more relaxed, mood in recent weeks. Christmas and New Year had been tough times for him, alone at home with no wife or children. Christmas can be painful, certainly melancholic. You imagine the rest of the world enjoying life to the full. Some people seem to develop the ability to be happy. Others have to work at it. Most simply pretend, go through the motions of festive happiness, fulfilling the expectations of the group at the gathering. Not Peter.

Peter's wife had not only walked away with the children. That was bad enough. She'd also taken Mopps, the family's five-year-old Black Labrador. Peter felt guilty about missing his dog more than his wife in many ways. He could talk to the bitch. She understood everything. She reflected his mood. Wagged her tale. Listened attentively. Mopps had been more faithful too.

Matt was focused for tonight's drink with his boss. He wanted a pay rise. He needed more money. He deserved it. He'd earned it. There were bills to pay, debts to clear, a life to live, anxiety to relieve, tears to stop flowing from sad eyes.

Chapter Nineteen

Rage reaction...

Jane was alone, lonely at home. And in recent weeks, when alone, she was in danger, threatened by her own thoughts. Or threatened by him, someone unknown, somewhere, out there, free to return.

People play many parts, she often said at school in drama classes. We capture Shakespear's characters for one major production, a play called *Real Life*. With just one physical face we use different faces with different people. We smile, frown, laugh, cry. We act differently in different places in differing situations. We live a life of multiple roles. We respond; we cause responses. We react; we cause reactions. In a complex world we seek complex solutions. We become social chameleons to camouflage our personal thoughts and feelings. We are what we *are*. We also play what we *are not*. If we had two faces, one public, one private, it would be simple. But we have multiple faces because we live multiple lives playing multiple roles. Child. Parent. Adult. Teacher. Boss. Employee. Provider. Receiver. Consumer. Supplier...

Jane's train of thought hit the buffers. The radio newsreader derailed her. His voice in the background came to the fore: *"It's been revealed today by the Home Office that only seven per cent of men accused of rape in a court of law are found guilty."*

Victim. Jane added "victim" to the role she now has, but resists. She tried to concentrated hard on a *reason* for being attacked, rationalising the circumstances, as if words would take away the hurt, as if intellect could suppress emotion.

Jane, a teacher, educated in child psychology, experienced handling difficult children, provided rational reasons for her attacker's act. Whoever he was, he was a victim too, a victim in life. Probably violent parents, she imagined. Shouting. Hitting. Drinking. Broken home. Perhaps another man in mum's bed, another women in dad's. Poverty. High-rise estate. Maybe another man in dad's bed or another women in mum's. Who knows?

He would have come from a "problem family" with no positive role-model to emulate. Drugs. Maybe dealing. Twenty-four hour telly playing trivia in a house without a book, she envisaged. A house without love, just anger. Scarred mongrel. Dog dirt squashed in threadbare carpet. Cold chips on cold plates in cold kitchen. Learning difficulties undetected. Low self-esteem. Bullied. Bully. Another male who copies his mates, as they him. Aimless. Hopeless. Frightened, with only soccer stars to worship and brand named t-shirts and trainers to desire.

Jane, mother of a child waiting to be born, believed the rapist was a victim of rape too. Did it help him in any way? Did he feel remorse? Guilt? Did her rape prevent a worse crime? Did the relief he released through her stop the death of a pensioner, or violence towards a child in a park or back street?

If only she had resisted with nails slashing face, fingers poking eyes, knees in groin, shoes scraping shins, would she still be alive? Violence begot violence. You don't teach a child to stop hitting by smacking, according to the research. Fighting back could have caused her death. Murder follows rape. Read the newspapers. But now, with his benefit from bullying, his success, his conquest, his satisfaction, his freedom, will he be encouraged to assault again? If crime pays, crime pays twice over for the unpunished.

She switched off the radio to help focus her thoughts. But the phone rang.

"Mrs Collins?"

172

"Yes."

"Mrs Jane Collins?"

"Yes."

"It's the counsellor from the hospital?"

"Oh, you have my results."

"Ah good. It is you. Sorry I was being a little vague. We have to be very careful on the phone to make sure we're talking to the right person. I'm sure you understand. We have to maintain strict patient confidentiality, especially in these matters. 'Mrs Collins', even 'Mrs Jane Collins' could turn out to be your mother-in-law."

"Don't worry. It's the real me. Do you have my results?"

"Normally, as you know, we'd ask you to attend in person for feedback on these matters. But as you were anxious to know as soon as possible I thought you'd appreciate a call..."

"Well?"

"The results so far are *negative* but..."

"Oh that's fantastic. What a relief..."

"But, Mrs Collins, HIV infection takes time to build up remember from initial exposure. Antibodies against HIV are not yet detectable in what we call the window period. We can sometimes, depending on the patient, detect other signs of infection a few weeks after exposure. But it's very early days. It can take up to four months before any infection can be detected. We would strongly advise you to take a second test, perhaps towards the end of March or the beginning of April."

"I know. But that's great news – well, for now."

The nurse hadn't finished. "When we met at the clinic you said the teacher you had a relationship with had 'been around a bit' I noted, and that he'd visited Africa."

"That's right."

"Have you talked to him about your test? Did you suggest he might have one? It would be very helpful for him of course and on the grounds of public health."

"Well it's a little embarrassing…"

"I realise that."

"But he could see his GP. Or come here to the clinic. Your names are not and will not be connected in any way. So please do have a word."

"Yes. Okay."

Jane played out the story to the clinic's counsellor. They didn't need to know what really happened. They can do their job without the details. The truth had to stay with Jane. It was her exclusive experience. There had been no fling, no naughty teacher, no philandering adventurer from Africa – and certainly no "relationship".

In many ways a one-minute grope with a colleague would have been preferable to what really happened. The true source of contamination had been unknown, an anonymous male who invaded Jane and threatened her life and her baby's. Bad from birth, she suspected, or someone good turned bad by circumstances. Nature versus nurture: that old chestnut discussed at every university and teachers' college in the land.

Jane walked to the crime scene from her living room. The old bread bin had finally been removed. "Didn't you notice the mould," she'd said to convince Matt it was time for a replacement. His argument to save a bit of money by giving it a good scrub with a wire brush was too late. This time she smashed it with a hammer, crushed it to pieces under her foot, put it with the rubbish as the collection truck approached the house. It would gain no reprieve. Matt would not – could not - be allowed to rescue the bread bin again. She watched it tipped, swallowed, crunched and taken away forever by the Biffa truck to a dump, hopefully miles away.

Bad memories are harder to get rid of. There is no landfill site for them to be buried. The replacement enamel breadbin didn't stop recall of the kitchen attack either. How could it? It was silly to think by crushing a stupid wooden bread bin flashbacks of a violent attack would end. It was a futile gesture. A token act like throwing away the clothes associated with that moment - the ripped jeans, the stretched jumper, the snapped bra, stained knickers. The shower had also failed to eradicate the memories of his touch, his smell, his act. The soapy sponge wiped his fluid from your legs, but you never forgot. Memories retain feelings, not just facts.

BREAD was still emblazed on the side of the new bin, painted in bold bright blue letters instead of a carving in the wood, beech wood, Matt had observed, as if such detail was important. Jane opened the door to the fridge, poured milk into a cup and microwaved it. In the 60-seconds that gave heat to her drink, she vented anger on her attacker. Sudden, uncontrolled, unexpected, frightening rage overwhelmed her. It came from inside, deep inside. Fists bang worktop. Feet stamp floor. Teeth bite lips. Towels flung across room. Slammed cupboard doors in this outburst from hell. Heart pounding. Fast breathing.

The voice inside had started soft, controlled, through the teeth, but ended shouting. "Bastard. You bastard. You no-good bastard. Rot in hell. Sod you. Damn you. You...you..."

Tapping on the kitchen window caused Jane to take a sharp and deep intake of breath. Her rampage switched off as instantly as the microwaves.

"Jane, it's me, Ray, I've just come to drop off some stuff for tomorrow."

Had he heard?

"Oh, oh, okay Ray. Did...did you want a cup of strong brew?"

Regain composure. Deep breathe. Get a grip.

"No love, I'm not staying."

Had he seen?

"What you up to next?" she called through the kitchen door while turning the key, sliding the bolts and trying to appear calm.

"Won't come in. Muddy feet as usual. As you can see most of the brickwork's finished. Roof shouldn't take too long. Then..."

"The electrics, plasterwork, flooring..."

Brilliant performance. He didn't suspect a thing.

"So you did learn the tricks of the trade. We just thought you were larking around. Your time with us as a kid on the sites wasn't misspent then."

Ready for a smile and joke now. "That's right Ray. I've watched you and Dad put up dozens of extensions, I could do it all myself."

Award the Oscar.

"It's one thing watching lass. It's another doing."

"Like plastering."

"Yes, like plastering."

"Looks easy, but it takes 'the knack'."

"Yer right there girl. Well I'm off. Will I see you in the morning?"

"No, I'm in school first thing."

"So you'll miss my new apprentice then."

Remember your Oscar performance. In acting you're only as good as your last show. Keep it up.

"Who's that then?"

"He's another young 'un. But the lad's tell me he's a much harder worker than the last one."

"Oh good."

"We heard that Paul Potts got nicked for something. Then got bailed, even though cops had been after him for some time apparently."

"Really?"

"Well Jane, maybe see you tomorrow afternoon if you get off school on time."

Jane sat on the sofa in the living room with her relaxing cup of hot milk. She put her feet on the coffee table as per Dr Khan's instructions to keep her legs raised as much as possible during pregnancy. We don't want varicose veins at your tender age, she'd said. "Tender" at 29, hardly.

She snatched a magazine from the rack. Seen that. Read this. Same stuff. December's tell you how to stuff yourself at Christmas.

January's tell you how to diet for your summer holiday. She looked at the clock. She looked again. It hadn't moved, well hardly. She couldn't settle or get comfortable to get thinking and find space for thought. She was trying to bring order to her mind, get things in perspective. She was searching to find the ideal emotional balance between past, present and future. *What's gone has gone. Tomorrow's another day. Life's not a rehearsal.* She ran through the clichés, the one-line adages to find balm for her trouble.

Then the baby moved. Just a little. But it was a life. His life. Her life. Their life. The future. Matt's child. Exclusive. No-one else's.

She'd tried to trace the night, or the day, or the point of conception, the moment of love-making that made this child. She'd tracked the dates, the places and possibilities. She thinks she knows. It was Sunday, in her old bedroom at Mum and Dad's place on a weekend visit. They'd had a pub lunch. Mum was watching an old black and white weepy on TV. Dad was sleeping after beef and beer. Matt was willing and she suspected the timing was right. She can't be sure. She'd enticed him several times in the middle of the month at peak fertility. It had been quick. Fun. Functional. For that's what mattered then, for what was right for now.

Matt would be home soon. He'd promised. His New Year's Resolution had worked most nights so far. With the radio switched off and no phone calls, Jane found thinking time, more thinking time. In her calm she analysed the outburst earlier. She accepted that while the anger was retained, she would remain the victim. Do you forgive in the hope of forgetting? It's impossible to forget before forgiveness. That male body intruded only for a minute or so, if that, or so it seemed. She'd had men before Matt, a few, not many. Should this brief assault really affect the rest of her life? Can a minute last forever? Should it? He'd left scratches and bruises. They'd healed. Broken glass had cut her foot. But the blood had dried and the gash closed. Stitches hadn't been required. Outside help not needed. Medical intervention not required. Psychological stress counselling not wanted. And, to date, no infection and her baby is safe. Rape was more a mental intrusion than physical violation. The books and articles were right. Her body had healed. But her mind had not.

* * *

At home Ray called Bob, still working in the office at Chislehurst. Doris was about to serve sirloin steak, mashed potatoes, carrots and cabbage. His favourite crumble with Bird's custard was to follow, she'd promised. It had to be Bird's, the supermarket's own brand didn't taste as good. Cornflakes can only be Kellogg's. Bacon has to be British, never Danish. And New Zealand lamb compared to British was rubbish. Ketchup has to be Heinz. Beer at home had to come from a bottle, never a can. After 40 years of marriage the wife of Ray Sykes knew every detail of her husband's likes and dislikes. She'd worked out years ago he never ate the apples she packed. But she always popped one in the Tupperware. And she always would while he went to work, until the day he retires and they move to their cottage in Somerset. There was always someone on site who'd eat a spare apple, she told herself, one of those growing lads probably. It would be a healthy addition to their diet of chips and crisps.

"Your tea's ready Ray," she shouted. "How many more times do I have to tell you?"

"Shut up woman. I'll be through in a minute. I'm on the phone to Bob. Bob Straw."

"I know who Bob is you silly bugger, I've known him nearly as long as I've known you, more's the pity. You're as bad as each other. Tell him your tea's on the table."

"Shush."

"Don't you tell me to shut up Ray Sykes. Your tea's on the table and it's getting cold. I won't tell you again."

"Thank God," he muttered on the phone in the hall waiting for it to be answered.

"Bob, it's Ray. I was round your Jane's…"

Bob interrupted immediately sensing from Ray's tone this was far from routine. "What's wrong? Something's happened? We've not heard from her for a few days, Maggie said. Is she..."

"I don't know mate. I turned up unexpected like this afternoon, just dropping some stuff off. She was really upset at something. Saw her through the window. Couldn't hear exactly. But she was shouting something, saying strange stuff, slamming cupboard doors and so on. God knows why. There was nobody there. Well, I don't think so. At first I thought she and Matt were having a row. But he weren't there. And she threw something across the room, a towel, a dishcloth or something."

"What did you do?"

"Well I knocked on the window to see what's up. She opened the back door after a few seconds but then she seemed all right, as if nothing was wrong. She just looked a bit flustered, but perhaps the baby's causing that. I thought I'd been seeing things Bob, no kidding. But I'm bloody sure I wasn't imagining it."

"I'll get Maggie to visit after work tomorrow. See if her Mum can find out what's wrong. I'm at a meeting in Birmingham about this Bull Ring redevelopment, hoping to pick up a building maintenance contract. Anyway, thanks Ray. Don't worry, I'll sort it."

"Look mate, my tea's on the table. I'll see you later."

"Right. Try and remember what she was screaming."

"Okay Bob, I'll do that. I'll keep an eye on her when I'm round there, you know that."

"I know you will. Cheers pal."

Chapter Twenty

There's a time to talk...

They were onto their third bottle in the low-lit basement bar with sawdust scattered across the stone paved floor. Matt had persuaded Peter away from their local watering hole to avoid colleagues from Henderson-Strutt. Matt handed over two tens for the overpriced Chianti, and nibbled a lump of cheese presented free on a saucer at the counter.

"Would you like fresh glasses?"

"No thanks, we'll make do."

"And here's the penny change sir."

"Thanks a lot. Why do they still bother with this 99p trick?" Matt challenged the barman. "Why don't you just charge £20, a nice round number? Everyone knows it's a con. Nobody's persuaded to buy anything just because it something 99p instead of the round pound."

"The management set the prices sir."

"Sure. I know. I'm not getting at you personally. It's just irritating hanging around for a penny."

"I agree," the barman said handing over the wine before placing both hands on his hips slightly irritated. "But the management tell us it still works with some customers. They think they're getting a bargain. And giving change gives the impression you're getting something back in addition to the goods you've just purchased. It also means we can set up physical contact, literally, with the customer by placing change, even a penny, into their hand. Well, the management tell us it's good for customer relations."

Matt carried the bottled to the quiet corner as Peter ended a call on the mobile.

"Business?" Matt inquired.

"Client's media monitoring team. We've heard no more about the project. No media calls. No stories. No more noise from our German journalist."

Instinct and habit ensured Peter and Matt never mentioned a client's name or any vital word in public – however much alcohol had been consumed.

"So it's all quiet on the western front. Good," said Matt as he settled into his seat, a replica 17th century high-backed winged church pew. It even had a Tudor Rose, the royal badge of England, carved into its back to provide authenticity and a sense of history. It appealed to tourists and indigenous sentimentalists, Matt could imagine "the management" say.

"So Matt, what's this evening all about? Or would you like me to guess?"

Matt was clever, Peter experienced. They made a good team. Matt never tried to outsmart Peter because his experienced counter-balanced intelligence. And he was the department's director. Matt didn't mention money. He didn't need to. He cut to the chase knowing Peter was sharing his wavelength. "Well, what are the chances?"

"Good."

Matt blinked. "What, really?"

"Sure."

"Despite the redundancies? Despite the overall picture? Despite our new owners wanting their pound of flesh?"

"I've recommended a £6,000 increase for you. And, as you know, what I recommend gets accepted."

Matt blinked again, looked skywards, clapped his hands and held them together as if offering a prayer. "What can I say? Thanks. Thanks a lot Peter. That's great news."

"You deserve it. I'm sorry we couldn't fix it before. But since the takeover you know there's been a pay and recruitment freeze in every office."

There was a lull in the conversation as they both enjoyed another mouthful of wine. Peter felt satisfied at giving good news, Matt happy in receiving it. Then Peter's head moved towards Matt across the small round table. Matt was paying full attention as his boss whispered. "We've also had a little extra help from our new client. They've agreed an additional £100,000 on top of our income projection. That puts our department even further into the black. We're quids-in over budget expectations."

"I thought we could only extract another £75k at most from them," Matt said, still excited by his rise.

"Jenni was in a generous mood," smiled Peter. "I've told you before Matt, and I'll tell you again, long lunches work wonders with clients."

"Obviously. An extra hour for lunch with the client and you extract a further £50,000 on top of budget. That's brilliant."

Peter sat back, relaxed in his pew and gulped down the wine in his glass. He poured out what remained of the Chianti into Matt's glass, stood and walked to the bar with the empty for a fourth bottle. But Peter had a change of mind.

"I'm starving," he shouted across from the now empty bar to Matt. "Fancy a sandwich here or shall we go and find somewhere else?"

"I don't mind. You decide."

"I'll tell you what. I'll phone Bert. He can pick us up in a few minutes. Know a nice Italian place. I've never taken you there. We'll have pasta or a pizza. Hey, we could have both. The night is young. I'm off for a pee."

There was no way out tonight for Matt. It was already past nine. Peter's committed to a boy's night out on the town, and Matt was the only company around. Matt recognised the signs and symptoms and had learnt the routine. After the wine they would turn to whisky as a nightcap. Peter would talk about his children, life, dog and wife. He'd talk about companies who had done stupid things to attract bad publicity. He'd talk about how the royal family screwed up after Princess Diana's death and "missed a great public relations opportunity". He'd talk about Prince Charles who simply failed to understand the media machine, despite an army of advisors. And at some point tonight Matt would hear Peter conclude his attack on the royals with, "...that's because the press offices at Clarence House and Buckingham Palace are ran by a load of upper crust snobs or people who are in training to become them."

He might mention Chechnya and his work for the Russian President. But this was one project that, for now at least, Peter was playing close to his chest.

Before Peter returned, Matt took out his mobile, scrolled to HOME and pressed the green icon. "Jane."

"Where are you?"

"Look, I'm with Peter. We're in a bar. He's set in for the night I'm afraid."

"Oh no. I was expecting you back ages ago. It's horrible being here all alone."

"I know. But he's really up for a drink and a chat tonight. There's no way I can leave him now."

"I wish you were here."

"I'm sorry. But he'd be insulted if I cut and run now, I've left it too late."

"I thought you weren't going to do this any more."

"Tonight's different. I've done it. He's done it for me..."

"What?"

"The pay rise. I've got it. Six thousand extra. Good news, eh?"

"Yes. Good. But I'd prefer you here."

Matt didn't hear excitement or pleasure. "Six thousand extra's good, isn't it?"

"It's not going to make that much difference after tax. And you know we'll have to pay a lot more tax for the BMW..."

"Jesus Christ Jane! Aren't you ever satisfied? Look, I'll see you later. Peter's coming back, I've got to go."

The call was not only terminated, the mobile was switched off, in anger at Jane's unenthusiastic response to his good news. Anyway, the battery was low. Save its power for later.

"Bert will be here in 10 minutes. He's parked in the NCP off Trafalgar Square. Shall we have another glass?"

"Why not." Matt wanted an excuse to forget Jane for the rest of the night.

"Why not indeed." He turned to the barman, bored by an empty bar and eager for closing time, and ordered two glasses of red. "Why don't you have a glass too?"

"No thank you, sir," the barman told Peter. "The management don't allow us to drink alcohol on duty. But I could have a juice."

"You do that," slurred Peter.

The M3 was quiet and Bert, tonight sporting his chauffeur's hat in the Mercedes, soon reached the Italian near Bracknell. The area attracted a sophisticated clientele who could afford to pay central London prices well away from the city centre. Yellow ochre stucco and neo-Roman pillars made an impressive entrance to the restaurant's marble reception. A small stone fountain provided the discreet sound of trickling water. The *Il Vaticano* was just a few minutes walk away from Peter's elegant home, a modernised farmhouse with converted stables set in three acres. Peter in recent months had clearly become a regular visitor judging by Giuseppe's warm welcome and firm handshake. "And tonight Mr Jones you have guest. Good. Good. Very good," he said directing them to "your usual table Mr Jones" with that inimitable sweep and flourish that only Latin-blooded waiters possess. The pasta was exceptional, the portions generous, the wine wonderful.

After Giusepp'e excessive bowing gratitude for Peter extravagant

185

tip, they walked briskly to the large house in the cold drizzle of late January. Bert had been stood down for the night. Wherever he had gone, wherever chauffeurs live, he would be in Peter's gravel driveway at six-thirty in the morning for the drive to Bloomsbury Chambers. Infrared security senses charged a string of spotlights up the semi-circle drive to the doorway after detecting their body heat. The house was already lit up, but not for anyone inside. No longer did Peter's children, dog or wife reside there. Matt felt its emptiness as Peter deactivated a very elaborate security system as they entered the hallway. Matt smiled at one of several CCTV cameras surveying the farmhouse and garden, and immediately regretted his stupidity. He blamed the drink.

It had been seven months earlier when Matt last visited Peter's place, a perfect English summer's day in June during Royal Ascot week. The racecourse was, to a betting man like Peter, a convenient 20-minute walk away. "From the loft with the binos you can watch the bloody gee-gees from here," he'd always tell guests, in the days when guests were frequent.

Henderson-Strutt always hired a private box on the top tier of the Queen Elizabeth II Grandstand overlooking the Royal Enclosure opposite the winning post. Several staff members had been invited back by Peter after a day of corporate hospitality at the races.

Many companies use such events to entertain clients, build relationships, win contracts and talk business while having a very pleasant time. Vintage Champagne, fine wine, cigars and food provided from arrival to departure – all paid for by the company. Henderson-Strutt also entertained at Wimbledon for "tennis posers and visiting Americans", as Peter described them, Twickenham for "rugby schoolboys and real women", Glyndebourne for "older clients, bankers and the gentry" and Silverstone for "boy races and bimbos". But in Matt's experience you found the same fun-loving senior clients at all of them.

Peter's housekeeper had kept the log fire burning before retiring to her room in the converted stables. "She'll have thrown a branch of elm on, smoulders for ages," Peter said, prodding the cinders into flame with a long black poker and providing fresh wood for the hungry flames to feed on.

It was midnight and the mood was mellow. Wood smoke scented the oak-beamed room. Although Peter was Matt's boss, socially they enjoyed each other's company as friends and equals, despite the age difference of nearly 20 years. It had been a good night. Great food. Excellent conversation. Matt had drunk too much. They both had. But that was a small sacrifice to suffer for a substantial pay rise, despite Jane's negative response.

Peter had already placed four tumblers on a well-worn leather-top table between the black chesterfields. At the back of the large square room, behind the Bechstein grand, with its yellowing ivories that Peter's children used to play when this house was a home, stood his glass-fronted oak cabinet with five shelves of malts. Peter stood back to survey the pleasure to come and to make his choice.

Peter meticulously arranged his whisky in alphabetical order, starting with his 15-year-old Aberfeldy to his 10-year-old Tullibardine. "By the time whisky makers had tasted up to t, they've forgotten the rest of the bloody alphabet," he quipped. "There's no scotch I've heard of beginning with the letters u to z. Funny thing that, isn't it?"

Peter took a little while to decide on tonight's selection and he selected two bottles.

"Now," he paused while pushing his index finger into the dimple of his chin, "this one first I think and... yes... this one second."

Peter placed both bottles gently on the table, like a priest about to bless holy water, before fetching a bottle of still water from the kitchen to splash in the malt. Matt read the labels of the Lagavulin, a single Islay 16-year-old malt, and The Macallan 25-year-old.

"To be consumed *not* in alphabetical order," he said returning to the room and handing over the first tumbler. "The Macallan you'll find is full, very dry and wonderfully smoky. Right? Good. Enjoy.

Then we'll turn to my whisky of whisky's, my absolute all-time favourite, Lagavulin, the 16-year-old."

"How do you pronounce that again?"

"Lag – av – oo – lin," Peter stressed the syllables with a slight slur. "Can you taste the peat, smell the salt?"

The fire crackled into flame making the walls dance with soft light. There's a time to talk and a time for peace. Good whisky tastes better drank quietly; receives its greatest praise though silence. For the next minute or so, while the whisky was being appreciated, the silence was savoured by the second, marked by the ticking of the tall ornate grandfather clock.

"How's Jane?" The question was posed gently.

It took a few seconds for Matt to break the atmosphere's spell. "She doesn't look pregnant yet. You'd never know. She still looks her slim self."

"Good, eh?" Peter held the tumbler of Lagavulin against the light of the fire to admire the pale amber of pleasure.

"But she's not the same women. Moodier. Tetchy sometimes. Jane's never been like that ever since I've known her. Always smiling, she was. Laughing. Bouncy. It's as if the pregnancy has sapped her energy."

"It's early days Matt. Early days. You've got to expect changes."

"Suppose so. But at first she was really high, almost ecstatic about the baby.

Then it all stopped, literally turned her back on me. Went cold."

The ticking of grandfather time was listened to again, the fire looked at, the peat and salt appreciated on what whisky connoisseurs call "the finish". This was the hour of midnight in a grand isolated house, not The Strand in rush hour. Time went slowly, just as they wished.

"Hormones," the silence was broken, "women can't control 'em". Peter poured another tot and added a splash of water. "They want you close one minute, then want you arms length the next. They'll screw

188

you silly when they want a kid, then virtually abandon you when you've given them one. They spend all this money on clothes and cosmetics to look good. Then, when it pays dividends and you show interest, they don't want to know. Nothing's changed since we were teenagers Matt, it's a game of tease and tempt, look but don't touch. It's called man abuse."

A third shot of Lagavulin oiled Peter's mouth. "They don't mind you looking at them. You're supposed to say how stunning they are when they're all dolled up. But look at *another* woman who's done herself up to look good, especially if it's a younger one, and they kick your shin."

"We're only doing what comes naturally," Matt said encouraging the diatribe.

"Exactly. We can't help it. Don't women understand that? Are they too stupid to realise men do appreciate the beauty of a good-looking woman?"

"We're biologically conditioned to do so," Matt continued as if Peter hadn't paused. "I've said it for years."

"Exactly. A women is a work of art to a man."

"Exactly. Couldn't have put it better myself Peter."

"They're so prejudiced about men, saying stuff like we're all the same, when it's patently not the case. They're so bloody prejudiced against us. If we said half the things about women they said about men, we'd be up before some bloody tribunal. Have you ever listened to that *Woman's Hour* programme on radio? Listen to it one day. Just go over all the things they say and reverse the gender language from 'his' to 'hers' and you'll be amazed at the stereotyping. Even if it were called *Man's Hour* they'd be an outrage."

"Not all women are like that," Matt added trying to bring balance to the debate. "Lots of them think this political correctness stuff's gone too far too."

"Sure, exactly, especially the younger ones. They just get on with it. It's that lot in their late forties and fifties, the left-over lefties who burnt their bras in the 1960s and '70s, then realised bras had a very important function."

Peter stood up and dragged his feet to the whisky cabinet. He asked Matt if he wanted to try another variety. Matt declined saying he couldn't soak up any more "barley water".

"It's a women's world and make no mistake," Peter went on as Matt's eyelids momentarily dropped. "They've got it all. The power of yes or no over men - they can let us do it or not. They can turn us on or switch us off far easier than we can them and..."

"Sure," Matt slurred in his tiredness.

"They have the power of pregnancy – well, unless they've got a gynae problem – and the final say to retain or reject the kid. They can have an abortion, we can't. You, me, fathers don't get a look in you know. We have no bloody rights over the baby, no bloody rights at all. It's bloody wrong...bloody wrong."

"Well, the kid is inside the woman's body Peter. That's the biological fact. Can't be helped."

"Sure. But we put it there, as men. But fathers-to-be have no bloody say."

"Can't see that changing," Matt struggled to speak fighting off sleep. "Anyway, with all this stem cell cloning stuff we're going to be surplus to requirements in another few years, as far as fatherhood is concerned."

"Well it cuts both ways Matt. Works for us too. Women haven't realised that yet. When the artificial womb is perfected, and they've cracked this stem cell stuff, men will be able to have kids without women," said Peter as his fourth - or was it fifth - tot swirled into the glass. "There's no way we can tell what women want, because half the time they don't know themselves. Then when they think they know what they want, they change their bloody minds...."

Matt's eyelids this time failed to open. He slumped across the sofa where he would spend the night. Peter managed to remove the empty tumbler from his employee's hand and spread a blanket over him. He sat with another tot listening to the crackle and watching the flames in the fire. He could hear Matt's breathing, disturbed at times as if experiencing a bad dream. It made him think of his dog that, at this hour, would always drop at his feet, fall asleep, and dream of retrieving pheasants.

Peter had kept talking, quietly, although he knew nobody was listening. He didn't care. It didn't matter. He wasn't speaking for anyone to hear.

Matt didn't see his boss and mentor stagger to his empty bedroom with a full glass in hand. Peter hoped this night he would sleep without dreams. But, as he had discovered, you don't have to be sleeping to suffer nightmares.

Chapter Twenty-one

SPRINGTIME

Strangers at the funeral...

White daffodils lined the steep road toward the crematorium as the flower-filled cortege drove at walking pace. The hearse driver could see the funeral ahead running behind schedule. Undertakers knew the problem of conveyor-belt cremations, and the previous service had overrun.

With two scheduled funerals each hour it was considered bad management to let one set of mourners hog the chapel. When the coffin's gone behind the curtain, and the final "earth to earth, ashes to ashes, dust to dust" speech delivered, you can't afford to let guests linger. Modern crematoria are designed more for the arrival and departure of the living than the dead.

"It's one-way traffic for all, stiff or standing, car or pedestrian. Get 'em in and get 'em out," the crematorium's director whispered to time-wasting undertakers and coffin bearers. "Bodies in boxes are easier to move than mourners stood around after the service. Look sad and sedate if you like, but always keep your mourners moving."

It was standing room only for the late arrivals at the funeral of Ray Sykes. He had made many friends in his life as a Master Builder. Mrs Sykes and close family sat on the front row as they heard his employer pay a short tribute. Jane, six months pregnant, sat directly behind Ray's wife between her mother and Matt.

As a mark of respect Bob Straw had closed his company for the day. A prospective new client in Birmingham had "insisted" Bob attend a meeting today, "funeral or no funeral". Bob gave him a direct two-word response before ending the call. Ray was worth more than any profit margin on a maintenance contract. Bob was pleased every one of his staff turned up to the funeral, even the new apprentice, although he hadn't ordered anyone to attend. It's your choice, he'd told them. Not everyone likes funerals.

Doris and the children had asked Bob if he'd like to say a few words. And although he didn't like making speeches, he appreciated the opportunity to pay his last respects in public. Bob cleared his throat nervously. Before the service Matt told him Winston Churchill's rule for speaking in public: stand up, speak up, shut up, sit down. So Bob stood up and spoke up. He'd intended to read from notes scripted last night on his PC. But tears welling in his eyes prevented his focus. He screwed his notes into a ball, squeezed it in the palm of his hand, and spoke from the heart.

"Ray was the best bloke I've ever known in the building trade, and I've known hundreds of fine men. Some of you are here today. Ray was a devoted husband and a loving father and a great workmate." Bob turned to Ray's wife and their three children, a girl and two boys, as a lump swelled in his throat. "You know Doris he was the best a wife could get. He really loved you. He was the best dad you kids could get. He was really proud of you. He probably didn't tell you often enough how much he loved you or how proud he was of you. We blokes hide our true feelings too much. But I promise you, everything he did, every penny he earned, he did for you."

Jane cried, quietly. Her father fought back the tears but continued talking to the mourners. "Like many of us in this trade, Ray was tough and hard – like a piece of English oak, his favourite wood. But underneath that powerful exterior he had a heart of pure soft gold. He

194

was a brilliant craftsman, totally reliable and a great teacher. If he said he'd do a job, you knew it would be done, and done well. I'm sure every bloke in this room who worked with Ray will remember some skill you learnt from him. In that way, Ray will live on in all of us."

Bob turned to the coffin. "Ray, your family and friends will miss you for ever. You'll never be forgotten. It's a great tragedy your retirement time has been so cruelly stolen from you, because nobody deserved a rest from hard work more than you. Ray, my old pal, the world is a better place because you made it a better place. We are better people because you made us better people. Losing you takes something away from all of us. Let's hope happy memories of you will fill some of the gap you've left in each and every one of our lives. God bless you mate. And thanks for everything, from everyone here today."

Bob walked passed the finest coffin of solid English oak and returned to his seat next to Maggie, who squeezed his hand in a way that whispered "well done". A local vicar completed the service, committing his mortal remains to the furnace. Ray was not a religious man. He didn't believe in "all that mumbo-jumbo". But Doris held her Methodist faith in God "despite all the shenanigans in the church what with child abuse, gay vicars an' everything".

Eight days earlier Ray suffered a massive heart attack. He'd been giving his lawn the first cut on the year and collapsed. Despite the fast action of the paramedics he was pronounced dead on arrival in casualty. Ray's heart was so severely damaged there would have been little hope of successful resuscitation even if the attack had happened in hospital, according to the consultant.

"When you're dead, you're dead," Ray often said throughout life. "You can do with me whatever you want. Bury me, burn me, makes no difference to me love," he'd tell his wife over the years, and she'd chosen cremation.

Doris had just one niggling regret at the funeral. She knew it was irrational, but the feeling remained. She couldn't forget her final words to her husband. She'd told him to "get out from under my feet and go do something useful in the garden". He did, and he died doing it. No amount of reassurance from the doctor, family and friends would rub out the memory of those final words to her husband of 40 years.

Ray's sudden death had meant no proper goodbyes, no deathbed words to his wife, children or friends. Sudden death always left life incomplete. No Last Will and Testament either. So the lawyers would grab a bigger slice of whatever was left to his beneficiaries, although Bob would keep a watchful eye to make sure Doris never went short.

Matt and Jane's house extension, built by Ray, was a testimony to his all-round skills as a builder. But the additional mortgage payments had started. Jane could not wait to decorate the spare bedroom especially for the baby, even though it had been freshly wallpapered and painted a few months earlier. A cot, pushchair and other items for the baby had pushed each credit card to its limit. But credit card operators, banks, building societies, like debt. They grow rich on customers' poverty. Financial institutions don't heed warnings about over-heating the economy and fuelling Britain's mounting personal debt crisis. They simply keep raising the ceiling on your so-called spending limit, extending your credit without saying, as if doing customers a favour. Matt and Jane received the offer of a new credit card virtually every week in the post. They all promised to take on your existing debt – and give you some more money to spend. Some of those early offers seemed to help at first. But then, in turn, they become difficult to clear. As Matt always complained, the term "credit" card should be banned and changed to "debt" card. Mr and Mrs Collins owed thousands of pounds, excluding the mortgage. Matt's pay rise had been largely absorbed in interest payments. Jane had been right. His pay rise didn't feel "substantial" any more. And funerals fuel depression.

As Ray's mourners left the chapel by the side doors, relatives and friends for the next ceremony entered at the back. The crematorium's director was determined to get back on schedule. Among Ray's mourners were two men, dressed respectfully in dark suits with black ties, who sat at the back during the service. Talking at the reception in a nearby hotel, it emerged they were not known to anyone. The family believed they were somehow connected with Ray's work; Bob had assumed they were family friends. Bob later made inquiries among his workforce, but they couldn't be identified. "I bet they turned up to the wrong funeral," Bob's secretary suggested.

Chapter Twenty-two

Carnal therapy...

Good news. Great news. But it could not be shared, only celebrated in silence. Jane's second and more accurate test for the human immunodeficiency virus proved negative. The genito-urinary clinic also gave her the all clear on the tests for other diseases. She knew it was a crazy word to think, but Jane was *grateful* her attacker had been clean, or at least failed to pass on any infection. No HIV, chlamydia, gonorrhoea or syphilis. She wanted to shout the news from the rooftops, but nobody knew, because nobody could know or would know.

In over four months not a day had passed without some reminder of the attack. Once sensitised to rape you're sensitive to the word and associated words such as *assault* or *crime*. Images on TV, or in movies, even advertisements for clothes or cosmetics, can become stimulants of traumatic recall. Someone makes an innocent remark during a meal - "pass the *bread*" - and it all comes flooding back. Jane could now be flashback free for several hours, and that, she knew, would eventually extend to days.

The pain had transformed into bitterness. The rage had reduced. Time, Jane concluded, had not, would not, could not and should not heal. What happened happened. It cannot be undone. You cannot be un-raped or de-raped. It could not be forgotten. Jane had come to believe that the attack should not be forgotten because that would be repression of reality, self-deception and self-denial. One evening Jane heard an American feminist writer on TV saying, or at least implying, that if a girl gets raped she should pick herself up, dust herself down, and get on with life. Jane agreed.

If Jane had been HIV positive a plausible explanation would have been needed to tell Matt of his likely cross-infection. There was no way of concealing it. She had planned to keep the story simple. She had already worked through her alibi making sure there was a respectable time gap between "the affair" and her pregnancy. The prime objective would be to ensure Matt was left in no doubt *her* child was *his* child.

Conveniently, a weekend conference she'd attended last July at the University of Reading on child psychology, provided the time and place for her cover. She simply adapted her story told to the nurse-counsellor at the clinic and rehearsed her lines a hundred times.

"*Matt, I love you,*" she'd scripted as the opening gambit. Telling someone you love them just before you criticise or admit a transgression is usually very disarming. "*It was stupid. Meaningless, I know. It was just five-minutes of madness that went too far. We'd had too much to drink. You know how it is. It only happened once. And it will never, never happen again. I'm really sorry. I didn't want to hurt you by telling you. Knowing is more painful than not knowing. The truth isn't always best. Ignorance is bliss. But you had to know about the HIV.*"

She had thought carefully about how to handle forgiveness. "*If this had happened to you, a one-night-stand with some woman, an impulse thing, I'd forgive you, I know I would, you know I would. Sure I'd be angry and upset. But I would forgive. I hope you will do the same for me now. If the circumstances are right, it can happen so easily.*"

The truth of true pain is harder to handle than acting in a make-believe scenario. It seemed easier to admit a fictitious affair than a real attack, although you have choice in one but not the other. It was simply impossible for Jane to disclose the assault in her own home

200

before Christmas. The reality of her rape, Jane now rationalised, was that the attack was actually a brief, boring and bland event – an opportunist random attack.

Jane believed that what happened was, for Matt, for any man, about territory. However it happened, voluntarily or compulsorily, another man had imposed himself on the other man's territory. She saw it as animal instinct, domination of the dominant male to impregnate *his* female or females. Her body had belonged exclusively to Matt by choice, her choice. It wasn't marriage vows or social expectation. It wasn't lack of opportunity. It was love. Love for Matt. Love for one man.

Her attacker broke the magic of exclusivity, the spirit of one woman for one man. Her body had been invaded. Territory had been trespassed upon. The way it happened, in Jane's view, was irrelevant, the reason confusing, his words unfathomable. It was the love for Matt that guaranteed her silence. Learning she was now free of infection reinforced Jane's vow of silence, allowed the secrecy to continue. The secret was even more secure.

Jane's self-administered therapy, her strategy of secrecy, was clearly working - slowly, but certainly. If everyone had been told, the suffering would have been multiplied like a virulent infection. The pain would have spread like ink on blotting paper. More people – her mother, father, sisters, Matt, friends - would have needed more healing instead of just one person. Jane did not want anyone to feel sorry for her. Never had, never would. As a child, falling over and scraping a knee raw, or banging her head after falling from the swing, she never ran to mum or dad for a reassuring kiss and cuddle like most children. She cried alone then. She cries alone now.

* * *

Pregnancy had been uneventful for Jane. The clinic's latest ultrasound scan had indicated a healthy baby growing at the correct rate. None of the nasty things her mother and friends had warned could happen did happen: no constipation, haemorrhoids, heartburn, craving for unsuitable food, swollen ankles or varicose veins. The little morning sickness of the first few weeks had abated, and that hadn't been too bad. She still suffered revulsion of tea and coffee, although that too had decreased in recent days. Her breasts were "voluptuous" according to Matt and her nipples had enlarged and darkened. In three months their child would be born healthy and hungry. The baby could now derive goodness from Jane's body instead of inheriting disease. She could look forward with optimism rather than dwell on a painful past.

Jane heard the key enter the lock. The door opened, then closed. She was stretched out on the sofa, keeping her legs up to avoid varicose veins and swollen ankles. She turned as the living room door opened. Matt had not removed his coat.

"How are you darling?" she chirped.

He resented her happiness with a seemingly artificial and exaggerated bounce in her voice. It rubbed against his feelings.

"You look absolutely knackered. Clients giving you a hard time?"

This was home, so this was personal. Work was in a city far away. *Doesn't she understand the difference by now?*

"Why don't you get changed and I'll get supper. I've been waiting for you. What do you fancy?"

Fuck food. It's not important. Why's she so bloody happy?

Jane adapted quickly to mirror Matt's mood. She had wanted to reflect the day's news, share her happiness - although she couldn't disclose the reason for it. She'd planned her moves, visualised a cosy evening. She'd wanted to be nice to Matt tonight. Touch him. Love him. Seduce him. Make up for several tetchy months where she had rejected his moves more than accepted. Although, since announcing her pregnancy, she'd noticed Matt had been less interested, more reluctant to touch her. A couple of girlfriends had warned her this might happen.

202

"Do you know how much money we owe?" Matt asked Jane angrily as she stood up.

"We'll manage," she said in conciliation.

"You said that six fucking months ago, and we haven't. It's worse."

"Look we can..." moving closer wanting to calm him but daring not to touch.

"We can't do anything Jane. You're not getting any more money. But we're spending more for some reason. The additional mortgage is breaking us. And now there's the baby. We shouldn't have gone ahead with that bloody extension. You were right about my pathetic pay increase, you'll be pleased to know. It's hardly made a blind-bit of difference. In fact with that fucking expensive car sat out there I'm paying more in tax and bringing home less. Bloody government. All chancellors are thieves."

Matt opened his briefcase, took out an envelope and slung it at Jane. She unfolded his payslip.

"Look," he shouted. "Less than last bloody month. More tax, more national insurance. And the stupid incompetent rail company that keeps us waiting virtually every day for dirty trains has announced a massive 15% rise in train fares."

He pulled London's Evening Standard out of his briefcase and held up its front page headline: SHOCK INCREASE IN RAIL FARES

"I can ask Dad to..."

"That's the *last* fucking thing I want you to do - blurting it out to every fucking one that we can't fucking manage. It's got nothing to do with them, apart from the bloody fact they encouraged us to have 'more space' and 'I'll do it at cost' tempted us to be so stupid."

In two years of going out together and three years of marriage, this was the most distraught she'd ever seen Matt. Jane quietened her voice in the same way she controlled a rowdy class. Apply psychology and experience, use his name, remain friendly and be supportive.

"Matt, they won't mind. You know they won't. Bob and Maggie aren't 'everyone'. They've always said they would help us out. They'll understand. Dad's got a fortune stashed away. A lot of money to us is peanuts to him..."

Matt was not consoled. "I'm *not* sponging off your family. And we *can't* sponge off mine - because my mother doesn't have any and my Dad's dead and he left her and me with nothing. This is *our* problem Jane. *We* have to sort it."

Jane's instinct was to put the kettle on - always her mother's response when Dad was upset. Tea for Matt might calm the storm. But he stood in the doorway looking at the floor as if into a large dark hole. If an abyss had opened up Matt, at that moment, would have jumped. Jane placed a reassuring arm around his shoulders, as he had supported her at Ray's funeral a week earlier. She guided her husband to the armchair and sat him down. She knelt in front of Matt as his head slumped forward into his hands.

Matt's eyes looked down and dejected. Jane could have spoken, but she decided touch could do the talking, allowing body language the freedom to express emotion better than words. She combed his thick black hair with the fingers of one hand and gently stroked the outside of Matt's hand with the other.

"I just can't see a way out of this pit Jane," he said softly, slowly, sadly. "How can we stop spending? I can't see where all our money goes. Life cost so much bloody money."

Jane maintained the healing rhythm of her touch. But Matt's depression continued. "We have no savings, no spare cash. At the end of each month we owe more than we did at the beginning. I discovered two unpaid final demands for the council tax and the water company stuffed behind the microwave. Why do you hide them away Jane? It doesn't make them go away. You can't hide bad news for long. You can't pretend they are not there to pay. And now we've this."

He looked at Jane's baby bulge.

"How can we bring a child into this world with not a penny to our name? What induced us to have a kid? We must have been crazy." Matt's head sank again to search for darkness below.

"Matt. Matt. Look at me. That's better. We'll cope. Somehow we'll manage. We have to. We can't just give up. I'll cut back spending as much as possible. I promise. We've got most of what we need for this little one."

"But we hardly spend money on treats now," Matt insisted. "Holiday's are out of the question. We're in a mess Jane and you don't seem to realise it."

He'd started to wind himself up again and she wanted him to relax. She needed to take control again. "Matt, imagine yourself as your own client. What would you advise them to do? You'd say go through the books. Look at income. Look at costs. What is the gap between the figures and how can we reduce it and reverse it? Look, tomorrow or at the weekend, we'll go through all the books, look at all the outgoings and see what we can do."

Matt managed a brief smile, even a little laugh. She'd picked a good line of argument. "That's good. You should come into my business."

"Well it certainly pays much better than teaching," she said encouragingly.

"But I can't see how we can bridge the debt gap. The fact is we have more going out than coming in. We can't square the circle," said Matt.

The smile had vanished and there was no longer any chance of a laugh. Matt returned to his state of sadness. Jane decided action would speak louder than words - action therapy not word therapy. She kissed him on the lips from her kneeling position, laid herself on the carpet and pulled him by the hands to join her.

"No, not now."

"It's all right Matt. The baby's safe. You can't hurt it. You can push as hard as you like."

"I know. But it's uncomfortable for you. Let's do it later. I'm really not..."

"Don't worry. I'll let you know if anything hurts. It's been ages. I've missed you, and I know I haven't been very nice to you recently in this department. Let me make it up to you..."

She pulled her top over her head and the new maternity bra conveniently opened from the front.

"I don't understand you," he said truthfully. "For the first few months you didn't want to know. Pushed me away half the time - most of the time. Treated me as if I had some disease. Now there's 'the lump' in the way and you want to do it. Women, eh?"

The word "disease' stunned Jane for a second. She froze. *Bread. Bread. Bread.* Shock. Fear. Injury. Pain. Dryness. Intrusion. Penetration. Pushed. Pulled. No, no, not now.

Matt started to respond. He started to remove his clothes, kicked off his shoes and failed to notice Jane's sudden upset. But she was determined. Determined to look forward and not dragged back by memories. Determined to please her baby's father than recall the pain of her assailant. Determined to see a bright future than a dark past. Determined to go through with this act of carnal therapy.

Jane turned her back towards Matt to hide her anxiety. She made the perfect excuse that this position would work better in her "condition". But it bought a few extra seconds to hide her distress, until she could return her mind to the good things in life.

"That's better, oh yes that's nice, very nice, isn't it?" she said as he slipped inside, subdued her anxiety, and provided a pleasure that had been missing for many months.

"Steady on a little, they're very tender, so be gentle," she informed him as his hands naturally moved across the unfamiliar landscape of her pregnant body.

Chapter Twenty-three

Why did they die...

All companies say the same: our people are our most valuable asset. But when recession strikes, the second a few bucks have to be saved, jobs go. Downsizing, rightsizing, head-shrinkage, redundancy opportunities and career realignment are the euphemisms of modern management. With China and the former Soviet states undercutting established chemical companies in Western Europe and North America, AestChem Inc had suffered a torrid time – until 22XP.

This "breakthrough technology", as the US press dubs it, has reversed the company's fortunes. It holds exclusive patents. 22XP technology is several years ahead of its nearest rival. Lawyers are briefed to be eagle-eyed for infringements. They will take aggressive action against intellectual property theft. The company is determined no one else will steal its research and development work. Marketed correctly, FFresherFood will make a killing. Many shareholders, not all, will make their fortunes provided they buy at the right price and sell at the right time.

Spies work for corporations, not just countries. The company had hired specialists in counter-intelligence to curtail industrial espionage. Theft of ideas for products, advanced knowledge of your rival's marketing, public relations and advertising strategies is big business. Knowing a competitor's chemical formulas and technological processes can mean the difference between success and failure, wealth and poverty. Industrial theft costing a few hundred thousand can save you millions in research costs.

Knowledge is power. Power, in business, is money in the bank. Acquiring intelligence makes good business sense. Directors who fail to find out what rivals are up to are incompetent. Ignorance is negligence.

AestChem's senior scientists and technologists working on the 22XP formula were loyal, long-term, highly paid staff. For new researchers, or for other employees who directors had doubts about their loyalty, routine checks and surveillance would be carried out. What did they *really* do in their last job? CV's rarely contain the whole truth. Have they *really* left their loyalty behind? Could they *really* be working as a mole? Would they return to the competition with a bagful of secrets and be rewarded with a large bonus? Even if they are genuinely loyal now, could they be turned? Will they learn too much and be tempted to sell the information they know? Do they have debts? Is their lifestyle too lavish for their salary and how is it being funded? Are they still phoning and meeting people in their former company? Are they using the photocopier more than they really need to? What company documents do they take home to work on over the weekend? Do they try to see confidential documents? Do they appear to have additional interest in other sections of the business? Is this natural curiosity and enthusiasm? Or is this eager employee trying to find out more than they need to know? If so, why?

Company security would aim to reassure directors. They would monitor suspect individuals to ensure "integrity of personnel". Specialists, including private detectives, are contracted for additional tasks to try and achieve the virtual impossible: to keep the affairs of a public company private.

Only a handful of senior directors understood how 22XP's processes worked together. The President and CEO had devised the strategy that way. Different parts of the company, each with its separate director, held a different piece of the jigsaw. If divide and rule was the blueprint for the British in India to keep the factions fighting, AestChem's boss had copied it to build and maintain his own empire.

As Senior Vice President for Communications, part of Jenni Tallow's management remit was to make sure the company's employees communicated efficiently. Alongside the firm's Human Resources Department, which had the task of maintaining and improving staff morale, a conference was arranged to involve the company's senior managers from around the world. Factory managers, scientists, technologists, engineers, senior managers from all departments would attend the five-day conference to discuss the future of the company. The Board of Directors and major shareholders had already decided the company's medium to long-term strategy. "But we've got to give the shop floor troops the impression they're participating in the key decisions," the President had confided to Jenni. "If our senior and middle managers were left to run the business, we'd be ruined in months," he laughed as he approved the generous budget and gave Jenni the go-ahead for AestChem's Global Strategy Seminar. She'd suggested the working theme: "Snakes and Ladders – kill the competition and climb to success." Jenni believed this title would appeal to the President and she would attribute this excellent title to him. She was right, and she did.

War Games were on the agenda. Teams of AestChem staff would pretend they worked for rival companies and given tasks to complete in small working groups. Imagining themselves as executives from their rivals, they would devise plans to damage 22XP and other products made by the company. Later, back with their AestChem hats on, they would develop plans to defend against these likely attacks. They were bringing to the chemical industry a routine practice from many other areas of business – cosmetics, detergents, food, ice cream, beer, lager and spirits. For years war game battles have raged between Pepsi and Coca-Cola, each trying to gain dominant market share. The Cola Wars are part of marketing folklore, becoming case studies at management colleges around the world. And the bitter rivals not only resent each other but also resent anyone else supplying any drink to any mouth anywhere on the planet. Some executives are so obsessed with selling their cola they would, if they could, replace mother's breast milk with fizzy brown sugary water.

Crete, the largest Greek island, had been chosen as a suitable venue by the conference organisers. Around 400 AestChem employees flew to Athens from its chemical plants, research laboratories and sales centres around the world. Australians mixed with Argentines, Indonesians with Indians, Belgians with Brazilians. The voices of the world gathered on a charted ferry that whisked them to their hotel and conference centre in the picturesque town of Aghios Nikolaos. Hand shakes, back-slapping, cold cocktails, fine wine and excellent food on board the white cruiser guaranteed delivery of the delegates in the right mood for management's message.

At the luxurious hotel, set overlooking the dark blue Aegean Sea, the company faithful would hear presentations from all key directors. They would be praised for the business objectives they had achieved. Egos would be massaged. Awards presented. In graver tones they would be warned about "challenges" facing the company - "problems" being a banned word in 21st Century management-speak. Complacency within the corporation could not be tolerated. That's why new targets had been set for each employee. Rewards and compensation, the company's word for salary, could only be based on each employee fulfilling clearly defined management goals.

After the carrot and stick, faith in the firm would be reaffirmed. AestChem's President and Chief Executive Officer William J. Morgan II would deliver a rousing speech to rally the company's troops. Unfortunately, because of his heavy schedule of commitments, he could only fly in for the second day of the conference to deliver The President's Keynote Address.

Jenni, on the waterfront balcony of her room late at night, was putting the finishing touches to the speech. In the distance she could hear the delegates drunk on a cocktail of jet lag, alcohol, ego, self-doubt and high hopes. They were to live like millionaires for five days, all expenses paid. It was an excuse for the delegates to have a great time on company money. Every employee knew it. But no one would admit it. Why spoil a good thing? Listening to speeches, taking part in discussion groups and role-play exercises, showing loyalty to the company, was a small price to pay for a week-long party.

Middle managers are the active players of management's game. They have most to gain and most to lose. They have ladders to climb, but slide to the bottom if swallowed by a fellow snake. Most fake enjoyment of teamwork and cooperate with the very people they most want to dominate. Team building exercises, they know, in practice, lead to team breaking. But the game must be played. They must do what they are told, and tell others what to do, often not knowing why. If managers need to be told the big corporate picture, they won't understand it. And for those who understand it, they don't need to be told.

Crete will provide a good playing ground for management's game. The bosses will provide the board and pieces, shake the dice, and make the moves. The directors will watch the managers and decide who is promoted, who's in, who has potential, who's sidelined. Company conferences always provide a stage for managers to jockey for the top jobs, and they know it. But how do you stand out from the crowd? How do you attract the attention of the directors without alienating your colleagues? How do you come across as intelligent without being arrogant? How do you demonstrate leadership quality when you're part of a team of equals? How do you show you're better than the rest when you're supposed to be a team player? How do you ask a question that is challenging without being threatening? How do you praise your boss or say something positive without appearing sycophantic? How can you highlight the company's cock-ups without offending the director who dictated the policy? Managers who find the answers will rise above their peers.

As Senior Vice President for Communications and Corporate

Affairs, Jenni was the top woman in AestChem Inc. She had reached the peak in an industry dominated by men. Working her way up as a Harvard chemistry graduate, and an Oxford PhD - although she often dropped the title "doctor" when it seemed to threaten a boss - she pioneered the chemical industry's awareness of environmental issues. From the beginning she stood out from most of her colleagues. Women in chemical plants were a tiny minority; attractive women rare, beautiful women exceptional. At a time when the chemical industry's reputation was sinking like a stone in water, as an exceptional employee, Jenni made the industry's grey men in grey suits realise they had to care for the environment. She made them sit up and listen. Greenpeace and Friends of the Earth should be our allies not our enemies, she told them. Working on the inside of the industry she became a one-woman environmental campaigner. Some said she'd achieved more than a million armchair critics, a thousand street protesters, a hundred demonstrations and a string of government ministers. For her the direction was clear. For the long-term interests of the chemical business, the industry had to stop polluting air, contaminating ground and poisoning water. The business itself had to become its own environmental watchdog.

When a former industry leader speaking at a major chemical conference declared, "the solution to pollution is dilution", Jenni, then an unknown graduate wet behind the ears, virtually tore his head off in public. Her answer in front of all the industry's leaders was simple. "The solution to pollution, sir, is prevention of pollution," she'd said when handed the microphone during the question and answer session. Jenni gained a ripple of applause, until they realised their bosses were monitoring dissent. Later as delegates filed out of the conference hall Jenni was cold-shouldered, even by some of her own colleagues. A few dared to praise her comments, but usually in quiet corners away from prying eyes. But one man had the confidence to speak to her, William J. Morgan II, then head of research and development at AestChem. He made her an offer she couldn't refuse. Her salary doubled overnight. She became part of a new team, AestChem's Environmental Monitoring Group. She had climbed three steps up the ladder thanks to one moment of courage, conviction and foresight.

Over the years Jenni on the inside, alongside outside pressure groups and government agencies acting after chemical industry disasters, played her part in making the world a better, safer place to live in. Industry generally and the chemical industry specifically should, she successfully argued, help restore the earth, replace what it could and correct mistakes. The industry must help educate the public about the role chemicals play in society, ecology and biodiversity. The chemical industry should "go green" and take responsibility to play its part in protecting the world's environment. It should, as far as possible, restore natural habitats, plant trees and shrubs, create reed beds, clean the water and replenish the earth.

Jenni had discovered her route through the management maze to join the men at the top.

Hard work too had underpinned her progress. And the habit is hard to break. As AestChem staff enjoyed their first night in Crete partying in the hotel's ballroom, Jenni switched on her laptop on the balcony of her room overlooking a moonlit Mediterranean sea. She needed to work more than play and party.

Beating bass speakers pounded in the background. She could hear the laughter and banter across the floodlit swimming pool and through the palms. AestChem's disco warmed up as the drink flowed freely after their five-course dinner. As always at company conferences new affairs would start, old ones rekindled. Marriage vows became meaningless and the first steps to divorce taken. Each woman, outnumbered by four or five men, would have their pick of the ones trying their luck. Some girls simply wanted to flirt. Others would go the whole way if Mr Right came along. All the men who tried it on wanted to be Mr Right. Flirting is a girl's game. Some women would stick with one partner for the conference. Others would play the field. The rest were simply having a good time making new friends and consolidating established friendships. The human resources department called it "facilitated bonding", "team building" and "sharing experiences". That way, presumably, the party became tax deductable.

But Jenni could always apply herself to work, whatever the distractions around her. She had learnt to live with men admiring her body as much as her brain, usually more so. She always stayed focussed on the job in hand and ignored the innuendo. She concentrated on the professional, not the personal.

Dressed in a simple short white cotton dress suitable for the tropical evening, she sipped a large gin and tonic packed with ice. The open sea, tamed by the harbour, lapped quietly on the rocks below her balcony. Gentle waves caused light from distant waterfront restaurants to ripple across the sea's surface to play on the white walls of her executive suite.

The President's speech was on the screen in front of her. One of her staff had drafted it following Jenni's guidelines for the conference in Crete. It was pretty good. The young man would be praised for his effort by a signed letter on the company's headed paper. An email would not have as much impact. But Jenni now needed to add subtle sentences, fine-tune words, condition expectations, set the tone and add emotion. The messenger would have to be on message.

The messenger phoned. "How's it going? All my senior staff pissed?"

"Hi Bill. No. I'm stone cold sober."

"You're always stone cold. That's your problem Jenni."

"How's Athens?"

"Smelly. Noisy. Crowded. Hot. And in a minute I'll tell you the bad news. How's Crete?"

"Scented with jasmine. Quiet – apart from a few hundred of our employees dancing the night away. And it's not too hot, thanks to a sea breeze."

The small talk always ended quickly between Jenni and Bill.

214

"Many changes to my speech?"

"A few. I'll email the final script in an hour or so."

"I think we should talk down the potential earnings from 22XP."

"I agree. That's one of the changes I've already made," said Jenni. "On the boat over here today a lot of them believe 22XP is already in the bag and it's going to make big bucks. But it isn't going to sell itself. And we can't have them thinking they can sit back and watch the cash pour in."

"My feelings too. And these European Commissioner guys haven't guaranteed approval yet. That Claude Perlemuter phoned this afternoon from Henderston-Strutt. Did he call you?"

"Yes, I told him to call you directly so you could authorise any action."

"The Commission is asking to see more research data, stuff from the animal trials."

"Claude says it's just routine. Nothing to worry about."

"You know me Jenni. When someone tells me not to worry, I start worrying."

"They want to make sure they're looking at the same research data as the FDA before they approved it," said Jenni.

William J. Morgan II sighed. "They didn't see all the animal stuff."

Jenni Tallow paused. "What are you saying Bill?"

"They've asked to see the LD50 tests."

"The FDA didn't request them. Lethal dose work wasn't necessary."

"You're right. They didn't request them because they didn't require them for the 22XP process approval. But we did some LD50 work anyway."

"I don't like the sound of what you're about to tell me Bill. Think carefully before you say any more. Do I need to know?"

"I don't know if you need to know? What do you need to

know?"

"I need to know only what I can say publicly. If I can't say it openly Bill then why don't you try mushroom management?"

The President and CEO laughed. "You've never liked been kept in the dark and had shit thrown at you."

"Perhaps this is the right time in my career to learn that ignorance is better than knowledge."

He thought carefully for a moment. And Jenni allowed him to without interruption. Mushroom management was rejected. "Three fucking rats died. Just three god-damn rats. That's all."

"But the hypothesis was surely a zero death rate? We couldn't expect any rat to die. You can't, theoretically, overdose on 22XP. So how can we do a lethal dose test to kill off half the experimental group in the first place?"

"I thought it would prove absolutely how safe 22XP was if..."

"But three rats died. Out of how many Bill? What were the raw numbers?"

"Ten thousand. Three dirty rats out of ten fucking thousand."

In the years Jenni had known Bill, since his offer of a job over 15 years ago at the back of a conference hall, this was the very first time she had known him to make a bad call. Momentarily, it knocked her confidence. Bill's judgement was always perfect. But the moment passed.

"Bill, you taught me years ago never to ask a question if we don't need the answer or if we don't believe the answer helps. This bags both. This was an unnecessary unhelpful question. So why the fuck did you authorise this study?"

"I said. I thought it would give us absolute proof of..."

"What did they die of?"

"Hearts packed up."

"Any pre-cancerous cells?"

"That's the good news Jenni. We didn't check that in this experiment."

"And we're not going to, are we Bill?"

"We don't need to."

"No," she underlined.

"Should we tell the Henderson-Strutt people about the rats?"

"No. They don't need to know. Is this particular study going to be submitted to the European Commission people?"

Bill breathed deeply. He regained the initiative. "Jenni, what study?"

Jenni heard the message. She regained her confidence in Bill.

* * *

The President and CEO's helicopter touched down in the hotel grounds at noon on Tuesday. All the President's men and women were there to greet William – "call me Bill" – J. Morgan II. The First Lady of AestChem, his wife, accompanied her husband to remind staff the company believed in family values. The delegates had spent the morning in small discussion groups working on plans to improve efficiency. Most of them also used the morning to sober up and replenish the fluids alcohol had taken away. At lunch the President and his wife visited every table in the dining hall to ask how they were getting on and enjoying Crete. Every employee expressed appreciation of the conference. They assured their big boss five days of debate and networking would bring benefits to the business of AestChem. They told him what he wanted to hear. He heard what he expected to hear.

The President missed lunch. He didn't like making speeches on a full stomach. His indigestion kicked in, despite the tablets. While the delegates enjoyed the rest of their lunch Bill and Jenni went to the main conference hall to make the final checks. They went over the changes to his speech for the last time. He was using autocue, where the words appear on glass screens to read, but appear invisible to the audience. The autocue operator would need to know the speed he talked and if he often went off script. Not that Bill needed the words to read. He could memorise most speeches after two or three readings. And he was a highly accomplished public speaker. They checked the microphones for sound level with the audio-visual technicians and discussed the opening and closing music. Bill always insisted on familiarising himself with the stage set. He liked to walk where he would be walking. He checked the height of the lectern. He made sure the lighting engineer kept the spotlights out of eyes. He also wanted some light on his staff. "I hate talking to a black hole," he told the man at the lighting controls. "I like looking into the whites of their eyes."

After lunch the delegates filed into the main conference hall with high expectations. They would hear their President and CEO. They would learn of the company's future direction and the challenges they faced. He would talk about ladders to climb and snakes that bite. The company's commitment to care in the community would continue. They would enhance their role as good corporate citizens. Social responsibility and environmental concerns would remain high. 22XP would improve the diet of millions of people in the western world and even bring hope to people of the Third World. But there were still several hurdles to jump before global approval. Chickens must not be counted while the eggs rest in the nest.

The President sincerely and personally thanked the employees for their hard work and commitment. He was confident they would raise their game even higher to achieve greater personal and corporate prosperity. They were assured they were the best people a company could get. Bill gave them praise and adoration. They gave him theirs: a standing ovation. Jenni planned a perfect presentation. Bill delivered one.

Somehow – an internal investigation is still underway to identify the culprit - parts of this confidential in-house speech at a hotel in Aghios Nikolaos, Crete, reached the media in America. Business analysts on Wall Street interpreted the CEO's comments as "pessimistic" or "downbeat" for 22XP's approval in Europe. One described the speech as revealing "a setback". AestChem's shares took a tumble. But by Friday they had regained Monday's price, mainly due to heavy trading on their stock raising demand. Some investors retained their faith in the company.

Chapter Twenty-four

The Law of Motherhood...

Matt sat there. Just sat. Thinking. But trying not to. He found it hard thinking of thinking nothing. He wanted to empty his mind because his mind was full, congested with confused thoughts. He wanted the simplicity of nothing, not the complexity of everything.

He lazily kicked the campfire into life and the smoke ignited into flame. Within minutes the water in the pan, suspended on a triangular greenstick tepee, started to boil. Two teabags thrown into the bubbling water would produce a brew to satisfy Matt's early morning thirst.

His attempt to clear his head failed and, in common with everyone, or so he thought, Matt set out his future on life's balance sheet: What was good? What was bad? What had he achieved? What could he achieve? Was he in the right job? Where would life end up, or is this it? And next? Debt. Growing debt. What could he do to clear it? How could he get ahead of the game, live in a state of credit rather than debit? Then, working with full lies, or half-truths at best, about Chechnya and how President Vadimov was "Western civilization's best friend", as he'd heard Peter brief many leading journalists. And perhaps Penny was right, the agency should not lobby for the approval of a chemical with the potential to cause cancer. Should he leak the health risk to the media? Should he tell the truth about the genocide in Chechnya? If he did, he'd never work again, not in public relations. And they would know, the men with bodyguards from the ministries and embassies who visited Peter and talked behind closed doors.

Things were getting worse not better.

In three months the baby arrives. Everything will change, or so everyone says. They should have waited. Waited for the right time, knowing the time is never right. But he couldn't tell Jane. Not now. Why hurt with truth when you can heal with lies?

Jane too appears to be over the shock of pregnancy and seems happier, more content, more confident, certain she can cope with a new life in her hands. Those early months had been hard for her. He witnessed how it drained her energy, sapped her confidence, transformed the extrovert into the introvert, perhaps because the focus of her life was now within. After that initial euphoria when the pregnancy test showed positive, Jane had distanced herself from him, mentally, physically. She too had suffered post-pregnancy shock syndrome.

Matt had moved to second place in Jane's affection. He realised his demotion just weeks after they'd learned of the pregnancy when Jane withdrew into herself, almost overnight. He'd come to accept the child inside had become the greater priority than the man outside who had helped create it. Child first, father second. It's a Law of Motherhood. Babies need feeding. Men can feed themselves. The baby was in Jane's body, the place of conception. It lived there, in her, for 40 weeks. Then it would feed from her. It was *part* of him, but not *in* him.

This was Jane's baby more than his. Fathers are estranged from their children from conception to birth. The chemistry of conception had taken place inside Jane. Then months of nurture cements the mother and child together for ever while the father lives in exile. Pregnancy provides the psycho-physical superglue fathers cannot achieve. Women have a nine-month start on men in the race for a relationship. Matt could not compete because he was only watching from the trackside.

Matt sipped his tea sitting on a log, one of three he had dragged with rope to form a semicircle of seating around his campfire, now burning brightly in the crisp air of early morning. He was preparing breakfast while chewing a stalk of vernal grass, his grandfather's favourite stalk to suck and spit out. Since childhood Matt had known its flavour was best in spring. Fat spat in the black iron frying pan sat on the embers. With long barbeque tongs he laid in several rashes of bacon, taken from the fridge an hour earlier as Jane slept. The fat crackled and snapped and sizzled. Jane hated bacon smell anyway, especially since the hormone upheaval of pregnancy. And Matt enjoyed breakfast in his woods alone.

Bacon. Pig. It made Matt think of the boar herd roaming somewhere in the woodland. Experts would say a "sounding" of boar, he'd learnt. Since his earlier sighting of them, the only signs had been their distinctive hoof marks in the soft earth at the edge of the pond and a wallow hole, where the boar rolled in the mud. He wondered if the "sounding" might seek revenge on him for frying a cousin.

Most trees had burst into their bright spring green. Bluebells were in full bloom delivering their sweet fragrance to the still air. Clumps of delicate long-stalked dog-violets with their heart-shaped leaves edged the grass clearing. Matt could sense the immense energy of the woods bursting into life after the sleep of winter. When he remained motionless and paused his breathing, he could actually hear the vegetation growing around him. Shoots were breaking through the ground and buds were opening leaf and flower to life's light. Birds were singing on wing or perch and scurrying on the ground finding succulent fresh-hatched bugs. Blackbirds, tree sparrows and magpies were among other birds fighting and scrambling in the branches to secure the best nesting sites. Wood pigeons, "woodies", were cooing in their wooing. Even the sombre brown Scot's pine, standing alone at the edge of the clearing, was tinged with joy of spring yellow as the year's male cones developed.

Over recent weeks King's Wood had become Matt's second home. Most weekends, and on the odd day off, he had worked through his woodland job list. He had roped off the enclosure near the centre of his land. Not that rope would keep anything out or anything in. But it was symbolic. Like an animal scenting its territory, he'd marked his private patch, not so much as a warning to keep out, but as a place to keep his private world in.

With a second-hand chainsaw and his toolbox he had built a log shelter using his own forest wood, both fallen timber and freshly cut. The cabin's four corner posts, and the two uprights to form the doorway, had been dug firmly into the deep fertile woodland soil. The floor made from wood boards - admittedly from a DIY store – was knee height off the ground to keep the damp out and restrict the bugs, rats, voles and mice.

It had rained hard but Matt's roof had done its job and kept the cabin dry inside. An old rug, a small round table, and a cheap rusty camp chair from the loft at home, completed the furnishings. A white candle sat in a jam jar on the table. The door had rope hinges looped through holes Matt had bored. A wood plank, supported by brackets on the inside and outside, kept the door closed from either side. It was dark inside the cabin except for fingers of light finding their way through the gaps between the horizontal logs bolted to the six upright legs. He'd seal them later with clay from the stream and pond bed. Now it was spring the urgency to stop drafts blowing through had passed. But summer's gentle ventilation would become winter's bitter wind. Matt had made sure the roof had a generous overhang, especially at the front, so he used the cabin's entrance as his main seat sheltered from any rain. That's where he went to sit and eat his bacon, laid between two thick slices of bread taken from the new enamel bread bin, washed down by a second mug of smoke-flavoured tea.

Matt was well aware the physical work in the wood contrasted sharply with his office life at Henderson-Strutt. Twelve hours earlier he had been at a meeting in the heart of London, shaved and splashed with aftershave, suit with tie and black shoes, paper files, pen-pushing, keyboard-tapping. Now, Saturday, Matt was unshaven and dressed in mud-splattered "camos", his hunting camouflage suit and brown boots.

Just hours ago he was surrounded by millions of people in the metropolis. Now, in the woods at dawn, there was hardly anyone for miles around. He could only be certain of Alice Campbell at Rose Cottage, who, he noticed through the trees when she was walking in her back garden, had started using two sticks to support her arthritic legs. He always promised to pop in and say "Hello" when visiting the woods. She liked to chat. But like many lonely people, once she'd started, she didn't know when to stop, as if the pressure of stored gossip had to be released. He'd taken to waving goodbye from the car as he drove away on the dirt track. Sometimes he lowered the window and mouthed see you next time. He always noticed her waving in the car mirror, even though she must believe he's looking at the road ahead.

The woods had become his place to think about not thinking, anything, nothing or everything. It was here he tried forgetting about work, crisis management, public relations, staff reports, billing, clients, 22XP and AestChem. To Matt, his woods were where depression about debt was forgotten. Or, at least, pushed back into the darkness of his mind. Here the focus was on the manual work not the mental. Here he could use his hands as much as his brain. Here he could construct useful things instead of London's public relations spin and froth. Here was real. There was false. Woodland was natural. Streets were constructed. Trees were truthful. Man dishonest. Woodland provided oxygen. Man abused it.

After the bacon sandwich and a third mug of tea Matt set about doing what he'd come to do. He took the rifle and walked to the eastern edge of his acres that bordered fields of farmland. He'd being practicing shooting and was hitting bull's eye consistently. The telescopic sight, once adjusted, made it easy. He aimed at the head. The rabbit died instantly. With the silencer, the rest of the rabbits just kept munching the farmer's crop, ignoring the death in the midst of their family breakfast. Matt quietly reloaded, aimed, fired, and a second rodent fell. This death didn't cause a stir either. It was not until Matt moved from the undergrowth to collect his kill the remaining rabbits scattered.

His grandfather always advised rabbits should be drained, hocked and hung up to allow them to cool quickly to avoid the meat spoiling. The razor-sharp sheath knife made it easy for Matt.

* * *

Jane's heart was pounding after the shock. He shouldn't leave dead rabbits unannounced inside a Tesco's carrier bag next to the bread bin in the kitchen.

"You don't expect me to eat them," she shouted upstairs at Matt shaving and showering.

"Why not? You're not a vegetarian," he called back through the curtain of water.

"I don't like rabbit."

"Have you eaten rabbit?"

"Yes... I think so."

"When?"

"Well, maybe not."

Matt stood at the top of the stairs drying his hair with a white towel. The rest of his body meanwhile was allowed to drip-dry onto the carpet. He resumed the conversation with Jane standing at the bottom of the stairs.

"When you taste rabbit you might like it."

"Doubt it."

"I was going to make a stew tonight. You'll love it."

"What sort of stew?"

"Jane, it's stew. Just stew. Stew's not rocket science. You just throw in whatever you've got around - potatoes, onions, carrots, thyme, rosemary - anything. Then some salt and pepper..."

"You know I can't eat peppery foods at the moment."

"OK. We'll forget the pepper."

226

Matt later that afternoon skinned the rabbits in the garden and prepared them for the pot. Jane was not normally the squeamish type but, as a precaution, he made sure Jane couldn't see the butchery.

Jane's parents, Bob and Maggie, arrived for dinner to the smell of the stew-pot.

"That smells fantastic," they said simultaneously as they entered the hallway.

"Two rabbits have perished to please your stomachs," Jane said, kissing both of them. "Matt shot them this morning up the woods."

"So they're fresh then," Bob said.

"They didn't have myxomatosis, did they?" asked Maggie as Matt kissed her in greeting.

"Two perfectly healthy young bucks," Matt reassured everyone.

"How can you tell?" Jane asked.

"What, tell the boys from the girls?"

"No, silly. How do you know they don't have myxomatosis?"

"Eyes as clear as yours, fur in perfect condition and free of mange."

They moved into the kitchen and the kettle went on for a round of tea for everyone except Jane. Skimmed milk was the strongest drink she now took. After answering the usual questions on the state of her pregnancy, Jane asked, "How did you know they were boy rabbits?"

"If you'd have seen what they were doing half a minute before I... well... before they said goodbye to the world, you'd be left in no doubt."

"They died happy then," Bob said, and they all laughed.

Then, suddenly and simultaneously as *died* sank in, they all remembered when they had last met - at the funeral of his friend and employee Ray Sykes.

227

Chapter Twenty-five

He's getting another gun...

"He seems to spend more and more time up the woods Mum," Jane explained on the phone. "They've become an obsession."

"But he should be spending more time at home with you now, not less. You're seven months gone," explained Maggie as if her daughter may have lost track of her pregnancy. "Believe me, after producing three babies, you need to start taking it easy."

"Matt's there every Saturday morning first thing. He always says he'll be just a couple of hours, but he usually doesn't get back until late afternoon. And he goes most Sundays."

"Really?"

"The weekend before last – remember the really cold windy one when it rained all the time - he actually slept up there."

"What?"

"I'm not joking Mum. He stays in some sort of shack he's built in the middle of the woods. He takes food up there and everything. He lights a camp fire and fries sausages and eggs and whatever."

"Is everything, you know, all right between you? You've not had a disagreement or anything? Some men find it hard when their wife's pregnant."

"Well, remember how he was at first, I thought he'd got over the shock of impending fatherhood. I felt he'd adjusted to becoming a dad and all that, you know, as good as any bloke. But..." Jane stopped.

"But?"

"It's as if he feels the baby will be a burden, too much to be responsible for."

"It will be Jane. He's right. That's what children are, a responsibility. But he knew what he was doing, didn't he? He knew you were trying for a child, off the pill and all that?"

"Sure. I didn't trick him. Well, we had talked about it..."

"Then he can't complain," said Maggie.

"It just happened sooner than expected, that's all."

"Just like me," Maggie smiled recalling happy memories. "Once we decided to try I only needed to look at your dad and, before you knew it, 'another baby in the bag' as he'd say."

Jane repositioned herself on the sofa to get comfortable. She took a sip of water from the glass on the coffee table. All three Straw girls, Ann, Heather and Jane, enjoyed an extra-special relationship with their mother. Maggie was a friend as well as their mother. Dad stood back and enjoyed his brood of girls knowing he could never join their magic circle, so he didn't try. Maggie cared for their emotions and Bob earned the income to provide for their needs and pay for treats. Maggie was always at home for the girls. Bob was working all hours everywhere building up the business to secure his family's future. It was the way it had to be.

"It's the money mum," Jane said resting her legs over the chair arm. "I'm sure that's what the problem is with Matt."

"I thought you'd got on top of that."

"Not quite. We took out one big loan to pay off all the little ones. We are budgeting better and we've shredded a couple of credit cards. But with one thing and another we haven't managed to get our noses ahead."

Maggie whispered as if the line was bugged. "Look, you know your dad and me will help you out. It's just sitting there in the bank. You're not going short on anything. You're eating properly and everything."

"Oh God Mum, of course I am. It's not *that* bad. It's not too bad at all. It's just that Matt would like more spare cash. Who wouldn't? But you know what he's like. He'd go ballistic if he thought we were taking more money from you. We've already had so much help from you. He'd feel even more undermined. He wants to stand on his own two feet."

"Just as your dad always wanted. Jane, I do understand."

"Men, eh?"

"Matt doesn't have to know, you know," resumed Maggie in her conspiratorial voice.

"What do you mean?"

"You could have an account of your own and he doesn't have to know about it."

"Oh mum," said Jane, "I wouldn't do that. It wouldn't be right. He'd probably find out one day. We promised 'no secrets'. We promised to share equally. I couldn't do that."

"Yes. Yes. You're right. I'm sorry Jane. Stupid idea," said Maggie. "But if there's anything you want, anything you need, just say the word."

"Sure. I know mum. Thanks."

Maggie had the afternoon off from the health authority. She'd planned to put her feet up and watch TV. But Jane clearly needed to talk.

"What does he do in the woods?" Maggie asked. "I thought you had contractors to chop the timber, plant trees or whatever."

"That has to wait because they cost money."

"He can't do all that forestry work alone."

"No, he knows that Mum. It's just that he likes being in the forest. He says it's the place he can relax and think. It's a complete contrast to London and the office. It's like he's recaptured his youth or something, gone back to boy scouting. Remember Matt and his mother used to go on holiday to his Aunt Sheila's. So he played in King's Wood for days on end as a kid. You know he's always been interested in wildlife and conservation and so on. And this gift has

231

given him his own private nature park to play in."

"But he needs to be taking care of you now Jane," said Maggie. "In a few weeks you're going to have the little one to care for. I know I'm coming down for the first week after the birth – if that's still okay – but you'll need all the help you can get after that. I hope he's not going to wonder up the woods all the time then."

"No, I'm sure he won't."

"He'd better not."

"But he's doing a lot of work up there. He's bought a chainsaw...."

"Heavens Jane – they're dangerous..."

"... a couple of axes and he's getting another gun."

"What? I thought he'd got one, that's what he shot those rabbits with last time we came over."

"Mum, that's just an airgun. A toy, he calls it. He wants a couple of *real* guns. You know, a double-barrel thing, a twelve bore or something. Then he wants a rifle. Apparently the twelve bore thing is no good for shooting deer, you need a certain calibre of rifle."

"My God Jane, it sounds like he's becoming the Clint Eastwood of Kent."

"He's applied for gun licenses and fixed a special metal cabinet to the wall to store the guns in. Even the police come round to inspect everything's secure."

Jane shifted her position again to something more comfortable for her back. But the baby inside protested and decided to register a protest.

"It's kicking or thumping Mum," she said.

"Ahh, that's nice," Mum said.

"No it's not. It's bloody uncomfortable. It kept me awake half the night."

"You're right. It's a real pain."

"What were we like? You know, during the pregnancy."

"Heather was the worst of you three. She never seemed to stop

232

moving all the time she was inside. Come to think of it, she hasn't stopped moving since she came outside, always on the move."

Jane laughed. "How active was Ann in the womb? Can you remember?"

"Off course. I remember every pregnancy very clearly. She wasn't too bad. Average I'd say. Now you Jane, before you ask, were by far the quietest. What was really interesting about you is that I felt you really early on, even after what seemed a few weeks, far earlier than the books or doctors say you can. You moved around of course. You kicked occasionally and so on. But you were far more gentle, a little more considerate on your mum's tum."

"I never knew that."

"Well Jane, people never got round to talking about lots of things."

Chapter Twenty-six

She was sugar to his eyes...

For most commuters Monday morning is hell struggling into central London. Delays north, south, east and west, on rail and road. But Penny Taylor had spent the weekend in her father's Georgian town house, a Grade II listed building off Savoy Street near The Strand. For her today, the usual train and tube delays from her flat in Wimbledon would make no difference. Henderson-Strutt's office would be a two-minute stroll after showering and dressing. From this central location it took only five minutes for her father to walk along the Embankment past Somerset House to his chambers at the Inner Temple, one of the Inns of Court and home to many of Britain's famous judges, barristers and solicitors. Some of the down and outs, the ones sober and conscious enough to recognise him, often said hello as he breezed by them each morning outside Temple underground. On Fridays, if he'd had a good week, he'd give one of the begging hands a £10 note "for a cup of tea, sir" accepting it would buy a few cans of Special Brew. But this weekend he had been with his latest girlfriend at his country home. At 24 she was one year younger than his daughter. Knowing Penny was going to be around the London house over the weekend, he decided it was better girlfriend and daughter didn't meet. He wouldn't feel embarrassed. But they might.

Penny and a friend had pulled their own partners at the club in Sloan Square on Saturday night before ending up at her father's house. Penny's lad was classic: tall, lean, dark and rugged-looking, as if he'd just stepped out of a magazine advertisement pushing some fragrance for men. He was a great ornament on the dance floor and on her arm. But, sadly she discovered too late, routine in bed. In the sober light of Sunday morning she also realised he was brainless and boring. Doubtless she'd made his dream come true and Penny endured the ride.

"His name was Darren or Dan or something," she told two giggling girlfriends in the office waiting at the drinks machine. "He put no imagination into it at all," Penny added as her colleagues encouraged more detail. "He just wanted to get it in and get it over with as quickly as possible." The giggles turned to laughter.

"Blokes should be forced to carry a certificate of competence around with them so we know what we're going to get in bed," one of the girls said, to yet more laughter.

"They should be given marks out of ten," suggested the other.

"Well this guy failed," said Penny. "Four out of ten at most."

After each of the girls shared their stories of the weekend, it was Penny's turn to press buttons 0 and 3 to order a white coffee without sugar. The machine dispensed the drink through a book-sized door allowing access to the white plastic cup. After a few sips Penny poured the remains into the sink. She had noticed Peter walking by and she wanted a word before he turned on and tuned into his emails.

"It's as bad as that, is it?" Peter said before turning to face her.

Penny looked surprised.

"You've closed my office door quietly," he explained with a wry smile. "In my experience Penny that means bad news, especially at 8am on Monday morning."

"It is delicate."

"Did you have a good weekend?" Peter asked, deliberately delaying the *delicate* matter.

"Do you really want to know?"

"No. Not really. But bosses are supposed to show interest in their staff."

"But we're in PR Peter. Normal business rules don't apply. The bullshit is only for the clients, eh?"

He laughed a little. "Matt and I have obviously taught you well."

"Too well."

"Fancy a coffee?" continuing to delay the delicate topic.

"I've just had one." But quickly she added, "Correction. I've just had a sip of some brown horrible substance purporting to be a coffee from that machine over there." She pointed across the workstations in the direction of the offending equipment.

"No, no, no, not that stuff. I'll get Sal to make us a proper pot."

After Peter made his request to his PA sat outside the office, he faced Penny. "Come on, out with it."

"Look, I feel really bad about doing this, saying this."

"Oh come on Penny."

"Well I like him. He's been a fantastic boss, always very supportive and helpful. And I really like him personally."

"Why the past tense, Penny?"

"Sorry?"

"He's 'been a fantastic boss' you said. So what's happened? Have you heard Matt's leaving? Or are you flying the Henderson-Strutt nest?"

Penny bit her lip. "I can't quite put my finger on it. But something's happened to him. He's changed. He's...."

She stopped. He stayed silent. She continued. "It's like he's... well...sometimes...it's as if he's not concentrating on the job. It's as if he doesn't care. No, sorry Peter, that's not right. It's more like he doesn't care so much as he used to. Something seems to be bothering him. And look at the way he dresses now. His tie is sometimes skew-whiff, or he forgets to wear one. And some days he's got mud on his shoes and pants. To put it frankly, he sometimes looks a mess, as if he's been sleeping in his suit and come to work without showering."

She bit her lip harder. "Look Peter, I feel really, really bad about doing this. It's as if I'm betraying him. But I do care for him. I think he's a fantastic bloke."

"Come on Penny," urged Peter. "Just say what's on your mind."

"I don't think he's looking forward to becoming a dad. He seems to be worried about coping after the baby's born."

"Has Matt said anything?"

"Nothing. Nothing really. It's just the odd thing he says occasionally. Nothing certain. It's the way he reacts to any mention of the baby. It's due in a couple of months but he's almost in denial. He doesn't seem ready or want to be. He's not what I would call the usual happy expectant dad. He doesn't even pretend to be. I don't mention the baby anymore. I don't even ask how Jane is getting on. I'm worried that…"

The door opened. Matt entered. He was carrying a tray with a pot of fresh ground coffee and a plate of biscuits.

"Here we all are, I thought I'd save Sal a job," he said acting a cheerful waiter. "I thought we were all meeting at ten." Then he sensed the tension. "What's wrong?"

"Penny is still worried we haven't been told the whole truth about 22XP by AestChem," Peter responded immediately.

The bluff appeared to work.

"Of course we haven't been told everything. A client would be insane if they shared all their information with their PR agency. I suspect they don't know themselves the full facts either. Anyway we can only work on the basis of the information we do have, not on what we don't have," Matt said, speaking so sharply it demonstrated he could still be on the ball, and slightly embarrassing Penny.

"So don't worry about it Penny," said Peter looking directly at her. She understood what his eyes had said.

The crisis and issue's management team meeting scheduled for 10am Monday morning was finished by 9am. The coffee pot had been drunk dry. The plate of biscuits was now a plate of crumbs.

* * *

In Brussels Signor Romani and Frau Schiller signed the approval documentation on behalf of the Commission. They processed many documents that morning and AestChem's 22XP was one of several new product categories receiving the official seal. It had taken many months – years in some cases – of negotiation, discussion, scientific review, health and safety assessment, re-submission, screens of emails and forests of paperwork before various companies had their novel or innovative products or processes approved. Ever-growing files shifted between various departments within the Commission and then between the Chemicals Directorate, officials in the European Parliament and at least one sub-committee of MEPs. In the end 22XP's submission documentation amounted to a 234-page report plus 1,250 pages of annexes. As these contained exclusive scientific data and were subject to intellectual property rights, most of their content remained confidential. The public would have to trust the judgement of officials.

Naturally the Commission had stipulated many conditions for the various companies to follow. If they failed to comply approval could be withdrawn and their license revoked. The firms would have to demonstrate ongoing correct use, comprehensive labelling, full training of operatives working with this new chemical and its processes. Each company would have to establish a reporting system, if one did not already exist, to ensure any adverse reactions are reported and assessed. Local health and safety officials would of course be required to inspect these records and systems on a regular basis.

But for EC staff that morning only one topic dominated the gossip across Brussels: corruption. Another scandal had hit the headlines. Not since 1999 when the Commission resigned *en masse* under Jacques Santer's leadership had Commission employees such juicy gossip. His Commission resigned after it had failed to deal with the corruption and nepotism scandal surrounding Edith Cresson, a former commissioner and French prime minister. Today's headlines had staff speculating whether the current EC President would fall on his sword too.

It had been revealed that Eurostat, the Commission's statistical agency, was in dire trouble. Its director-general had been "removed" from his post, other officials departed and contracts were terminated with four companies supplying statistics. The EU's anti-fraud criminal investigation unit, known as OLAF, had discovered a chain of wrongdoing.

None of this scandal came as a surprise to Signor Romani and Frau Schiller, apart from how long it had taken to be revealed and how little had been exposed.

"We must ensure these types of errors cannot occur in our office," the Italian said to the German in English.

"I have already tightened our procedures," replied Frau Schiller, dressed smartly in black with a soft pink scarf. "Also I have gone over every difficult approval in recent years and I am satisfied with our, shall I say, administration procedures. I have of course removed any confusing and unnecessary paperwork from several key files to ensure full transparency. Details can be misunderstood or open to superfluous questions. So I do not believe we could be exposed to such accusations."

"Good. Good," approved the overweight Signor Romani from his leather swivel chair behind the large desk. "Such headlines only fuel the stupidity of the Euro-sceptics and their claims that corruption is rife within the Commission."

"Nothing can stop the European project now," she said assertively. "Not now after enlargement with Poland, Hungary and so on."

"Ah...but the bigger the animal the easier the target," Romani said peering over the top of his spectacle frames. "And already we get the big boys - Germany, France, Britain and Italy - talking of the EU's first division, a premier league of major economies. They want to do things the smaller players cannot do or do not want to do."

Schiller walked elegantly across Romani's spacious office, like a swan on still water. The way she held her head high and pushed her hips forward revealed that, as a young woman, ballet had been her great passion. But she had grown too tall to make it professionally in the *corp de ballet*, according to several leading choreographers, and she wasn't quite good enough to be a soloist. She folded her arms and looked across Brussels through Romani's window on the top floor of the Commission building. She spoke while looking down at the activity in the streets, people hurrying in all directions and cars stopping and starting as commanded by traffic lights. "You know that we used quite a lot of data provided by Eurostat?"

"Yes, I understand so."

"Some of our data on the labour market, environment, the spread of new technologies, industrial competitiveness, sustainable development and health and safety came largely from them."

"So I gather."

Romani was pleased Frau Schiller was looking away from his gaze. She was sugar to his eyes. And, while she was looking outwards, he could look towards her, feasting on her femininity. But he would have to be tall and handsome to be in with a chance of attracting her to his bed. He was neither. He would continue gaining satisfaction from Eastern European girls now dominating the escort agencies of Brussels. Illegal immigration had its benefits.

Schiller folded her arms and her fingers tapped her tanned skin, slowly, rhythmically. "I see we have told the press in our statement today that none of the, shall I say 'scandals', that are now under investigation has affected the quality of our work."

"Yes, that is what we've said."

Then she turned to face him and walked towards his desk. "That cannot be true."

He took his glasses off and dropped them on the approved documentation. But she had, unknown to him, noticed his gaze – through the reflection in the window. She had notice his narrow eyes following her around before. He could look as much as he like, she

241

thought, but he'd get a slap if he touched.

"Statistics only play a small part in our decision-making process, Frau Schiller. Remember they provide broad guidance only. General trends. Indicators. Nothing substantial. It would be wrong to over-estimate the importance of figures. We must not be fooled like so much of the media into thinking figures are essential for our decision-making processes. The 'quality' of our work, I can assure you, has remained untainted by Eurostat's demise."

"I see." After a pause she added, "The Office of Economic Affairs that controls Eurostat has nearly 600 full-time officials and a further 120 seconded experts."

"And your point is?"

"You would have thought with all those resources someone would have noticed the missing millions of euros."

"Ah Frau Schiller, you are so German. If you were like me, full of Italian Mediterranean blood, you would know by instinct the more people we appoint to find a problem and seek a solution the less likely they are to discover it and solve it."

"But the anti-fraud office is going to expand substantially with more people and more powers."

"Not everyone who takes these decisions has Latin blood. They don't understand that in certain cultures some things have to be done differently. The definition of 'truth' and 'honesty' and 'reasonable behaviour' differs. Most of the world doesn't think like you Germans, or the British, and certainly not like Americans. Some of us take a more relaxed view on certain practices. I am certain, Frau Schiller, our colleagues who plan to expand the work of the anti-fraud office have made the right decision. Doubtless the new officers will achieve what we need them to achieve. They will find what we need them to find."

* * *

AestChem's share price had remained stable in recent months, despite the general downturn in the chemical market worldwide and further unrest in the Middle East and the Caucasus. At one point, a few weeks earlier, it dropped significantly for several days. Analysts had predicted approval in Europe of 22XP might be delayed or face difficulties. Unfortunately a number of senior staff had been indiscreet within the industry about its prospects following a company conference. This had leaked to the trade press and then the New York Times and business TV picked up the story. Rumours also became rife that a competitor had developed a similar product to 22XP creating a further fall in AestChem's share price. But, for once, the rumours were wrong. AestChem staff did not need to be so gloomy. Then a leading Wall Street analyst changed his mind and declared on CNN and elsewhere that AestChem was a "bargain buy". A rally of its shares soon followed. Meanwhile, in the dark days when the shares dropped, several substantial share purchases had taken place. This provided a clear indication some people believed in AestChem and 22XP. So these factors combined and stability returned to AestChem's stock. Within hours of the European Commission's approval of 22XP AestChem's share price rallied strongly. At the peak of that surge the very people who bought on a low weeks earlier sold on a high. For those lucky speculators millions of dollars were made.

* * *

Claude Perlemuter, Henderson-Strutt's expert on European affairs, was delighted to hear 22XP had been approved. It would be announced very soon, his former friend at the Commission confided. Perlemuter called Jenni Tallow at AestChem's HQ in Chicago. As head of communications and corporate affairs, she was pleased with the news. But Claude was surprised how unsurprised she sounded. After two years of preparation, months of intense work, weeks of lobbying and discussion, and days and days of meetings, he'd expected an almost ecstatic response. Tallow was a cold fish, he knew, but you would have thought she would have thawed at this news.

"It was a very cool response," Claude told Peter on the phone to his colleague in the London office.

"Do you think she already knew it had been approved?" Peter asked.

"At first I thought that. Then I believed she just wished to maintain the image of a cool client."

"You mean she was secretly punching the air and dancing round the office?"

"Exactly."

"I suspect she's a very passionate woman under that hard exterior."

"I wouldn't know, would I Peter?"

"You can still tell, can't you?"

"As you know my preferences do not extend to women," said Claude. "I've been happily related to the same man for nine years now."

"Is it as long as that? How is John by the way?"

"He's fine. Still teaching. Still adores me."

"Give him my regards."

"I shall. But you don't make me jealous," Claude joked.

"I would hope not. He's not my type anyway," Peter said. "As you know Claude I'm very old fashioned and conventional. As a man, I like women."

"You just don't know what you're missing," Claude said.

"Oh, I've got a pretty good idea and I'm really pleased to be missing it. But back to business Claude - when is the official announcement on 22XP going to be made by the Commission?"

Claude described the announcement procedure to Peter and the call ended.

Peter asked Matt to his office.

"Good news," announced Peter. Then he paused and smiled at Matt.

"Oh, I see. So it's really bad news," Matt played along. "Don't tell me. Which client has the problem? We have to handle the withdrawal a drug after killing hundreds of people. No?"

Peter shook his head and maintained his smile.

"Perhaps there's been a massive chemical spill and the whole of Liverpool has to be evacuated? Max Clifford wants to retire and he's asked us to try and persuade the tabloids it's really true? The porno video we thought we got away with at Christmas has finally been played and exposed?

Peter continued to shake his head.

"I know. I've got it. Princess Diana was not actually killed in the car crash in Paris. It was just an act, a scam to give her privacy. She's been living heavily disguised on a farm in Australia. Now she wants to make her public comeback and Henderson-Strutt has exclusive rights to handle all the public relations."

Peter broke his silence. "Now that would be good. But I can exclusively reveal that...that we've done it. FFresherFood has been approved. It's gone through. Claude just phone."

"That's great news," said Matt. "Let's tell the team."

Matt moved towards the door of Peter's office. But he was called back. "No Matt. It has to stay between you and me for now - price sensitive information, stock exchange rules and all that.

"Of course. But let's tell Penny at least."

"No Matt. Not even her."

"Okay. No problem. When do you think it will be announced publicly?"

"Claude thinks tomorrow morning, certainly while the New York Stock Exchanged is closed for trading. AestChem will have to suspend dealing and make an official announcement. The US Securities and Exchange Commission will have to be informed and they will have an input on how the announcement is handled."

"Have you told AestChem?"

"Yes, Claude called Jenni a few minutes ago."

"So it's all over for us?"

"For our department maybe. But Jenni told me weeks ago if

we secured approval it was guaranteed our general PR team will handle the business to business promotion and the public awareness campaign to promote 22XP-treated food. But, yes Matt, you're right, our work has ended. It is no longer an issue."

* * *

Jenni Tallow walked into the office of her President and Chief Executive Officer after checking with his PA he was alone. Apart from Jenni only one other person, the Chief Finance Officer, could walk unchallenged into the office of William J Morgan II. Even the President's wife – especially his wife – was not allowed to barge in. Every visit was strictly by appointment only. And nobody had ever sneaked passed his hawk-eyed PA unannounced. AestChem, like Henderson-Strutt and most organisations, operated an "open door" policy. It meant that anyone could go and talk to anyone else, whatever position you held inside the company. In theory the cleaner could complain to the President about her toilet brush being threadbare. But it never happened in practice. One or two junior executives had tried to go over the head of their immediate boss. But they hadn't lasted long before seeking career opportunities elsewhere.

Jenni sat down without being asked and leaned across his desk. "Bill, we can press green for go early tomorrow or even late tonight."

Morgan picked up the phone. He pressed one speed-dial key. "We're on. It's in the bag."

Jenni could hear the CFO's voice asking questions and making statements, but not his exact words. But the President's words were very clear. "Sure...not yet...hold back on that...officially we don't know...very sensitive don't go there...we've got to suspend...sure... Jesus, who knows what these guys do in Europe...sounds crazy to me too, but that's how they do it...sure, just get everything ready...sure... great job." AestChem's President replaced the receiver.

"Have we really done it Jenni?"

"We've really done it Bill."

"Tell me again. Have we really done it?"

"Bill, we've really really really done it. Believe me."

"But we haven't heard officially."

"It's signed. It's sealed. It's stamped. Relax."

"I guess we just have to be patient a few more hours."

"It could be minutes," she said.

"We could get to know officially in seconds."

The phone rang.

His hand grabbed the phone like a Colt in a gunfight.

"Jesus Christ Almighty" he yelled as soon as he understood the question.

Jenny edged up to the desk.

"Okay, okay. Sorry. Sure we'd like some coffee. Bring it in."

Jenny sat back.

The President took a pill to regulate his heartbeat.

* * *

On his way out of the office Peter caught Penny alone at the coffee machine.

"About this morning, about Matt, let's keep it to ourselves for now," he said after checking nobody was within earshot.

"Yes, of course. I wasn't complaining or anything. I'm just concerned. I still feel bad about telling tales about…"

"Don't worry. You did the right thing. I share some of your concerns. Just give me a bit of time to deal with it. Okay?"

"Okay."

"Must dash, I'm meeting someone." Peter left Henderson-Strutt's building and turned right walking briskly towards Whitehall. Bert would pick him up later in the Mercedes and drive him home. He would kill time meanwhile in his small room in the basement watching his small TV. Mr Jones, as he always called him even when Peter asked him to address him as Peter, would call when he was ready. Bert never minded waiting. Waiting is what a chauffeur's life is all about, he'd told his wife for years before she died. The clock was still ticking. The overtime was handy, even though he couldn't think of anything at the moment to spend it on.

* * *

Matt left work a little after Peter. He waved goodbye across the office to Penny and other members of the crisis and issues team still working. "See you tomorrow," they called to each other. As Matt walked on the pavement in front of Henderson-Strutt's office he noticed Peter's driver watching TV in his cupboard-sized room in the basement. He took it as a signal that Peter would be back to the office later or that he was meeting someone nearby, although Peter had said he was going home early. Strange, he thought. But Matt quickly dropped the mini mystery from his mind and headed towards the station. As he approached Charing Cross Matt realised something was wrong. Crowds of people were filing out of the entrance. Some rushed for taxis. Others jumped on buses. Most just hung around watching and waiting and phoning and complaining. Chatter from the crowd confirmed what Matt suspected from experience: a security alert. All train arrivals and departures had stopped. Police had evacuated the station and a search was being conducted for a "suspect package", the euphemism for a bomb. Nobody believed there was a bomb. There never was. Real killers want to kill not warn. Most commuters would rather take the risk and keep travelling. But the police have their procedures and the health and safety officials can flex their powers, look and feel important, complete forms on their clipboards.

Matt walked towards Whitehall for a pie and pint away from London's frustrated commuters. There was no point in getting agitated about the delay. If there are no trains, there are no trains. He bought a copy of the *Evening Standard* to ease the pain of waiting. He phoned Jane and told her about the trouble and he'd be home when the trains were running again. But after the beer came the wine and the whisky.

248

He completed both the paper's crosswords, even though he believed crosswords were a waste of time. At around 11pm as the pub landlord called "time" to encourage his customers to drink up and leave, Matt walked from the warmth of the bar into the crisp night air. Charing Cross was quiet, apart from the usual drunks, addicts and homeless, key characters in the late-night life of London's railway stations.

A few late commuters waiting for their trains devoured burgers and chips to counter their hunger and the effects of the night's drinking. The main backlog of frustrated commuters had been transported home hours earlier. No bomb had been found, because there was no bomb to find.

The departure board informed Matt he would have to wait for nearly an hour for the next train to Sevenoaks. Damn it, he must have just missed one. He looked at his watch. The calculation was easy. In less than seven hours he'd be back on a train returning to the station in which he now stood. It was pointless going home at this late hour. He walked back to Henderson-Strutt to make the office sofa his bed for the night. As he approached the entrance to Bloomsbury Chambers he noticed the light from Bert's TV dancing around his little room. But from the way his head was slumped forward it was clear the chauffeur was asleep. Matt rang the bell to raise the night security guard. The speakerphone crackled into life. "Hello?"

"It's me Jim, Matt, I need to do some work."

Two bolts slid across the back of the door and a key turned the lock.

"How you doing mate?" Jim said. "I though it might be Mr Jones. Bert's been waiting for him to call all night."

"Yes, I see he's in his room. I think he's nodded off."

"You going to have a little lie down after you've done your work?" Jim asked with a grin.

"I think so," Matt said as he pressed the lift button.

"I won't disturb you when I do my rounds as usual."

"Thanks. I appreciate that."

"You've had quite a lot of night work recently," Jim said as Matt walked into the lift and the doors started to close. "Don't your wife want to see you anymore?"

There was no reply. But Jim wasn't certain his question had been heard.

Chapter Twenty-seven

Animals don't smile to disguise a snarl...

The grey mist of morning turned into the bright yellow light of late springtime. The woods were alive with animal movement and bird song. Overnight the late buds finally burst opened on the trees and a further layer of green shoots carpeted the forest floor. Winter's straw brown had been overshadowed by spring's emerald green. Last year's grass, now dead, replaced by this year's growth. Day by day, as dawn follows night, spring was turning into summer. The taller trees gently creaked swayed by the slight breeze refreshing the Kentish downs. Matt's head emerged from his well-worn sleeping bag. Inside the wooden hut Matt filled his lungs with morning air. He feasted on the moist mossy smells of the woodland he loved. Jane would be upset. Another night away from home, she'd complain. But after that frosty greeting they'd get on with the routine of married life the rest of the day. He'd go home soon, after cooking breakfast on the campfire. Matt felt guilty about spending the occasional night away from her. With the baby due in June she needed his support more than ever before. But the logic in his head clashed with the instinct in his heart, which urged him to the woods. Guilt, conscience, self-awareness, habit and even common sense were not powerful enough forces to break the call of the woodlands. It was a need as much as a want, a compulsion more than a desire.

Elm burns slowly and last night's campfire had retained its life in the warm ashes. With a handful of dried moss and twigs, stored in an old biscuit tin in the hut, and a gentle blow from Matt to rekindle the embers, the fire quickly crackled back into flame. He dropped the bacon into the blackened frying pan and the rashes spat and sizzled. Two eggs followed. Matt had already heated baked beans on the edge of the fire using the can as a pan. He served the eggs and bacon onto his plastic plate and scooped the beans from their tin.

On each visit over the months to the woods Matt had taken something to make his life more comfortable. Blankets, an airbed, spare clothes, an old chair, a small table, paraffin lamps, candles, torches and various tools. He acquired a large plastic barrel from his father in law, who thought it was going to be used in their garden, and had gradually filled it was fresh water. He used this sparingly, for drinking water only. For washing and general use he took a bucket of stream water. He had built up a small store of kitchen utensils and food, including a bottle of brown sauce. He'd used most of it. But by hitting the end of the bottle hard with his palm Matt extracted just enough to give extra taste to breakfast.

Sat on one of the three steps leading to the floor of his hut on stilts, balancing the plate on his knees, Matt ate his favourite meal of the day. Between mouthfuls he looked around to see if he could spy rabbit, deer or any new migratory bird that had made its way to Britain for summer breeding. He kept a special watch for the boar ever since the day of the charge by a herd of them, but they remained elusive.

A combination of last evening's rain and this morning's dew had soaked his smart black shoes, designed for city streets not woodland mud. They felt much tighter now than when he took them off before climbing into his sleeping bag last night. Usually shoes are loose in the morning and tight at night, thanks to feet swelling throughout the day. But the shoes had shrunk overnight to the point of pinching his toes. His suit trousers were also wet and spattered with mud. He then discovered a tear just above the knee on the left leg. Brambles have vicious thorns. On closer inspection of the site Matt found a cut on his leg where the barb had pierced his skin. He had grown so used to small cuts and abrasions in the woods Matt hardly noticed these minor wounds. The blood had congealed forming a two-inch brown line. His skin would heal. But the suit, or the trousers at least, was ruined. He usually put on his combat fatigues or casual clothing before venturing into the land. But last night had been different. He was desperate to escape the fast life of London and craved for the open air.

After walking from the railway station to home, he opened the BMW parked on the drive and drove directly to King's Wood. He didn't go home to change, deposit his brief case, eat, or brew tea. Jane wasn't there anyway, he remembered. She was attending a music concert at school, suffering the scraping violins and out-of-tune singing of the less-gifted pupils. The house was dark and empty and he didn't want to step inside. The woods were a far greater attraction, especially at night when the sky was starlit and peace pervaded the earth – or that part of the earth where he slept.

Woodlands provide open space, not enclosed within walls like at work or home. Matt was alone in the woods, but never lonely. To him life in the woods had become real, unlike the sham of public relations, press releases, politics, client meetings and corporate positions. There are no smiles for votes, statements for shareholder confidence or team-building exercises to raise staff morale. In the woods there are no colleagues to stab you in the back, forms to fill, staff assessments or email addicts. Night brings extra security because people stay away from the countryside, preferring to live their life through television or movies at the expense of real experience. They prefer the bright lights of London, shops and streets. They won't trust the moon. They won't venture into the woods at night. That's far too real for them. Their fear provided extra security for Matt. His isolation was almost guaranteed during the hours of darkness. And unless someone had considerable experience of walking in woodland with exceptional stalking skills, Matt at night would hear anyone approaching within half a mile. The woodland floor during the quiet of night was better than any doorbell at signalling a visitor's approach. To Matt the countryside is natural in contrast to concrete, brick, metal and glass. Earth, fallen leaves, grass, heather and moss are better surfaces to tread than tarmac. The air is clean and always slightly scented, depending on the season and what aroma nature has decided to release. There is no need of "fresh air" from a can mimicking apple blossom, mountain mist or fresh pine.

Animal behaviour is simple and truthful, not the conditioned false friendliness of corporate life. They have not read Dale Carnegie's *How to Win Friends and Influence People* or attended a course in body-language skills in a bid to manipulate the rest of their species. When the owl hoots, a bird sings, a deer cries, they make the sound of truth, not the noise of management-speak or the false promises of politicians. They can't use words to lie, just sounds to reflect their true feelings. They can't smile to disguise a snarl. What you see is what is. Fear is fear, food is food, escape is escape, copulation is copulation, birth is birth, care is care. They focus on now not the future. They do rather than think. They act on need not greed. Eat when hungry, drink when thirsty. It's animal survival not human pleasure. There is no façade, no falsehood. Matt wanted to live with life as it has been for thousands of years, not the pseudo pretence of office politics and city survival. The woods, and all they contain, represent the life he wants to live. His woodland was freedom. Work was drudgery and home had become a burden and the place of bills and debt. And Jane?

The thought of her urged him to hurry. He'd left a message last night on voicemail promising he would be home early, probably before she woke up. It was now around six o'clock. But as the pregnancy progressed she'd started to wake earlier. Matt finished breakfast and washed the knife, fork and plate in the bucket. Water was bubbling away in the billycan suspended over the campfire on its wooden tripod. He scooped out a cupful and dropped in a teabag. He'd started to drink tea without milk, primarily because he always forgot to bring it. There was just time to finish the cup before he rushed home to his wife and the urban world. Matt poured the washing up water in the bucket over the fire to kill it. A plume of steam and ash mushroomed upwards as its dying act of defiance. Matt raked his foot over the soggy embers to make sure no life was left to start a forest fire. His office shoes would need a good clean before they would be acceptable on the streets of a city or the carpet of a house.

As Matt approached the car, parked in the track near his aunt's former house on the edge of King's Wood, Alice Campbell called out from her garden at Rose Cottage waving her walking stick in the air. There was no escape. She came to stand outside on the verge. He couldn't just drive past as usual. She was a dear old lady and clearly determined to speak. She had been the closest friend of his aunt's until her death late last year. And it was Alice, after all, who had discovered Aunt Sheila's body surrounded by her cats.

"How are you Miss Campbell?"

"Very well, thank you," he heard as he approached her fence.

"Is everything all right?"

"Yes. Well, no actually. All the electricity has cut off. I've tried phoning the electricity board and all I get is one of those machine things asking me to press a star or something. Then the blasted thing just kept playing music. I couldn't get anyone to talk to."

"Well let's have a look. Perhaps a fuse has blown."

Matt followed the frail Miss Campbell up the crazy paving to her cottage. Her garden didn't follow the fashion dictated by designer gardeners on TV or in magazines. There was no coordination of colour or layout, no grand planting scheme following a sketch. Her garden was a patchwork of flowers, bushes, apple and pear trees and vegetables. But for over 50 years she had tended the same soil, putting a cutting in here, replacing a dead plant there. She'd deliberately let the

255

lettuce, cabbage and radish go to seed for replanting. And she always saved some peas and beans to produce fresh plants the following year. But when they lost their vigour she'd send off for a packet of fresh seed from one of the catalogues that dropped on her mat every winter. Her cottage garden had genuine Edwardian charm, because she followed the ways of her mother who had done what her mother had done. She had tulips and wallflowers and a few late-flowering daffodils between roses and other bushes. There were sticks here and there marking the spot where summer and autumn perennials would push through as the sun warmed the soil.

A handful of onion sets were contained in a small rectangular bed of bricks. To one side of this bed, which reminded Matt of a grave, Miss Campbell's carrots and spring onions were growing under glass cloches. She was certain there would be no frosts now before autumn, but they would grow faster in the gentle warmth under cover. Her broad beans were already half way up their cane frame and would grow as tall as Matt.

"You have to pinch the tops out of those beans you know," she told Matt as they walked by. "Otherwise the blackfly will have a field day."

Matt's eyes adjusted to the dark of the house as she took him through to the kitchen.

"It's here," she said, pointing to the metal box on the wall.

"Oh, this is one of those old fuse boxes Miss Campbell."

"Is it? Aren't all fuse boxes like this then?"

"No. Not any more. Fuse boxes nowadays have circuit breakers for each section of the house. Usually you just need to flick up the switch and it turns the electricity back on."

"My goodness. That sounds too good to be true. But look on top there, I've got some fuse wire, three amp, five amp and some thicker wire for the 13amp."

"Good. Well let's see which one needs fixing. What were you using before the electricity went off?"

"My kettle, about an hour ago. I switched it on and pop. Everything went. But it didn't stop me making my tea. I boiled a pan on the stove."

Matt opened the panel of the fuse box. "So it's probably this one," pulling the white enamel fuse out of its socket. "Bingo. See it's burnt."

"Now somewhere here I've a little screwdriver," she said searching through an old square biscuit tin full of antique tools, rusty nails and screws. She handed Matt a screwdriver with a wooden handle that looked at least a hundred years old. As if she'd read his mind Miss Campbell said, "It belonged to my grandfather."

"Before we put in some new wire we should check the fuse on the kettle." Matt pulled the plug from the wall socket and opened it. "Do you have one of these?" he asked showing the five-amp fuse to Alice.

"Oh, I don't think so," she fussed.

"Never mind. I'll bring one next time I come up. What I could do for now is take a fuse from another appliance that you don't need for now, just to check it is the kettle that blew the main circuit." An unused black and white television, standing in the corner of the back room, gave up its 5 amp.

Eventually Matt's role as an electrician ended and he drove home. The kettle was indeed the culprit; it blew the main circuit again. Matt guessed the heating element had packed up. Knowing Jane had planned a shopping trip that afternoon, he promised to buy a new kettle and would bring it tomorrow on his routine Sunday visit to the woods, so it would be no trouble.

"You spend a lot of time in the woods at the weekend," Alice commented as Matt was leaving.

"That's right. I love it up here."

"You should pop in here for a chat more often," she said, knowing he hadn't popped in at all.

"Yes, I'll do that. Anyway, I'll definitely see you tomorrow with the new kettle. Did you want a white one, a brown one, a stainless steel one?"

"I don't mind Matt. Anything will do. I've got some money here, shall I give you some now?"

"No. Don't worry. I'll let you know tomorrow how much it was."

As Matt closed the garden gate heading towards his car the old lady called out.

"Matt, remember, please do call me Alice. 'Miss Campbell' makes me feel very frumpish."

Chapter Twenty-eight

It was all so terrifying, dark, despairing...

"You're late," were the words Matt expected to hear as he arrived home. He wasn't prepared for Jane's soft and sympathetic attitude, making him feel worse about his absence overnight. Even wearing what she described as "a tent" of a maternity dress, she still looked elegant at seven months pregnant. She approached to kiss Matt's unshaven face. Shocked, she stopped. "God, you look a mess," she said, immediately regretting her honesty.

She was increasingly frustrated and, at times, angered by his aura of doom and gloom which she believed was unnecessary. He had a good job, a loving wife, friends that cared for him and a nice car. Sure, they had the stresses and strains of everyday life - commuting, road delays, bills, cold calls from telephone salespeople, unnecessary paperwork – but nothing extraordinary. Most importantly he was soon to be a father. Surely that would make his life complete. But venting annoyance was not Jane's style. Displaying anger was a weakness in her book. Something was clearly troubling him at Henderson-Strutt. And when you have stress at work you need sympathy at home. It was a lesson she had learnt from her mother dealing with dad after a bad day with cowboy builders. Jane was hoping Matt would pull himself together before the baby was born, relax and enjoy fatherhood. She wanted life at home to be settled and stable, routine and predictable, happy and ideal. Yet the more she tried to make his domestic life better, the more time he spent in his precious woods. The more she lined the home nest with soft feathers, the more it seemed Matt wished to fly away. The more Jane made home-life more comfortable, the more time he lived in what she imagined was uncomfortable squalor up the woods.

Life, to her, had never been better. The pregnancy had progressed well and an inner-calm had returned. Everyone around her, including Matt, had witnessed the return of the bubbly self-confident Jane. They all knew this was down to the confidence pregnancy instils in women.

Some days, she always noticed with pride, had passed without once thinking of her ordeal at the hands of the assault. When memories of the attack returned to haunt, the images were, at least, shorter, less traumatic. Time does heal although scars remain, as she predicted. She felt vindicated in keeping the rape secret. She was right. Silence had been better than speaking, secrecy better than disclosure. Knowing that nobody else knew of her suffering was now very comforting. In the early days she had done everything to disguise the damage. It had worked. Today she could face the world as she really is, as she really was.

"I forgot to change," he said as if defeated and looking down at his soiled clothing.

"But your suit, Matt. It's ruined." She returned her voice to neutral trying to avoid any implied criticism. But the "but" had done its damage. And she had condemned his suit to the dustbin.

"The dry cleaners will sort it out," not caring if they did or didn't.

She knew he was wrong. She also knew it was the wrong time to tell him so. The trousers at least were beyond repair and the mud seemed engrained in the well-worn jacket.

Jane decided to switch subject. "Do you want a shower before we go shopping?"

Matt's response was to simply walk upstairs like a contrite child in absolute obedience, her question interpreted as an instruction. Jane watched him ascend. He resembled a weary man with arthritis. Each step seemed a struggle, like the final steps in conquering a snow-capped mountain peak. Each leg appeared heavy as if the limbs were a burden to his body at high altitude. His breathing was deep, fighting to find oxygen in thin air. He gripped the banister in search of support as he took his tired frame slowly to the bathroom. But it wasn't his body that was weak.

At the top of the staircase Matt dropped to his knees. His head fell into the hands outstretched across his face. The sobbing started uncontrollably. Jane climbed the stairs and sat next to him doubled up foetal-shape. He rarely cried, crying made things worse. She placed an arm around his shoulders, rising and falling with each distressing convulsion. She didn't know it but her gentle touch made him feel more wretched, guilty for feeling sad. He had no right to feel depressed. Things weren't so bad. Many people face far worse: hunger, death, bereavement, disease, wrongful imprisonment, torture. Set against this plight of humanity he was, he knew, privileged. He suffered none of these. This pain was his, about him, of him, nobody else. Depression is self-indulgent and self-inflicted, a consequence of modern-day comfort. Caused by too much time in thought instead of in the primitive struggle for survival.

As tears were shed these thoughts were racing through Matt's mind. Yet he couldn't break this despondency. He was fully aware of the depth of the depression he now suffered. He knew it was irrational, without justification. But even with this ability to search his psyche in a rational way from the outside, it did not and could not stop the grief inside. In the same way a doctor is not immune from disease, Matt's awareness of the sadness, the irrationality of the anguish, did not protect him from it. Depression came from within. No intellectual barrier could prevent it breaking into his body and impacting his behaviour. He felt physically tired and mentally exhausted.

Jane's physical closeness highlighted Matt's psychological distance from her. Depression needs distance not proximity, isolation not integration. He wanted her arm around his shoulder, although he didn't deserve comfort. He wanted her love, although resented having to return the affection, so he resisted. He wanted her presence, but not the pressure of acknowledging it. He wanted her reassurance, but was blocked from responding. It was all so terrifying, dark, despairing.

He heard her through the confusion in his head. "Tell me what's wrong Matt."

He couldn't answer this distant voice through the anguished cries.

After a while she whispered to him again. "Has something happened? Have you had some bad news? Has something gone wrong at work?"

His face was wet with tears and his skin blotched from where his fingers had pressed. She noticed a streak of dried mud in his tangled hair and dirt behind his broken fingernails. She saw the state of his shoes covered in wet earth and matted leaves from the woodland. Jane could also detect that stale smell you accidentally breathe when passing a beggar in the shelter of a doorway. But this was Matt, the man always in control, her husband who always took pride in his appearance, Henderson-Strutt's up and coming crisis management guru destined to be a director, the young man many big corporations entrusted with their most vulnerable problems.

Slowly, rhythmically, Matt moved his head side to side. "No... no...oh no," he cried addressing some inner stranger's challenge, an intruder trespassing in the pit of his stomach.

With her lips close to his ear Jane whispered, "What's wrong?"

His wet eyes stared frontward focusing in the distance with nothing on the horizon. "I...I...I don't know. Nothing it's just... just..."

She waited patiently for him to complete the sentence. He couldn't. He didn't know what was wrong. He was just sad, very sad.

Sad about everything and nothing, tired and drained. After a long silence Jane quietly asked, "It's just what, Matt?"

His face fell again into his hands. In his depression he was driven to look downwards into the dark than ahead into the light. The full force of despair returned. His hands could not contain the tears and droplets leaked though his fingers. Each teardrop formed a small circle of damp in the dried mud on his trousers. Jane gently swayed Matt as if he were a baby struggling for sleep.

Matt thought of his mother, very different to Jane. There would have been no touch from her, no healing arm around the shoulder. She would have no sympathy or understanding, or at least no concession to any, perhaps in fear of her own demons. A strident pitch would have shouted, "Snap out of it" or "Come on son, this is no time for messing about." Matt would have been left alone to seek his own recovery while his mother went to work or busied herself with housework. For days or weeks, at home and school, awake and sometimes in dreams, this dark fog of despondency would pervade every moment. Compassion to Matt's mother was weakness. And weakness cannot be shown to your children. Understanding was threatening because understanding is an admission of knowing and sharing the same depth of suffering. Like his mother's, Matt's sadness would never be talked about. Like his mother's, his inner anguish would remain taboo, locked uncomfortably inside the soul.

Neither Jane nor Matt would remember how long they sat together at the top of the staircase. Time, at this moment, wasn't important.

"Shopping," Matt said suddenly. "We were going shopping."

"That can wait," reassured Jane. "There's nothing we need urgently."

Matt became agitated. His head shot up and looked left then right, up then down. "Kettle. We need to get a kettle," he said accelerating his words.

This worried her. There was nothing wrong with their kettle. ·

"It's all right Matt. Just rest. Take it easy."

"No. It's not. We need one now."

He stood bolt upright pushing Jane back. "I've got to go. I've got to get a kettle."

Chapter Twenty-nine

SUMMER

Suicide is selfish. But living is hell...

"It's a girl," the midwife smiled.

"Let me hold her," Jane pleaded instantly forgetting the pain she'd suffered.

"Well done. She's beautiful, just like her mum," the midwifery sister said while checking all was well after cutting and tying the umbilical cord. "Here you are. She's fine, absolutely perfect."

Jane savoured that precious moment when she held her baby for the very first time.

"Hello little one," she cooed. "It's nice for you to pop out and see us at last."

A perfect face seemed to smile at her mother. Ten tiny wax-white fingers and thumbs, on gyrating arms, waved a welcome to the world. Ten perfect toes curled and uncurled themselves on two chubby feet.

"She's absolutely wonderful," Maggie said. "I'm so proud of you." She kissed the forehead of her daughter, then her grand daughter, the first of several she longed for.

No birth is easy, but obstetrically speaking it was "a textbook birth', according to the midwife. Jane's first signs of labour were the regular progressively painful contractions. Then her waters broke. But she remained calm at home with her parents, who had moved in for a few days to be on hand. Maggie and Bob drove Jane to hospital after alerting the maternity ward over the phone. The hardest challenge had been climbing into her father's Range Rover. During labour she used some of that magical cocktail of oxygen and nitrous oxide to ease the pain. But no caesarean, forceps, nor an episiotomy was required.

Throughout the delivery they hadn't spoken of him. But Maggie couldn't contain her annoyance any longer. "It's wrong, you know, it's all wrong. He should have been here."

"I know mum, I know."

"It's outrageous to miss the birth of your child."

"He said he couldn't face it."

"What's to face? It's not the men who suffer the pain for hours on end."

"I know mum. But he's still down."

"What's he got to be 'down' about? He just needs to get a grip, get on with life, pick himself up and stop feeling so sorry for himself."

"It's more complicated than that, mum."

"No. No it's not Jane. Everyone's made it more complicated. We've all been too nice, treating him with kid gloves. You've been too patient with him. So have those people he works for."

"He just needs time, mum, that's all."

"How much more 'time' does he need? He's already had plenty of days off work to sort his mind out."

"Just give him a little longer, mum, please."

"I suppose he's back living like some wild man in the woods."

A gurgle came from the bundle in Jane's arms. Matt, for the moment, was forgotten as his daughter demanded attention for the first time in her life. Maggie's scowl turned into a broad smile. "Ah, you're so gorgeous I could eat you all up," said grandmother with delight in her eyes.

"Thanks mum. Thanks for staying with me."

"I didn't do anything."

266

"You didn't have to. You were here. That's what mattered."

During those first minutes of her life the baby had captured the full attention of her mother and grandmother. They had been oblivious to the midwife and her trainee completing the clean up of the bed and the birth suite.

"I wish all our mums were as good as you Jane," the sister said, experienced enough not to take offence at becoming no more than paint on the wall in the eyes of parents in the minutes after a child's birth.

"Thanks for all your help," said Jane. "You were all terrific."

"Yes, thanks very much indeed," Maggie echoed.

"It must get very boring delivering babies day in day out," commented Jane.

"Now please don't say that or my student here may decide to pack in midwifery before he really gets going," the sister said as she continued to check equipment. "And we're already desperately short of midwives, even females ones, never mind males."

"Millions of mothers have shared the same experience of giving birth, Mrs Collins," the student midwife added pompously while arranging a trolley for the next delivery. "But each baby is unique to its mum."

"You're right there," said Maggie keeping her eyes firmly on the baby and not upset by the young man's statement of the obvious.

As everyone surrounded the bed in admiration, reminiscent of some modern nativity play, the baby's nose nudged Jane's swollen breast. The midwifery sister was ready to intervene with help and sound advice to the new mum. But wisely she held back and watched to see if nature would do its work without a medical hand. Instinctively mother and child responded to each other's need. Nature's impulse moulded them in a single embrace. Both received nourishment: one for the body, the other for the soul.

* * *

He shouted each word as if they were unconnected, "Are. You. There?"

He stood still to hear a reply. No voice could be detected on the warm wind. So he struggled on through thickets of bramble and blackthorn with their long, hard, hooked spikes ripping his clothes.

"Matt, where are you?" Bob shouted again hoping his son-in-law was nearby in this expanse of dense woodland.

Matt's car was parked on the dirt track just down from The Bower House and Rose Cottage as Jane had described. But, he'd asked her, did Matt stay in his land or did he stray into the thousands of acres of woods and farmland? A needle in a haystack would be easier to find, he'd said. Look for his hut, Jane told him as the labour pains gripped harder in the back of the Range Rover as it sped to hospital.

She'd managed a few vague directions to help find Matt, although it had been many months since she last visited King's Wood. And Bob had concentrated more on reaching the hospital in time than his forthcoming search for his son-in-law. I don't suppose this hut is painted fluorescent orange by any chance with signposts right up to the front door, he'd said trying to ease the tension. Maggie scowled through the driving mirror to shut him up. Jane's pain had moved past the point where her father's sarcasm was funny.

Now, tramping around in this wood with no real idea of where he was – and with even less idea of where he was going - her plea was ringing in his head: *"You've got to find him dad, please, you've got to find him. He's got to know I'm having the baby."*

Bob walked into more open woodland where the ash stood tall. Knee-high soft summer grass ebbed and flowed in the breeze as waves breaking on a beach. Further through the soldier-straight ash trunks Bob could see green grass turn to gold. Surrounding trees had been felled so the sun touched the forest floor directly without diffusion through a canopy of leaves. When he arrived at this golden clearing Bob saw the trees, prostrate, awaiting further work from the chainsaw. Branches had been hacked from their trunks during winter and dragged to one side where the twigs had turned brittle. It was simply a matter of time before the long logs would be stripped of their bark and turned into planks or pulp or timber for builders. Some of the felled trees had already been prepared to meet their fate as firewood. Fresh shavings on the forest floor, the lingering smell of freshly sawn timber and several stacks of newly cut logs made it clear to Bob someone had been working this part of the wood in recent days. Perhaps it was Matt? Perhaps he'll return to the site soon? But maybe it was the contractors he knew Matt still retained for the heavy forestry work?

"Matt, it's Bob, can you hear me?" he yelled in four directions with his hands cupped around his mouth to concentrate the appeal. But not one reply was returned from any quarter of the wood. Bob tried Matt's mobile again. He phoned out of frustration more than expectation. Jane had told her dad that Matt always switched it off in the woods. "What, even when his wife's expecting a baby?" said Maggie rolling her eyes.

Bob sat on a stump to rest and call Maggie to report his progress, or rather the lack of it. "How's Jane?" has asked reflecting his main concern.

"Everything's fine, the midwife thinks it will be a few more hours yet."

"Look, I'm sure he's here somewhere. The car was parked up near that cottage and his Aunt Sheila's old place."

"Keep looking. Jane really wants him here for the birth."

"I know, Maggie. I know. I've been searching and shouting everywhere. Someone's been here recently where I am at the moment, the ground is well trodden and someone's been chopping trees down."

"You'll just have to keep trying."

"I will, I will. I wondered about calling a few of the lads in to help me look, hiring a helicopter or something."

"That might scare him off."

"Exactly. So I'll just keep looking and you get Jane to hold on."

"Yes love," said Maggie. "You may have noticed, with our three, the woman giving birth doesn't get much of a say in the matter."

"Give her my love. Call me if there's any news."

Maggie told her husband that mobile phones were banned in the delivery room, but she'd take breaks outside whenever she could.

"If you find him Bob, just grab him and bring him in," were Maggie's final words before switching off the phone.

Bob put the mobile away in his shirt pocket unaware that Matt had watched every move. Bob stood up and turned a complete circle on the same spot deciding which way to walk next. Should he backtrack or risk getting lost? Should he head towards those hills in the distance or follow this meandering stream? Matt was standing in the shade cast by dark conifers, watching, waiting, ready to respond to Bob's next move. Dressed from head to toe in camouflage kit Matt knew he was invisible to Bob's eyes. If he could deceive deer, rabbit and hare of his presence with their highly sensitive senses, he could easily stalk an ill-equipped human without woodlander skills.

After wiping the sweat off his brow using the forearm of his shirt, Bob decided to head towards the conifers. He was thirsty and cursed himself for not bringing a drink. He also needed a pee. His instinct was to head for a tree to conceal the act. But, what the hell, nobody's around. Trouble was it splashed his shoes. He then realised that's why you use a tree – to help it trickle down, and quietly.

Matt had observed his father-in-law for nearly an hour. He'd picked up his first calls from a distance and tracked him to this new clearing of timber. He gathered Jane must have gone into labour. What other reason would there be for him to come trampling through the woods? But what should he do? Go? Stay? Could he cope with hospitals, equipment, nurses, doctors, procedures, fuss and bother? Did he want to be surrounded by people, people looking, people talking, people doing things?

Bob started shouting again. "Hello. Matt. Jane's in hospital."

Matt froze as he strode towards him.

"She's having the baby. She needs you there."

She *wants* me there. She doesn't *need* me, Matt argued inside.

Bob approached.

Matt's body went rigid. He stared ahead. Even a glance could give him away. The white flash of an eye can be a beacon in a forest of brown. Stillness means survival.

Matt could smell Bob's aftershave, Aramis, the only brand he used. Artificial perfume and natural woodland don't mix.

"I can take you to the hospital," were the next words absorbed by the woodland. "You should see your child born."

Why? Who says? Why should I? What use would I be?

Bob entered the conifer darkness, a different wood world where the grass didn't grow.

"Come on Matt, please. Jane's gone into labour. There's still time to get there. They say it will be a few hours yet." His voice sounded different here in this dimness. The pines were so densely planted Bob could touch two trees with outstretched arms.

Matt wondered why Bob was shouting these things. As far as Bob knew he was alone. Nobody could hear. Matt wasn't around. Bob accepted his words died in the woods. But the more he shouted the more he felt he was doing the best for his daughter. Her heartfelt plea to find Matt was still ringing in his mind. Shouting was all he could do.

Matt watched his father-in-law walk by so close that, had he whispered, like a thief in a church at night, Matt would have heard every word. But Matt's tree-patterned hood, face veil, jacket, trousers and boots kept him concealed. And he hadn't blinked. And he hadn't moved a limb. And when he breathed through his mouth it was long, and deep, and slow, and silent.

Bob marched deeper into the pines crushing the fallen needles and releasing their resin scent. He didn't know it, but Bob, striding south, was further away from Matt's camp. What he did know was that he felt very, very sorry for the anguish of his son-in-law. To be here, instead of at the bedside of his wife about to give birth, whatever the attraction of the wood, demonstrated just how low Matt had sunk into himself.

Matt stopped stalking the intruder and headed north. At the edge of his camp, around the back of his hut, he kicked away a covering of dead branches. You could see him use a short chestnut stake to lever open the lid of a concealed container buried underground. Cunningly, the lid had a tray bolted to its top in which sods of earth had been laid. He bent down and reached inside the secret store, an abandoned fridge Matt found dumped on the roadside months earlier. Matt lifted the rifle out of its underground store. He unravelled an oil-soaked rag wrapped around it to prevent rust.

The Finnish Sako 75 was no kid's air gun. This shot bullets, not pellets. This was big game, not child's play. This was the gun of gamekeepers hunting deer, not the fairground pop gun for plastic prizes. This had a calibrated scope to hit, not skewered sights to miss. Matt reached into his pocket and extracted his bullet wallet. After standing the rifle against a tree he took one cartridge out of a small cardboard box in the subterranean store. He placed the brass bullet carefully in the leather wallet before dropping the wallet back into his pocket. Returning the box of bullets into the underground store Matt hesitated for a moment. Something made him think a second bullet might be needed. Perhaps the memory of his grandfather's words returned. "Now lad, always take more ammo than you think you need," the gamekeeper routinely said before a day's shooting. "And you never know, you might not always get a clean kill first time."

Matt made his way to one of several observation platforms he'd constructed high in selected trees throughout the wood. He'd spend hours on them watching wildlife with the naked eye and through binoculars. This particular platform, overlooking a small valley, was supported by three thick beams just above where they had grown out of the main trunk of the oak. It had become a favourite spot in the wood with superb views of the surrounding territory. He climbed the tree and loaded the rifle with a 6.5 x 55mm calibre 140-grain bullet. It would kill virtually anything at 200 yards with ease. But this bullet's destination would be much closer.

He thought of Bob, probably still scouring the woods in his vain search. He recalled good times with Peter at Henderson-Strutt and a night in Chicago with Penny. In seconds it seemed hundreds of scenes and people from his twenty-nine years played in his mind like memories on fast-forward.

He remembered how he was and compared that to what he is. The problem-solver had become the problem. The suppressor of corporate crises had transformed into the creator of a personal crisis - for his wife, family and friends. Ambition was dead. Gilt over 22XP and Russia rife. The future was now. The past was now. Time had merged to this moment.

The mind of the depressed is the mind of the confused. Matt didn't know what to do, what to say, where to go, what to think and – most painful of all – what to feel. His mind was a blur of contradiction and conflict. Life could end; or it could go on. Life was important; life was irrelevant. Planet earth is significant; or a mere spec of dust in an infinite universe. Perspective and perception can make a grain of sand massive or microscopic. Do you view it as an ant or an elephant? People care. People don't. Love is real. Love is false, a fool's gold, emotional self-deception.

Jane was in the midst of childbirth. One feeling tells him to go, to be at the bedside. But fear keeps him back, although he doesn't know what he's afraid of. Time is ticking away. He can't decide. To be there would accept he had a reason for being present, for being. To have purpose means you have value. Matt could not accept he had worth because he felt worthless. He couldn't decide what to do, or do anything. He forced himself to think, think through what to do. But how can you concentrate when dark forces inside are creating chaos?

How can you focus when inner demons are stabbing inside the pit of your stomach? He pleaded with them to leave. Cursed them to depart. Cried for them to go.

As if responding to Matt's plea, a few seconds of calm descended. The demons allowed a temporary freedom for his mind to think of Jane, valuable moments of relief and respite from the self, an unwanted ego. Matt knew it was time to make a decision; go to the hospital now or be somewhere else.

The gun rested across his legs as they dangled over the edge of the observation platform. Then, slowly, deliberately, he placed the bullet into the breech of the barrel. His right hand cocked the firing-bolt. The other grasped the walnut stock. Matt's thumbnail anxiously scraped the diamond-shaped chequering gun makers cut into the barrel's woodwork to help the shooter grip. He stood the weapon between his legs, the barrel pointing skywards. Life could end. Now. Later. Or it could go on.

A finger on a trigger has a choice too: squeeze or release. Death delivered in an instant. Painless. Easy. Here, in the wild woods he loves, all life's conflicts could end in death's hands. Suicide is selfish. But living is hell.

Chapter Thirty

It took a moment to recover...

"Now settle down quickly children. We have a lot to get through this morning," the Head said standing at the lectern opening his notebook. Most of the 500 pupils responded to his demand except for a group in year 10. A prefect tried to shush them quiet. But he lacked authority because he lacked respect. Severe acne and a skinny body with a voice like a soprano did little for the prefect's confidence.

"I have four very important announcements to make." The Head paused and glared towards the girls still chattering. His eyes silenced them.

"To the first announcement I want no applause. No jeers either please. I can confirm the rumours – yes, I've heard them too – that I shall be retiring at the end of this term."

Breathy whispers could be heard across the hall.

"The second is more important. Your new head is to be…." He stopped again and silence descended quickly. "The new head, I'm delighted to announce, is the current Head of English Mr Tinkler." He started to clap and the school dutifully copied. "The school's board of governors confirmed his appointment at last night's meeting. The governors did of course interview and consider several other candidates. But I'm delighted to say our very own Mr Tinkler was head and shoulders above the rest. At 6' 4" that was also literally the case." Everyone laughed. "I know he will do an excellent job at taking this school from strength to strength."

The Head stepped towards Mr Tinkler and shook his hand and gripped his shoulder.

"That means of course we have a post to fill as Head of English. Again we considered applications from other schools. But the governors last night offered Mrs Collins the post when she returns from maternity leave in the autumn." The Head put his hands together again and the pupils and teachers responded.

"That brings me to my final major announcement this morning. This also concerns Mrs Collins. I'm sure everyone will be delighted to learn that yesterday she gave birth to a beautiful daughter."

A loud round of spontaneous applause and cheers came from the school, especially the girls. Some of the lads just used it as cover to push and shove each other and couldn't see what all the fuss was about. As the applause faded the Head continued, "For some reason it has become tradition to describe new born babies like boxers before a fight - everyone wants to know what they weigh. I can tell you the baby, named Susan, weighed in at 7 pounds 11 ounces – or as we should say nowadays – about 3½kilos."

As assembly broke up several girls formed a gaggle in the corridor to catch the overnight gossip. The usual giggles and titters were going on as so-and-so was revealed to be going out with so-and-so. "He didn't," someone gasped loudly. "Well she said he tried to," another reported spicing up the story. As Jane's friend Sarah was returning to her duties in reception she overheard gossipmonger Claire Thomas, "He's gone stark raving bonkers apparently". And Jessie McAleavy went on, "Buggered off and left her with the kid to look after". Sarah pretended she hadn't heard a word. But she was amazed how quickly so-called secrets circulated.

* * *

"I'm really sorry to hear that Peter," Penny told him. "It wasn't anything to do with what I'd said a few weeks back?"

Peter Jones closed his office door as Penny sat down. Gossip was already rife at Henderson-Strutt and he wanted to get the story straight. He didn't want quarter sentences and half phrases to be misheard and pieced together incorrectly.

"You did the right thing," he said. "Several of us who knew Matt realised over recent weeks something wasn't quite right with him. You work most closely with him and compensated for a lot of his little mistakes – and a couple of big ones."

"I'm sorry Peter. I was just trying to..."

"I'm not criticising Penny. You really helped him. You made sure he got through the day. And it was good the clients didn't get to know about the state he was in. You did the right thing. But his work went downhill, he looked an unshaven mess some days, and then all the odd days off without any explanation. We couldn't ignore it any longer."

"So he's been fired," said Penny.

"No."

"Really?"

"No, he hasn't. Is that what they're saying out there?" He looked through the translucent glass.

"Yes."

"They're wrong. The management team, on my recommendation, have placed him on extended sick leave."

"So what's the difference between that and the sack?"

"Everything. He needs time to recover. And we're going to give him that time. He's a bloody good operator and we don't want to loose him. He's had some sort of breakdown, some personal crisis or other."

"Why? What's caused it?"

"We're not sure. His wife thinks pressure at work. We think pressure at home. New baby? Bills to pay? The usual. Who's to say?"

"He's not had the baby to give them sleepless nights."

"They have now. Jane gave birth yesterday. I called this morning to speak to Matt and his father-in-law picked up the phone."

"And?"

"Matt is spending most of the time up those woods of his. Days on end..."

"Peter, please. And..."

"Eh?"

"Men! The baby. Boy? Girl? Details. Come on Peter."

"Oh, it was a girl. Jane's dad says it's called Susan."

"Her," Penny corrected with a smile. "Not 'it'."

"Anyway," Peter returned to his track. "Matt hasn't seen it – *her* – yet. He's been up these bloody woods day and night."

"You mean he wasn't there for the birth?"

"That's right."

"That's wrong. He's well out of order."

"Penny, Matt's sick. Sick in some way in the head. He's become a recluse, paranoid or something. He's not thinking straight so he's not acting straight. Anyway, fathers being present at the birth is only a recent introduction society seems to have imposed on men."

Penny didn't rise to the bait. There were more important issues to handle. "What can we do to help him?"

"I don't know Penny. I don't know. I'm going to drive down to Sevenoaks over the weekend and talk with him. That's if I can find him."

"What do you mean?"

"Well yesterday, Bob, that's Jane's father, spent the whole day scouring those woods trying to find him to let him know Jane was in labour. He drew a blank. He said he knew Matt was up there somewhere. Bob said he was sure Matt heard him calling out, but he just refused to answer and avoided him.

"What does he do in these woods all the time?"

"God knows. He just likes studying nature, managing the wildlife and woodland, planting trees and so on. He told me ages ago he just likes generally messing about. He hunts too. He's got a very nice rifle and a couple of shotguns. I know - I provided the references to the police for his firearms certificate and shotgun license."

"Jesus. Was that a good idea?" she challenged.

"Well, he was fine then. I didn't know he was going to go all depressed on us then, did I?"

"Suppose not. Nobody did."

Peter started to tell Penny about the camp Matt had built and that, according to the father-in-law, he spent nights on end there.

"He pops rabbits, pheasant, woodcock and deer. In fact I'd planned on joining him one weekend for a good shoot," added Peter. "Apparently Matt's freezer's full of skinned rabbits and venison. Bob said he heard shooting yesterday. So I presume that was Matt..."

The phone interrupted Peter, irritating him. He'd asked Sal his secretary to block all calls. But this one got through. It must be important. Sal was a pretty good judge at sorting substance from spin. Peter put the phone to his ear. Penny sank back into the sofa to let Peter deal with the call. She was feeling sorry for Matt, and his wife, and his baby daughter.

"Tell me you're joking Jenni," Peter said seriously. Penny tuned into the conversation immediately sensing Peter's anxiety. "Permanent? Temporary? And the reason behind their decision?" Peter listened hard. "Let's try. Sure. Same here. Talk later."

Penny was smart. She kept quiet. She'd never witnessed Peter Jones, who when speaking at conferences was usually described as "one of the world's leading crisis communicators" in a state of shock before. Whatever this crisis, it took him a moment to recover before he could speak again.

"They've banned it," he said softly in total disbelief, as if describing a spaceship landing in Trafalgar Square. Then his voice became gradually louder and faster as the words poured out. "The fucking Food and Drug Administration have put an immediate ban and recall on all 22XP-treated products across the whole of the United fucking States."

Peter needed to think and act. Fast. Alone. A race was on. "I'll see you later," he told Penny opening the door for her leave. And when she left, he smiled a satisfied smile.

Penny needed a drink. A stiff one. But coffee would have to do. As she stood alone at the drinks dispenser she re-ran from memory the parts of Peter's phone conversation she'd managed to overhear. She was sure – well, pretty sure – that Jenni had said, "Love you" to Peter at the end of her call. No. Couldn't have been. Perhaps it was "Would you?"

Chapter Thirty-one

No time for mercy...

It was the car door Alice heard outside Rose Cottage before the engine revved into life. She'd become accustomed to Matt coming and going at odd times. But this early morning hour was strange even for him. The bedside clock confirmed 3.15. It was almost mid-summer but the night sky was still dark and the land was darker. There was no point in getting out of bed just yet. She'd try finding an extra hour's sleep. Then she'd totter downstairs to the kitchen and put on her nice new stainless steel kettle for a cuppa. But after nearly 90 years of life Alice Campbell found sleep more elusive. And once the rising sun slipped through the slits in her curtains to flood her bedroom with light, sleep would be impossible anyway. In summer, at least, she was always out of bed and usually in the garden by 5 o'clock. In winter she'd try and stay in bed longer. It saved on the heating. Like her former neighbour and friend, Sheila Chamber, whose nephew now lives the life of a woodsman, Alice treasures every moment she's awake. Sleep, to her, is a waste of time. And time was running out. She accepts each day could be her last, but hopes it won't be. Alice doesn't fear death. She fears the loss of her independence. She'll never go into one of those old folks' homes. Never. She'd rather die than be dependent. Death is sleep without dreams. And she would miss her dreams. Death has no sunrise or sunset, no twilight time for remembering. Alice would miss her memories, recollections of the war years and the good old days when people had time to talk.

Miles away a man stopped a car on a housing estate. A brand new car would normally catch every eye here. Local thieves don't park new wheels in the open street. They invite cops. Even your mates will nab your car given half a chance. "Honour among thieves?" Don't make me laugh. A nicked motor would go straight to a garage lock-up for instant re-spray and modifications before sold for cash up north. But at this hour the streets were still. The man's car also hadn't been washed for months, covered in mud and heavily stained with bird droppings: rural produce making urban disguise.

He knew the estate now. Scrap yard gardens. Car parts scattered over "pocket handkerchief lawns" as some 1950's architect full of idealism described. Broken fences. Smashed windows. Some boarded up. Some bricked up where the boards had been ripped away. Roaming dogs depositing their mess on the streets for the unwary to spread on their shoes. Council housing left to rot out of sight of respectable England. Even *Guardian* readers wouldn't want reminding of this problem too often. Terrorism, the intractable Arab-Israeli conflict, global warming, ozone depletion and Third World exploitation and starvation make more comfortable reading.

He'd watched. He'd observed who was coming and who was going. Four high-rise blocks dominate the estate, each with sixteen storeys of squalor. They had been given names to provide the pretence of a rural idyll: Park House, Garden House, Heath House and Lake House. Residents would have to dream about parks, gardens, heaths and lakes. They might even provide memories for the old. But they're unattainable for the unemployed, unimaginable for the low-paid, and unknown to the youth. And none was a "house". These were concrete and breeze-block boxes, high-rise containers to stack low-down people.

The man risked leaving the car a few streets away from Garden House. Not many street crimes take place at 3.45 in the morning, even here. And he knew it took exactly five-minutes to reach from this spot. He'd walked the walk. He grabbed his long bag from the boot and walked, hood up, head down, watching for the dog mess. This morning, miraculously, the lifts were working at Garden House. On his previous visits to the block both lifts had been "Out of Order Due to Vandalism". Why not "vandals?" He thought "ism" excuses the bastards.

He tried holding his breath for two reasons as the lift creaked upwards. First, it helped settle his nerves, or so he thought as it stopped the shallow breathing for a while. Second, it prevented inhaling the acrid smell of stale urine. Someone had recently sprayed the walls like a dog with a cocked leg and a pond of piss had formed on the floor. A half-eaten burgher bun and abandoned chips were soaking up the human waste. This aluminium cage was used more as a public toilet than a means of elevation to the higher floors.

The lift rocked to the fourth floor. The doors of this cesspit opened to an empty corridor. One resident wanted to make Garden House live up to its name with a pot plant opposite the lift. Someone had to try making the estate nice for decent people again. But someone else, a vandal, in an act of vandalism, had kicked over the little table on which the red-flowered Christmas cacti stood.

From previous visits he knew the flat he wanted was to the right, six doors along. He was certain the person he'd come to see would be alone inside. Sure, he had a few mates on the streets. But here, and much of the time, the lad was a loner. Went alone. Came alone. Paint was pealing off the door to flat 422. The number had been casually daubed in white gloss on that pale blue emulsion made on mass for council building departments everywhere.

Nobody should share a car with a loaded 12-bore. He knew he'd broken the rules, even with the shotgun's safety catch engaged. He removed the double-barrelled Beretta from its canvas sleeve. As safety was no longer required, he flicked off the catch. He drew in a deep breath and glanced left then right. The corridor was empty, apart from a tabby cat prowling for rodents at the far end. Surprisingly, the doorbell worked. He'd planned to knock with his gloved knuckles.

Although he could hear the bell from outside, there was no response from inside. Nothing. No movement. He pressed the button again, maintaining the pressure a little longer, but not long enough to cause concern to the resident. The ring was loud enough to penetrate sleep. And this time it did. A light came on, yellow, low wattage, bare bulb. In its shadow, through the panel of frosted glass, a tall figure approached the door.

"Yeah, who is it?" a sleepy voice sounded.

The man outside mumbled, "Me".

"Wot yer want? Do yer know what bloody time it is?"

"It's me."

"Who the fuck's 'me' supposed to be?"

"Come on mate."

Street-smart kids usually know better. But at this hour who's thinking straight? Doors never open for strangers on this estate. And cops never knock. They just kick in doors. But the chain slid off and the Yale turned. As his sleepy head peered around the door it was blasted from his shoulders. No debate. No discussion. No time for mercy. No time for mitigation. No time to hesitate. The naked body jolted backwards spread-eagled across the floor. Brain, blood and shattered scull-bone slid down the spattered walls.

Before, planning, watching, waiting, he'd told himself many times that after the deed he'd quickly slip the gun into its sleeve and walk away. He wouldn't - mustn't - run. No need. Nobody here will chase you. Heads will stay down. If it's not their business, it's not their business to know about it. Neighbours see nothing. And they'll all tell the police they didn't hear anything either, although the shot shattered the peace of night like an exploding grenade.

He was dead. Objective achieved. Walk away. Go. Stick to the plan. But the gunman stayed. He looked down without pity or shame or regret at the corpse with only half a head. Slowly, in one smooth movement, he pointed the barrels at the soft flesh, squeezed the trigger and discharged the second cartridge. This he hadn't planned. This was stomach-twisting fury despite the appearance of cold-blooded calm.

The police won't ask why the killer or killers shot away the young man's manhood. It was standard practice. Not until forensics confirms the shot to the head was fired first will they start to think about it, and then not too deeply. Even a fresh-faced constable on this case will work out which shot was fired first. With head flesh embedded 6-feet up the wall, the victim must have been standing when the first shot was fired.

What's unusual is that drug-dealing gangs normally like to inflict pain before delivering death. It's good to get 'em on their knees screaming for mercy. It's fun to give 'em a kicking first. It's great to hear 'em promise they'll never cheat you again. It's amazing that some think they'll be allowed to live. It's power, absolute power over their life.

And when your head's full of heroin, your heart's full of hate, your hand's full of gun, mistakes are made. Anyway, who cares how another low-life street-corner dealer died in a shabby suburb of South London?

* * *

It was three weeks after Ray's funeral back in April when Matt called. "Well this is a surprise," she'd said. "Come in lad, make yourself at home." Doris hadn't yet touched a thing of her husbands even though their two boys and daughter had encouraged her to have a clear out. She liked his things about the place - now. When he was alive his overalls, tools and bits of wood he left lying about were of course a nuisance. They were always under her feet when cleaning. She couldn't move for all his clutter and mess. It should all have been left in the shed.

After the funeral the children stayed as long as they could, a few days. But they had jobs to get back to and families of their own to bother about. She'd manage, she told them. She'd have to. They'd visit more often and bring the younger grandchildren. The teenagers have a will of their own nowadays. You can't force them. Meanwhile, her life and house would seem empty. Ray's boots, as always after years of marriage, were left standing on the kitchen doormat. Doris knew he'd never fill them again. No man could walk in Ray's boots. But looking at them sometimes she could imagine him standing there. She'd complain about the mud he brought in the house. Leave them outside, she'd always bark. And he'd always say he'd take them outside later after tea.

Today, in that hollow time after death when the fuss of the funeral is over and the bereavement cards are placed in a drawer, his physical things filled an emotional gap. A toolbox here, old overalls there and a neighbour's chair waiting for repair in the corner, were reassuring symbols of his presence in her life. Each item evoked a picture, a sign of his time on earth. Every room in the house held at least a moment's memory of him suspended in a past time. In his mess her memories now rest. That's the way she liked it. That's the way it would stay.

They'd planned to go to the cottage in the West Country. But it wouldn't be the same without him. The mortgage was already paid off and there was the assurance money and a pension from the company he'd served faithfully. Bob Straw had always treated Ray well, and she'd never forget the kind words he'd said at the funeral. And now Bob's son-in-law is on the doorstep.

"Would you like some tea Matt?"

He hesitated before changing his mind. "Oh, go on then. Thanks."

"You in a hurry then?"

"Things are busy at work."

"And how's Jane? Just a couple of months to go before the baby's born."

"She's fine and the hospital says everything's progressing according to plan."

"Are you ready for becoming a dad?"

"As ready as I'll ever be Mrs Sykes."

"Good. Good. Now I'll pop on the kettle and you can tell me what you want."

"Well, as you know, Ray built our extension..."

"It's all right, isn't it?" Doris interrupted sounding worried.

"Sure. He did a fantastic job, as always."

"Good. If a job's worth doing it's worth doing well, was one of his pet sayings."

"You may remember Mrs Sykes that for a few weeks he had an apprentice working with him at our place. A tall thin lad."

"The lazy one?"

"Yes, that's probably him."

"What on earth do you want to know about him for?"

"We found a brand new electric drill in the shed. It's hardly been used. It's not ours. The only person we can think of is this apprentice and we want to return it. We're pretty sure it's not Ray's because he marked all his tools with his initials, Jane said. Anyway, Ray would never leave tools behind."

"You're right there. He always knew where every single piece was, even if it looked like chaos to everyone else."

Doris went to the kitchen and returned with a tray of tea and biscuits and put them on a small table. Ray had made the tray from beech wood and the table from oak many years ago.

"I know Ray used to pick him up before they came to work at our place. You wouldn't happen to know if Ray kept a note of his address?"

"Now, let me think. Drink your tea while I go and have a look in his notepad."

Within a minute Doris was back in the living room with Ray's blue-covered notebook, the type a reporter would use. She flicked over the pages without success shaking her head after searching each page.

"Was that the notepad he used earlier this year?" Matt asked, suspecting it wasn't.

"Oh, silly me. That's the one he was using until...." Her face grew momentarily longer in sadness. Then with a half-smile she said, "He's got a little pile of them in the cupboard. I'll go and get the last couple he used."

Doris returned clutching a few pads.

"You have a look at these two, and I'll go through this lot."

After several pages had turned, Doris suddenly stopped and looked up. "Wouldn't Bob have the lad's address on file at the office?" she asked.

This was the question Matt didn't want asked. But as a PR professional he had a prepared answer.

"Yes I knew I could do that. But Bob's been very busy with a big contract recently. Then I realised it would be good to call in and see how you are. And there's a third reason," he added hoping to totally convince Doris. "I want to visit that big furniture store just up the road from here. So, three birds with one stone, so to speak."

At that moment Doris's eyes lit up. "I think this is it. I remember Ray saying he'd have to go round that horrible estate to get to it. There's a mobile number here too. They start with 07, don't they?"

Doris watched Matt make a note of the address. It wasn't until after he'd gone she realised Matt hadn't taken down the phone number. Perhaps he was simply going to post the tools back to him or deliver them personally.

Matt didn't stay long. He hardly touched the tea and he certainly didn't have a biscuit. As Matt was driving away she tried to signal to him. "Turn right not left," she mouthed without speaking. But he wasn't looking at Doris as he drove the wrong way for the furniture warehouse.

Chapter Thirty-two

Resignations and threats...

"The headlines killed him," she insisted. But the wife of W J Morgan II was wrong. AestChem Inc's President & Chief Executive Officer had died, like his father and grandfather, of a weak heart and arteries full of fat. With one first class honours degree in chemistry and a second in pharmacology, he knew more than most about taking exercise to maintain health. He knew all about cholesterol, free radicals and anti-oxidants. He knew about eating fresh fruit and vegetables. He knew aspirin thinned blood but exacerbated ulcers. He knew about executive stress and work-life balance. But he drafted company strategy sat behind a big desk for long hours. He held business breakfasts often starting at 6am to kick-start action. Tactical lunches checked on progress with senior managers. Dinners cemented relationships and usually ended with bourbon after midnight. He held meetings between the meals. And whenever he had meetings throughout AestChem's worldwide empire a plate of chocolate biscuits accompanied every pot of strong coffee that was served.

Newspaper headlines had been cruel. But headlines don't kill. It was knowing he would be standing before a Congressional Committee in Washington DC and facing a high profile court case that twisted the knife. To suggest Morgan alone was to blame for a "cancer time-bomb" ticking under millions of consumers "exposed" to 22XP-treated food was probably media exaggeration. Despite the shocking stories, American and European experts investigating what had now become "a scandal to rival mad cow disease" said it would be at least 10 years before the full impact in humans could be assessed scientifically. But newspapers want sensation today, not rational debates a decade away.

AestChem's executive board members were hanging on to their posts resisting calls for their resignation. Stockholders at next month's extraordinary general meeting might oust them anyway, according to television and newspaper pundits. Dismissal was more lucrative than resignation; money was preferable to honour.

They blamed Morgan for running a secret ship with an iron hand. He didn't consult, they accused. Neither did they challenge his decisions. His death made blame easier: the dead can't sue for slander. People realised Morgan could not have worked without accomplices. Others must have helped him hide the laboratory research demonstrating 22XP caused cancer in rats.

Three senior directors had already jumped the corporate ship before it sank. They had sold their shares in the company for a good price and gone to live the rest of their lives in luxury away from corporate life, or so the newspapers said. In media interviews they claimed "coincidence" and "luck" about the "fortunate" timing of their stock sale weeks and, in one case, days, before their value dropped deep south. The Securities and Exchange Commission and Europe's financial regulators might discover the timing of their share sell-off was more than mere luck.

* * *

"You don't need to resign," Peter Jones told her. "Just because I'm leaving doesn't mean you have to go."

"I know that," said Penny. "But the department won't be the same without you."

"Thanks. I'll take that as a compliment. Look Penny, this takeover of Henderson-Strutt doesn't mean the company's abandoning issues and crisis management. Far from it. It needs people like you. You do a fantastic job. I'm sure you'll get a promotion and I'll do everything I can to secure it. The new company say they want to expand public and government relations work, not contract it."

"Why are *you* leaving then?"

Peter came round from behind his desk to share the sofa with his young executive. "I helped set up this company years ago. I was even younger than you at the time. A kid. Fresh down from Oxford. Got lucky. Got a lot of shares at bargain basement. I've been offered a really good price for my shares. I'm 50. To paraphrase mafia language, 'It's an offer I can't refuse'. I'll be able to take life easy. It's a great opportunity. I might do a bit of consultancy on the side. I'll see how life pans out."

"But you love your work."

"I did. But some of the stuff I've been involved in recently has become very messy. It leaves a bad taste in the mouth."

"I knew this 22XP process was fishy. But I wouldn't have thought it gave you nightmares."

Peter couldn't tell Penny about Chechnya, Myanmar, East Timor or other projects. The cover-ups. The lies. He didn't want Penny to react the same way as his wife. She'd already poisoned the hearts and minds of his children against him. Peter had thought he could trust his wife with the truth. But she couldn't live with a man who made excuses for dictators, child-killers and torturers. And when a nice man came along...

"Why South Africa?"

"Sorry?"

"Why you going to retire in South Africa?"

"It's warm. It's spacious. It's politically stable now. It's economically sound. Great hunting and..."

"Jenni's there."

Peter's breath was taken away. "How on earth did you know that? I didn't tell you. I didn't tell anyone about..."

293

"One and one makes two," smiled Penny. "Call it female intuition. We've watched you and her over the months. You couldn't stand each other at first. But now the body talk screams 'l o v e'."

Peter laughed. "Christ, was it that obvious? I thought we'd kept it under wraps."

"You didn't disguise it that well, especially as Britain's top PR guru."

"No, obviously. Okay Penny, fair cop," Peter said recovering from realising his team had been openly gossiping about their secret affair. "Jenni's been fed up with AestChem for a long time. Hated her boss who ran the place like a dictator. So she's sold her stock options, fortunately before the shares collapsed. Made a mint. And her mother's South African. They're very close. So it's all fitting into place."

Penny was still holding her resignation letter because Peter refused to take it. He'd told her to tear it up.

"It doesn't look as if Matt will ever come back to work," Penny said sadly.

"We don't know that Penny. He might return."

"He must have lost his marbles. You say he's still living like some hermit in those woods, eating rabbits and deer and pheasant and god knows what."

"That's what his father-in-law tells me. Matt's not been home in weeks. He's not even seen Susan, his baby daughter."

"That's so, so sad," said Penny. "What happened? What caused him to flip like that?"

"I don't know Penny. I really don't know. Stress? Marital problems? An affair?"

Penny kept her face in neutral expression as Peter paused, apparently to see if she knew anything about Matt's private love life.

"But," he continued without any added gossip, "that wouldn't have sent him to live in a wood hut in the middle of a forest. Money worries? God only knows."

Peter, temporarily at least, persuaded Penny to think again about her decision to resign. Wait and see what the new owners of the company do, he'd said. She returned to her desk and placed her unopened resignation letter in the drawer. Was Peter right to encourage her to stay? Wouldn't it be better to gain experience in another company? Did she want to stay in public relations at all? Considering the ban on 22XP, the coincidental death of AestChem's President, and the resignations of Jenni and now Peter – not to mention Matt's mental breakdown – Penny felt distinctly uncomfortable, isolated.

Staring at her screen, Penny instinctually opened her email and found herself deleting letters and notes, especially where she'd questioned the safety of 22XP. She knew, of course, this was next to useless. Emails were forever there, somewhere, in cyberspace, on files elsewhere. But she felt better distancing herself from the failed project. Her desire to efface all Project 66 matter was driven by her sense of shame rather than any knowledge of wrongdoing. Out of a retained sense of loyalty she also logged into Matt's email – she'd known his password for months – and cleared all Project 66 matter. He wouldn't care now, even if he knew. Right or wrong, legal or not, Penny erased every document she could trace on their system about 22XP and binned AestChem's disks. Waiting until her colleagues left the office, Penny extracted documents from the filing cabinets and shredded them. If anyone asked, especially Peter, she would deny culpability.

As a final check, rummaging through Matt's desk, she discovered a red wallet folder under the usual desk-drawer rubbish of staplers, hole-punchers, paperclips, pencils and scraps of paper. Inside were two printed notes without addresses or dates. She read the first.

Peter

I can't go on. It's wrong. You – we – I - can't keep lying for Russia. We know they've committed atrocities in Chechnya. We've seen the evidence. The world should know too. Truth, you've always claimed publicly, is the best public relations. But secretly we've been telling

bigger and bigger lies, going deeper and deeper into deceit. We're
not simply denying truth but creating excuses for ethnic cleansing.
We're providing alibis for Vadimov's mass murder. You said once I
started I couldn't stop, no backing out. There'd be "consequences" if
I quit. But there will be bigger "consequences" if I continue. I can't
go on. I can end it. There is a way out. I can say "No". Sorry.
Matt

Penny knew of course Peter's travelled regularly to Moscow.
She'd been told it was routine "reputation and image" work. But
Chechnya was never mentioned. The second note, on a sheet of ruled
paper that had earlier been screwed into a ball then unravelled, was
more disturbing.

Collins

Your wife did not warn you. If she did, you failed stopping your
poisonous work. What we did to her was just symbol of suffering our
people go through every day at hands of New Soviets. They usually
kill afterwards - by slashing throat – or worse. But we wanted wife
to tell you stop. But your stupid wife kept quiet. For money you will
tell great lies. Now you must tell truth to media about what New
Soviets doing in my country. If you fail tell media about slaughter of
innocent people of Chechnya, let me promise you, we will not give
your wife second chance. Why, you ask, do we not silence you? We
could cut throat easy or put bullet in head or bomb you. The answer
is obvious - from now you must work for us.

We demand you:

1 - call press conference of international media with CNN and
BBC etc

2 - confess your lies against our country with full details of your
propaganda on behalf of evil dictator Vadimov

3 – tell whole truth about attrition and suffering of our people
If you refuse work for us, you and wife die after we give pain.
Signed: Dzhoxhar

Penny felt sick. She gripped her stomach with both hands. "Jesus

296

Christ," she cried. "What the hell have you been through Matt? Why for Christ's sake didn't you say something?"

Chapter Thirty-three

This murder was different...

Bob Straw was always last to leave, especially on Friday. When it's your business, it's your baby. You conceive it, give birth to it, nurture it, see it mature and constantly protect it. It doesn't matter how old the business grows, it's always your kid. Running your own business is as much a vocation as a job.

At fifteen Bob became a builder's apprentice. Now, forty-five years on, he was founder, owner, chairman and managing director of a thriving business. The last few years had been good, very good. A boom time for builders as punters put their money into bank accounts made of bricks - thanks to falling equity markets. In recent years developments and redevelopments in London, Birmingham, Ashford and Bristol, had expanded his business beyond his dreams. His reputation for hiring good people, providing realistic prices, quality work and meeting deadlines, was second to none. Developers, unofficially of course, often approached Bob to make sure his tender was submitted at the optimum price. They went through the motions of competitive tendering. But Bob got the job if he really wanted it.

A year earlier he had been approached with a lucrative offer for his business. At first he'd said no, no way. You don't sell your children. But after the death in April of his life-long work mate Ray Sykes, and the birth of his first grandchild, he'd re-evaluated life. A business is a means to an end after all. The end is the benefit it brings to your family. Ray had deserved years of pleasurable retirement with Doris in the West Country. He had been robbed of those years, cheated of time. And Maggie increasingly reminded him "You're not getting any younger". It was time to quit. Get out while the going was good. Spend some of the millions he'd make on the sale and share the rest with his three daughters. He'd give them the financial security he never enjoyed. He was self-made and self-satisfied. Maggie still worked as office manager at the regional health authority. She didn't need to. She just enjoyed it. A world cruise would tempt her to retire too, especially now the nights were getting darker. She loves the house in the Lake District and the villa in France. But most of all she now has Susan. And, hopefully, there'll be more grandchildren.

When everyone was off the premises, Bob unlocked the shoulder-high document safe in his office. Two keys were required to open the heavy iron door. On the top shelf lay a buff A4 folder. Inside a newspaper cutting he'd kept since it appeared last Christmas in London's *Evening Standard*. He didn't want to see the face ever again, an artist's impression of someone the police had wished to question. With one strong builder's hand, he crumpled the cutting into a tight ball.

The police didn't know his name then, although the illustration was very good. Bob recognised his face instantly. So had Ray. They were in no doubt. The police didn't know his whereabouts either. Bob and Ray did. The police appealed for information about the alleged assailant, wanted for a series of rapes and assaults across south London. Bob kept quiet, and so did Ray. They'd remembered the lad, the face with the dull eyes and weak chin. Bob regretted - more than anything else ever in his life - the day he put apprentice builder Paul Potts on the payroll.

Ray had told him how he'd found Jane crying and distressed, pretending nothing had happened. He'd recalled how Jane had suddenly changed and lost her bubbly confidence. Bob had also witnessed how her husband had crumbled under the stress – and they thought it was pressure at work. What a shocking secret they shared and suffered. How terrible for Matt, knowing his wife had been violated by this pathetic piece of shit and unable to do anything about it. But Bob could. He had the lad's address.

After reading the news report with the lifelike artist's impression, it hadn't been difficult to work out what happened to his daughter. The pain, the degradation, the secret she and Matt had harboured from their family and friends. Something had to give: Matt caved in and Jane – made of tougher stuff – eventually got on with life. Bob said nothing and would say nothing – to Jane or Maggie or anyone, ever. And Ray died with their secret.

Bob couldn't rely on the police to secure a conviction. He wanted justice, not due process; punishment, not mitigating excuses. Even if they caught Potts, would the case reach court? How many women would stay silent because they didn't want questioning in public? How many rape victims would back down rather than endure recalling their ordeal in graphic detail? How many social workers would argue in Pott's favour with psychobabble blaming his upbringing? Who would say he's just an evil bastard that deserves banging up for ever?

Bob didn't want some fat-faced barrister sweet-talking a judge into a short custodial sentence with a bit of community service and therapy on the side. Pott's would testify she "asked for it" and some stupid jurors would be convinced the case wasn't "proven beyond reasonable doubt". As a law-abiding, hard-working, tax-paying citizen, Bob Straw believed it right and proper to fulfil his civic duty.

He closed the safe and left the office for a relaxing weekend. It had been a good day. The week's main contract had been completed to his personal satisfaction. On the way to his car, parked across the yard, he tossed a ball of paper into an open Biffa skip awaiting collection of his firm's rubbish.

* * *

The face under the *Evening Standard's* headline checked Matt's stride crossing the garage forecourt. He'd seen this police artist's impression before, many months earlier. It was a face he'd come to know very well. He'd studied its features intensely. It became the face to hate, to blame, to destroy one day.

Gangland killings rarely make the front page. But it had been a quiet news day. And this murder was different - the eighteen-year-old victim had been wanted in connection with a string of assaults against women across south London. DNA tests would soon confirm if he was the guilty man. Although most of his head had been blasted away, police had, the report said, positively identified him.

"Do you want that *Standard* then?" the girl in the garage asked when Matt went to pay for the petrol. "You know, now you've read half of it."

She'd watched him grabbed by the headline and eagerly read the shocking tale. Judging by his dishevelled state and black mud-splattered BMW, she assumed he'd taken avid interest because of the drugs link, probably his supplier. But Matt had seen enough, mumbled "No" through his beard to the girl without looking at her, and paid cash for the fuel. He left without waiting for the receipt.

Stunned by the news Matt drove home fast. He went directly to his secret store beneath the forest floor to find it. He carefully removed the newspaper, soggy with damp. He looked at the police picture again for the very last time. Now he'd been murdered, the artist's impression could be destroyed. With two hands, resembling an act of religious ritual, Matt placed the limp pages on the campfire's embers. Intense heat instantly crumpled the newsprint and, through the smoke, the distorted facial image of builder's apprentice Paul Potts burst into flames. Burnt pieces of paper rose into the air and floated away on the woodland wind like black snowflakes.

Matt was relieved Jane's attacker was dead – and pleased the way he died. It helped close a chapter on this secret tragedy. "Vengeance is mine," recalled Matt from some Biblical text. He hoped, without guilt, his killers made him suffer before they blew off his head. Back street drug gangs usually did toy with their victims like cats with mice.

Sadly the *Evening Standard's* report had been scant with details. He would read *The Daily Telegraph* tomorrow knowing that, if any paper were to print the gore, it would be this.

They had murdered the right man, but for the wrong reasons. It didn't matter. There was no mistake. Matt knew Potts was the youth detectives were after and the genetic testing would prove it. The police drawing had been as good as any photograph, maybe better than some. Their description of his character and physique was vivid and almost worthy of Dickens.

The hazy sun of early August was gradually fading over the horizon when Matt left the woods. It would be a red sky tonight, and a better day tomorrow. Before leaving he rubbed the campfire's dying embers with the sole of his boot. There were no remaining traces of burnt newspaper. The image of Jane's rapist had been obliterated, the ghost exorcised.

As Matt approached his car on the track Miss Campbell waved from her garden at Rose Cottage. She expected his usual "Hello, see you later" response. But Matt walked the few yards up the track towards her. In recent months he'd noticed she'd grown unsteady, relying more on her sticks and sometimes a metal walking frame. She seemed smaller, probably because the arthritic bend in her back made her stoop forward further.

"How are you Alice?" he inquired.

"Oh, you know, not so bad. Could be worse." She was pleased he'd called her Alice instead of Miss Campbell. It was the first time he'd done so despite several requests over the months.

"You seem in a good mood," she observed.

"Yes, I've had some good news." But he didn't elaborate. "Can I get anything for you tomorrow in the shops? Potatoes? They're always heavy to carry."

"No thanks Matt. I'm growing my own, see." She pointed to three neat rows of earthed-up potato haulm. Despite Alice's frailty, she could still wield her hoe as good as any gardener. "Great Scot they are."

"Sorry?" Matt thought he'd misheard.

"Great Scot. It's a variety of potato. Best baking one there is. I don't think many supermarkets sell it."

"Okay, I'll be off then. See you soon."

"Drive carefully," she said as Matt sat behind the wheel, started the engine, and drove into the summer sunset.

* * *

"Hello," said Jane.

But the phone stayed silent.

"Is it you again? It is, isn't it?"

She knew he was listening.

"Look, how many times do I have to tell you? He's not working for Henderson-Strutt at the moment. He's ill. Out of it. Whatever he was doing – whatever you say he was doing against your country – he isn't doing it any more."

His heavy accent broke the silence. "We warn you. We tell you to tell him. We tell him. But you took no notice and he keeps telling lies about our people. He must tell truth or there be consequences for you."

"Please..."

"No! Enough is enough. Our patience run out. If he no tell truth soon, we get you – and your baby."

"Oh...oh god, no..."

"Our people suffer worse every day and..."

"Please, please listen to me. He doesn't work at the moment. He's, he's..."

"We watch him leave the office nearly every day..."

"Impossible. He hasn't been there for weeks."

"Lying cow. We saw him yesterday. He got in big Mercedes. Went to airport. Got on Moscow flight..."

It took Jane a second to gather her thoughts.

304

"That *wasn't* Matt. That's not *my* husband. That's...that's his boss!"

There was a short pause before an angry outburst at the end of the line. The caller was shouting at someone in a language Jane couldn't understand and several voices were shouting back. A long tone sounded as the line died.

Chapter Thirty-four

Sleep without guilt...

Susan slept in her cot undisturbed by the doorbell. Matt still had a key but believed it wrong to enter Jane's home uninvited. The seconds seemed like hours as he stood waiting for the door to be answered. Concerned about waking the baby, he was reluctant to ring again. He was sure Jane was in. Ten o'clock at night was not the time to go walking with a month-old baby – and the lights were on downstairs.

A new Golf GTI was parked in the driveway. Unknown to Matt, Bob had recently presented each of his three daughters with £50,000 as "a little treat" to celebrate his retirement and forthcoming sale of the business.

"My god, it's you," Jane said placing both hands on her heart in surprise. "I wondered who it could be at this time of night." She unhooked the door chain. But Matt hesitated before stepping inside, half-expecting the door to be slammed in his face. Jane would have been within her rights to reject, insult and condemn. He deserved it for missing the birth, for abandoning her in her greatest need, for not facing up to what had happened. But he was most ashamed of his inability to share the suffering with Jane - and the cowardice of silence.

Matt had planned a hundred things to say when he saw Jane for the first time in weeks. But now could say nothing. He froze, both arms hanging limp, like a man on the gallows. The guilty should be punished, but Jane's warm smile delivered a verdict of forgiveness.

"Well don't just stand there, come in." She held out a hand to help Matt step over the threshold. He took it noticing she still wore her wedding ring. They walked towards the living room, Matt's boots leaving a trail of woodland mud on the cream carpet. He apologised. Jane said it didn't matter.

"Have you come to see our baby?" she asked softly. "She's sleeping at the moment, but it'll be all right."

He'd come more to speak to her than see the baby. He had much to say. But where do you to start after weeks of virtual silence living the life of a recluse? If he started, would he stop? Would he say things he would regret? His head remained down, his eyes searching for pointless detail in the carpet, providing more time to choose his words, avoiding risks, evading the chance of failure.

"You've lost weight," she observed, hoping small talk would help Matt.

"Have I?"

"You've grown a beard."

"Yes, suppose so. It's easier, you know, up the land. Nobody's ever around in the woods. Well, the odd walker. Doesn't matter what you look like."

"Suits you."

"Thanks."

He lifted his head and glanced at her for a second, eye contact relieving the tension a little more.

"Although Matt, I must say, I prefer your naked face."

"I'll shave, if you want. If...if...if my things are still in the bathroom."

"Of course they are. Why wouldn't they be?"

"Well, you know."

Jane held his hands. "Look. Look at me Matt. This is *your home.* This is where *you belong.*"

He looked around the room as if confirming it was home and not a house. Nothing had changed in the weeks he'd been away, apart from cards of congratulations for Jane's new baby on the table, a baby rocker, a plastic changing mat propped against the wall and a big yellow plastic box already full of toys. A teddy bear sat looking at him from the corner of the settee. He felt it looked more "at home" than he did.

"Have you come to take some more clothes?" she whispered.

"Hadn't thought about it. But suppose I could, now I'm here."

There was a pause, each thinking their own thoughts, each considering carefully what to do, what to say and who should speak next.

Jane broke the silence: "Would you like to see Susan?"

Susan. A girl. That's her name. A daughter.

"You had a girl?"

"Yes."

"Did everything, you know, the birth, go okay?"

"Yes. Everything was fine. Mum was there. Dad was pacing the hospital corridor. He tried finding you. Went looking round the woods."

"I know. I saw him. But I couldn't Jane. I couldn't come. I'm sorry. It's pathetic, I know. But…"

"It's over now Matt. Whatever it was, it's finished. Don't beat yourself up. I wished you had been there, of course. But I understand. Well?"

"Well, what?"

"Do you want to see Susan?"

"Yes. Yes please. But I came to see you, explain things," he said.

"You've seen me now. There's time to talk later. Come and meet your daughter. She's gorgeous."

Jane took Matt by the hand and they tiptoed upstairs. The door to Susan's room was half-open. A low orange light from a small lamp cast sufficient soft light to see her face. Her tiny hands were touching as in prayer, although she didn't need forgiveness. Her lips were closed together, content, fed. Susan's breathing was shallow and rhythmical, causing her blanket to undulate like gentle waves on a calm sea. Her eyes were gently closed in sleep. Baby sleep. Sleep without guilt. Sleep without nightmares. Sleep without regret.

Matt's eyes filled with tears - of joy and sadness.

"She's just magnificent," he whispered. "She's perfect. She's just perfect. She's beautiful, like you."

"She's not always this way you know. She does cry and fill nappies."

"I know... I know," Matt said as tears trickled down his face.

Jane and Matt found themselves holding hands, sharing a special moment.

"Will you come home? Are you ready to come home?" she asked, as softly as their baby's breathing. The question turned into a request. "Leave the woods. Come home to us. She needs her daddy, and I need you."

"But how can you forgive me? I left you. Abandoned you. I went at the wrong time, the worst possible moment..."

"Matt, I love you. Susan is yours as much as mine. And she loves you too, I know, because you are part of her. That cannot ever change."

"She's bound to love you more. You carried her all that time. You gave birth to her and I wasn't even there because...because...because I was selfish and stupid and..."

"Matt, listen. You were ill. You've had a breakdown. We understand. We all understand."

Matt dropped to his knees grasping the white wooden bars of Susan's cot. He pressed his face against them, like a prisoner pleading release from his cell. Jane stood behind him massaging her husband's shoulders. Her hands offered strength, support and sensitivity. Susan slept as her father wept quietly by her side. And her mother shared his feelings. The phone rang in the hallway. They didn't answer.

THE END

ISBN 1-41205488-5